By Nathan Goyer

Copyright © 2017 by Nathan Goyer

All rights reserved. No part of this publication may be reproduced, distributed, or transmitted in any form or by any means, including photocopying, recording, or other electronic or mechanical methods, without the prior written permission of the publisher, except in the case of brief quotations embodied in critical reviews and certain other noncommercial uses permitted by copyright law.

This is a work of fiction. Names, characters, businesses, places, events and incidents are either the products of the author's imagination or used in a fictitious manner. Any resemblance to actual persons, living or dead, or actual events is purely coincidental.

Nathan Goyer

nathangoyerauthor@gmail.com

Prologue

Gusts of sand battered Derek's face as they rode through the wasteland packed into a Jeep that had seen better years. Dunes stretched every direction, and three supply crates pressed into his back. The relentless sun bore down, causing him to steal another sip from his water jug, but even that couldn't break his smile. The Jeep bounced, and water spilled through open lips.

"If you keep grinning like that, your mouth's going to fill with sand!" Julia quipped, a sly grin on her face.

Of course I am. This is it, the find of century. This is what I've been waiting for.

He pulled out a handkerchief and wiped off his face and the fronts of his teeth before stuffing it back into his vest pocket. "All better now?"

The Jeep finally slowed to a stop. Its passengers wasted no time climbing down from the vehicle. Before them sat a deep hole in the ground hardly wide enough for a grown man to squeeze through.

It was the only notable feature in the land as far as Derek could see. Aside from a few large rocks and various weeds the land was bare. A wilderness that should house nothing.

"In there?" Derek turned to Eliot, the oldest on the team of scientists. He was larger, though not at all fat. His eyes widened as he peered down, followed with a deep gulp. Eliot wasn't the bravest of the seven, but his knowledge of ancient languages made him a key member of the team.

"Don't worry, it gets wider very quickly," Said Derek "Claustrophobia is the least of your worries."

"The cavern is still open? It hasn't been filled in with sand?" Peter was an architectural historian, one Derek brought on many of his expeditions. With just a glance Peter could tell who had built an ancient structure and during which time.

"As far as I could tell, it's held up surprisingly well." Derek pulled his rappelling gear from his knapsack and anchored it to a secure boulder near the opening. The others did the same.

Peter nodded then switched on his headlight. "No use in waiting, then."

Derek returned the nod as he locked himself into a harness and connected it to the rope. The fear of the dark unknown could not stand against his excitement, he climbed into the pit without a moment's hesitation.

He sucked in a breath of air cooler than outside, fresh almost. It didn't make sense. He'd been in hundreds of ruins, and they all smelled of age and dankness.

He glanced downward and was surprised to see his rope hanging just above the ground, swinging slightly with his movement. He'd been sure it would reach the ground *This is a 50-yard rope. How big is this place?*

With the limited vision his headlight offered, he barely made out designs on the walls that filled the room from ceiling to floor. Carvings twirled up the walls like ivy before meeting together at the peak in a massive spiral.

It was a breathtaking sight, and Derek released a relieved breath that their entrance hole hadn't harmed anything important. His eyes widened as he lowered himself, and his headlamp penetrated the dark. Goosebumps rose on his arms. The marks had been left by a master whose carving knife matched the skill of any artist's paintbrush.

"Of all your finds, Derek, this is by far the best!" Eliot called from above.

"I never imagined such a place existed. Truly incredible," Petra echoed. A real compliment, as she had seen just as many ruins as he had, if not more.

He shrugged. This wasn't about him. Discovery shouldn't be about fame, success, the big grant.

Near the bottom, he let go of his rope and dropped the few feet to the ground. He moved over to one of the walls, examining it. Intricate designs of dashes, arches and swirls repeated themselves in an uneven pattern as a mysterious text.

Eliot dropped a few feet away, staggering for balance.

"What can you make of it?" Derek asked.

"Nothing." Eliot righted himself and coughed awkwardly, pretending that his embarrassing landing hadn't happened. "It's not even remotely like any other language I've seen. I wouldn't know how to begin deciphering it."

As the other team members reached the bottom of the cavern, Derek turned back to the writing on the wall. With another linguist, Derek would have taken the man's words as a lack of knowledge. But he knew Eliot. He'd never been stumped before.

"But how could that be?" Derek dared to ask. "Who could have erected this place?"

A loud bang split the air from behind. He swirled to see Peter smacking the wall with an open palm.

"Some civilization we haven't discovered would be my guess." Peter removed his hat and ran his fingers through his hair, shaking his head. "It's sturdy. Only the slightest amounts of dirt are making it through its walls. It's holding hundreds of feet of dirt above and making it look easy."

A new civilization ... and a highly advanced one at that.

It seemed the only option. There was no known city anywhere near here. The most they'd found nearby was a nomadic campsite. This place might have been lost for the ages were it not for the nomadic traveler who spoke of a pit that swallowed his cloak in one yawning gulp. Derek reached down and plucked the nomad's garment from the floor.

Can't forget you down here. You're filled with luck, no doubt.

"This place is as massive as you thought." Julia's voice quivered in awe.

"It's big, yes," Derek said, "but what was it built for? As far as I can tell it's not a tomb, and I haven't seen any obvious signs that it's a temple. People don't build things for no reason, especially in the middle of nowhere."

She gave no answer, and he turned to face her.

Julia's brows furrowed. "You sound worried. Would it be so bad for it to be empty? It's already an amazing find."

"Of course, it would be bad!" How could she ask such a thing? "This is going to be our greatest find! Our…" Irrational anger pumped through him, and he pressed his lips together.

He had spent his whole life looking for something great—greater than anyone before him. Nothing had satisfied him. Nothing had amounted to more than a headline in a few archeological journals. His life's work had left him empty. He couldn't bear to see this place empty too.

He turned from her and stuffed the nomad's cloak in his bag. As he zipped it back up, something caught his eye. A small image that sat between two bodies of ancient text.

There were many similar carvings in the room, but this one drew his attention. It resembled a man, his face intricately carved to show the smallest details. That alone made the carving seem important. The man stood in front of an archway, arms open wide as if to invite Derek in.

Maybe it was a religious carving, the man a god. Derek was strangely drawn to it. What did it mean exactly? Perhaps it was the look on the man's face, a look of adoration and love that he could only attribute to the closest of couples. Though he hadn't known that type of love personally, the picture stirred such feelings within.

"Derek," Julia called from behind.

He started, turned, and coughed, regaining his composure. "What is it?"

She pointed down a hallway. A faint glimmer of light flashed from deep within. The rest of the crew had moved on.

He nodded and followed in a quick, and what he hoped was dignified, stride to catch up.

As he walked, he scanned the walls for more depictions of the man, whoever he was.

His heartbeat quickened, and his chest tightened, as if someone had coiled his rope around him and pulled tight. There was something down here—something important. He knew it.

Julia's hand on his shoulder startled him, causing him to pause his steps. "Derek, I know this is important to you but—"

Derek pushed her away at the sight of another drawing. It wasn't of the man this time, but of a strange series of arches that connected. He let out a grunt of annoyance and searched the walls feverishly for another depiction of the man.

Julia prodded him with a playful finger. "We're getting left behind, Derek."

Sudden anger rose and Derek slapped her hand away. "Do I look like I care what the others are doing?"

"Calm down back there," a voice called from ahead.

He looked down the passageway. Lantern light illuminated Eliot's smug grin. He wagged his finger at Derek. "We wouldn't want to 'forcibly dismiss you from the mission,' now would we?"

Derek feigned a laugh. They were his words coming back at him. He'd pulled together seven willful people, and they'd formed an unlikely team. He was the glue. If he caved, they all would.

Pushing the tension from his gut, Derek shrugged it off and hurried after them. The corridor ended, and the group paused before what appeared to be a large door on the side of the hallway.

It was tall and sunken deep into the wall, blocking their progress. Derek pressed between his teammates and examined it. He touched the frame and slid his fingers along it. There seemed to be no way to open it short of prying it apart from the middle. But they hadn't brought the tools for that.

"Looks to be the end of the line this direction," Peter said.

Derek held up a hand and kept studying the door.

How was this possible? The door didn't appear to be able to swing in any direction, nor did it have space to swing upwards.

But the builders went through the effort of building this corridor and door. Why would they do that, if the door didn't open?

The rest of the crew moved down further into the hallway. But Derek moved closer to get a better look.

What am I looking for?

He couldn't answer, but he felt a *need* to find this place's meaning. His normally renowned patience did not seem to be present. Only anxiety. A need to know.

There. He spotted a small circular stone sticking out a few inches from the wall.

It can't be that simple ...

To humor the naïve child in him, he shoved on the stone piece. The button slid in smoothly.

Derek let out a yelp as the entire door groaned and scraped against the surrounding walls. Each side of the door slid perfectly into the walls beside it.

Impossible.

The sound echoed down the halls, and the rest of his team rushed back. They watched as the door slid until it was even with the wall and then stopped.

Julia's words escaped in a gasp. "Derek, what did you—?"

A wave of blue light along with *something* rushed out of the room, washing over them like a warm wind.

The sensation sent shivers through his body. Not uncomfortable, but instead almost ... relaxing, welcoming.

He knew at that moment they'd made the discovery of a century, of a lifetime. Derek was about to change the world.

Chapter One

It's a strange feeling when someone in your life vanishes, never to be seen again.

It makes you realize how much people affect each other. And, whether the interactions were good or bad, how much the loss of a single person can change your entire outlook on life.

This feeling is one that most people get at some point in their lives; it's inevitable. But my question is, why do I feel it?

More importantly ... why do I be feel it now?

Eric Dunst sat behind his post watching the same people move past his station as he did every day. He looked alert—that was his job. The people would sometimes comment on how he paid close attention to their every move as they passed by, making sure they weren't breaking any codes. He would usually play along and hold up a pointed finger as they passed.

Truth was, he was lost in thought during these long shifts, and he paid very little attention to his actual duty. In his defense, he'd thought that a top-secret research facility would be more ... exciting. They had their inventions, but most of the time the scientists talked and schemed and theorized about things they were too fearful to attempt.

Even worse, he wasn't a scientist himself. Merely a Marine who'd been asked to secure the facility. It was secure. No one attempted to get in. His biggest adrenaline rush had come from a few squabbling researchers who'd been far too easy to wrangle.

What am I doing here?

This wasn't his passion. He'd joined the military because he needed a job, an income.

He wasn't even sure *what* he wanted from life. He'd be willing to search, if he knew what he was searching for. Was finding a purpose in life too much to ask? And maybe a pretty girl to share it with?

Eric relaxed his shoulders, his spine. When no one was looking, he released a sigh, hanging his head. *I wish I could have stayed back on the aircraft carrier. At least there I always had something to do.* It wasn't a purpose, but—

"Hey, Eric."

Eric started. He wasn't supposed to be at ease, no matter how worn out he was. Glancing up, he saw another security unit stride toward him. Just another macho guy who wondered what he was doing protecting secret labs of bubbling ooze.

Nick Barrier stroked his chin and paused in front of Eric's cage. "Couldn't wait a few more minutes to relax? Your shift is over, you know."

Finally.

"I lost track of time."

"Oh, I understand how time flies as this exciting post." The man playfully shoved him. Eric nearly tumbled off the stool, but he righted himself.

"Git. You shoulder the most boring shift. Go on and do something fun."

Eric nodded. Then he hopped off the stool and headed down the hallway towards the exit.

Something fun, huh?

He didn't normally do anything. He didn't have any friends in this town. Anyone he had previously called "friend" would not be someone he would associate with anymore. There was one person he tolerated more than others. And instead of heading back to his apartment, Eric made a snap decision and turned down a hallway, toward the offices.

The smell hit him first as he entered one of the labs, something he now referred to as "genius smell"—a mixture of body odor and the leftovers from a dozen different food items. He gagged and tried to cover his disgust as best he could.

Almost unchanged from when Eric first arrived for today's shift, James was still plugging away at his computer keyboard. The wrappers from yesterday's lunch cluttered his desk.

James was young, one of the youngest in the facility. From what Eric had been told, he'd been recruited while he was still only halfway through high school. A prodigy.

He was a nice enough kid, too. Eric had trouble understanding him when he started going into the details of his research, but he found they both shared a few common interests. He was as close to a friend as Eric had here.

But true friendship with James would require patience. Based on the volume of garbage scattered across the floor and his greasy unkempt hair, James probably hadn't left the office in days.

"James. You're leaking again," he said with a smirk.

The young man seemed confused for a moment, having not noticed Eric's arrival until he'd spoken. Then, with a smile, he twisted around in his swiveling chair, looking for the drink he had spilled. He found one tipped over on the floor and promptly tossed it into the already over-filled trash can.

"I swear," Eric said, "they're gonna quarantine your office one day. You really should clean up occasionally."

"I don't have time for that." The boy grinned, waving him over like he often did when he'd discovered something. "Look at this! I just found something *insane*."

"Oh yeah?" Eric tried his best to sound interested as he stepped the chair, looking at the screen. It was covered in various graphs that, while Eric was somewhat educated on the subject, were far above his intellect.

"I found these meteoroids just now. We didn't see them at all, and we should have, based on where they came from."

A chill traveled up Eric's spine. "That's comforting."

James turned and changed screens on his computer. This one showed images of the rocks. "No need to worry. They won't come too close. Close enough to see, but they won't hit us. But if they *did*, that would be devastating. There's a lot of them up there, enough to make us … well, all the USA would be wiped out for certain. The after affects would probably kill off the rest of the population in the following weeks as well …

James changed the window on his computer to a close-up image of one of the meteoroids. "Enough of that kind of talk. This is even more interesting—we've never seen anything like them. They look like they could be made of materials we haven't seen before."

"That *is* interesting. Could they have come from another solar system?"

"It's not likely, but that would explain why they're so different. We won't know anything for sure until we get a closer look."

"I hope you find out more about them and maybe see them coming next time." Eric laughed. "Not to be paranoid, but how close will they come?"

"Not close at all. We won't even be able to see them without a telescope on a day like today."

A window popped open on the boy's screen, instantly drawing his attention towards it. From the looks of it, Eric wouldn't be able to pull him away a second time.

Shrugging, he turned and headed towards the door.

He walked, feigning purpose—a charade to the rest of the office that he had important things to do. Instead, he'd head home and sleep, like usual.

This is my life, I guess. Eric exited the building and then hopped into his car with a grunt and half-heartedly jammed the keys into the ignition. The rusty old sedan started unusually quickly. It roared to life on the second try.

The skies above were a light gray, the clouds not allowing a single hint of blue through their canopy. Despite the warnings they gave, the clouds merely provided a drizzle over the city below. Not enough water to provide any real help for the vegetation, but the gray was as depressing as a real rainstorm.

A world of love, eh?

His mother often said that when he was a child. She dreamed of the world's potential. He had as well, long ago. But the pain of life had dashed those ideals. What love could there be when everyone who'd loved him was gone?

Eric turned and drove down a street. The sidewalks were covered by hundreds of people who scurried like ants over a rotting piece of fruit.

Eric looked up to the Space Needle in the distance, trying to recall the feelings of excitement it gave him when he'd first arrived. He looked at its magnificence, yet nothing inside him stirred. His soul felt as dreary as the streaks of clouds overhead.

Movement in the clouds caught his attention. A flash of red light that streamed in an arch. Even without a perfectly clear visual he could tell what it was.

Didn't James say they wouldn't be able to see them?

Another larger one tore at the clouds, cutting a wide hole through the cloud blanket above.

Catching his breath, Eric cried out then made a U-turn at the next intersection, cutting off a white SUV. The driver blared his horn, but all Eric could think about was getting back to the laboratory.

He had to get back. He had to tell James—warn the others. When was the last time they'd done an evacuation drill on the building? Would anyone even know what to do?

Eric gripped the steering wheel, weaving his vehicle around those who'd stopped to watch the sky. He sped past a police officer, who was, like the crowd, gazing upward.

Eric's heartbeat quickened. James's predictions of what would happen if they hit were on the forefront of his mind.

City-wide alarms blared, confirming his fears.

Something's wrong.

James was wrong.

James was rarely wrong.

The people seemed confused at first, but all it took was one man running for a building for all the others to start to panic. The sidewalks cleared as people hurried into buildings. The street clogged with cars as an unfortunate amount of people attempted to merge. Most were in a rush to get out of the city, not to get back to work.

Eric turned on the radio. The warning service played a lovely screeching tune before the announcement. It advised everyone to remain indoors. Eric pushed the car to its limits. He slowed briefly when a confused straggler scrambled down the street in a desperate attempt to escape. Eric passed the frantic man and then hit the gas again.

Finally, he arrived in the parking lot. The whole building seemed calm from the outside.

He ran up the steps leading to the front door, his hopes of a sane environment shattering at the top. He peered through the glass and watched as scientists ran from room to room, papers and documents in hand. They seemed to be looking for somewhere, *anywhere* to save themselves.

Eric swallowed hard. He pulled the glass door open, stepped into the chaos. He spotted James, wide eyed and pale, standing just outside his office. Eric approached. "What's happening?"

James's body trembled violently. "The meteoroids. They're going to hit."

"I know that already!" Eric grabbed him by the shoulders. "What do we do?"

James shook his head. "What *can* we do?"

"We've got to get underground, right?" Eric asked hopefully. "Just bunker down and hope for the best?"

"No, no ... that isn't going to help." James's eyes glazed over, and he looked past Eric. "From what I saw ... hundreds, and very large ..."

Anger, worry, fear rushed through Eric. He shook James harder. "James! *Will it help? Can anything help?*"

"It's better than nothing. But from what I saw, our very existence..."

"Attention!"

Eric recognized the voice of the director as it rang through the laboratory halls over the intercom. "As you know, a train of meteoroids have been spotted. They are on a direct collision course with earth. All personnel are ordered to stay in the building. Go immediately to underground testing section 703. Remain calm. All of you will be safe."

703?

It was the room he guarded daily. Every time he'd asked, he'd been told the room housed a new, highly theoretical technology. He'd once heard a rumor that the device was supposed to allow the user to travel through space and time. He'd laughed at that thought. He'd believed they were pulling his leg, but now he wasn't sure.

Could this be real?

Color rushed from James's face. "703? But ... it's not ready for trials, let alone human trials ..."

Did that mean this thing ... *was* real?

People continued to rush past. No one seemed to have even heard the order. One woman cried. A man kept stumbling backwards as he held a hand to his forehead.

Eric turned back to James. "Go to room 703 like the director said. Forget everything else. Do *not* stop by your office."

Surprisingly, James nodded and rushed down the hall. Satisfied, Eric turned back to the rest of the crowd. He spotted Nick. His co-worker wandered aimlessly in the center of the mob as if trying to figure out who to help first.

You would have been a lot more help at your post!

Eric ran up to him, shoving frantic people out of his way as he moved. "Nick! I need you to get the opposite side." He motioned to the far side of the hallway's entrance. "We have to direct the crowd to 703!"

Nick looked up, his eyes reigniting with life. He nodded and rushed to his designated location, tapping people on the shoulders and offering short directives as he moved past.

Eric moved back towards his spot, waving his arms. "People! Get to 703 *now*!" He grabbed a man who was frantically picking up papers scattered on the floor. "Leave those! Go to 703. Now."

Finally, the scientists started to get the idea, allowing themselves to be directed. The progress was slow. There were many people in the facility, all attempting to pile through a single hallway.

Soon enough, the crowd had almost emptied from the foyer its end. Optimism buoyed in Eric until one woman made a sudden break for the door. "My kids! I have to go find my kids!"

There's always one.

Eric chased her. The female scientist was no match for his speed. He came upon her before she made it down the first step out of the building. He grabbed her shoulders firmly.

She cried out, pulling against his grip. "I have kids, a husband! I have to get them!" Her trembling hand reached toward the parking lot.

Sympathy shot through him, but how could he let her disregard her own safety?

"Your only chance is to follow directions. There's no time."

"I don't care!" she wailed. "I won't live if they can't!"

Eric's face darkened, and he lost the will to fight the woman any longer. He released her, and she scampered to her car.

This could be it. He looked up to the sky. More flashes of light streaked across, only lasting a moment. They did no harm, but it heralded what was to come. *The end for everyone.*

Eric's feet moved on their own. His body's desire to live propelled him back into the facility.

What do I do now? He didn't have an answer, not now. But he still ran.

Eric entered the front doors of the large lab. He scanned the crowd. It appeared most people had made it into 703. He had to make sure though. With a jog that turned into a sprint, he moved from room to room to check for any stragglers. Thankfully there didn't seem to be any, but he knew that he had just wasted a lot of time. Everyone was gone now, everyone except him. Seeing that his task was done and all the staff had been corralled, he made his way to room 703 and stepped into the elevator, finally going past the station he had guarded for so long.

The elevator whirred to a start and sped downward. Anxiety tightened Eric's throat, making it hard to breathe. He'd wasted too much time. The meteoroids could crash at any moment. And if the facility lost power, he'd be done for.

Would it really be that bad? Do I deserve to live?

He allowed thoughts—memories—to push into his mind. Ones he'd tucked away behind a brick wall around his heart. Money wasn't the only reason he'd joined the Marine Corp—not really. He'd thought that maybe the only way to make up for his past sins was to give all of himself—to sacrifice his life for something useful. But it hadn't worked out that way. He'd ended up here. Too safe.

Too safe.

He looked to his hands, hands that had caused so much pain. Why did he deserve to be here? After all he'd done...

The elevator opened revealing a massive room. Four large cylinders, one at each corner of the room, were filled with energy rhythmically pulsating through them. Connected to them with thick cords at the room's center was a large machine.

It stood at least twenty feet high. Two large arches crossed over each other to form an X. A brilliant white light shone underneath them, giving the appearance of a large orb. The last stragglers of the crowd fearfully made their way into the light. Good, he hadn't been completely left behind yet.

Motion caught his attention, and he spotted Nick waving his arms from the machine's base. "Eric! Quick! They said it's unstable, we don't know how long it will hold!"

A loud crack sounded from above. A great force rippled through the facility, rattling everything in the room. The generators started to grind, causing the light to fluctuate sporadically.

Only one explanation crossed Eric's mind. *The first meteorite has hit.*

Eric frantically waved him forward, sprinting across the wide opening. Nick stepped into the light, melting into it during the last step as if he'd turned light himself. The sight stopped Eric in his tracks.

I'm supposed to walk into something like that? Are they crazy?

Cautiously, he made his way towards it—the sheer brightness of the device now making his steps difficult. He lifted an arm to shield his eyes as he tried not to stumble up the last step.

His foot touched the step, and then the ground boiled and shook beneath him. The sickening sound of rock meeting rock thundered. They were deep underground. What did that mean for the world above? Did Seattle even exist anymore?

All four of the generators burst in unison, showering the entire room in sparks. The teleportation device wavered. Light and energy ebbed from it, twisting unnaturally. Yet despite losing its power source, it continued to run.

Eric's whole body burned from the rivers of vibrations sent through him. It took all his strength not collapse. With a final effort, he threw himself forward, following Nick into the river of light.

White enveloped him.

And then, only darkness.

Chapter Two

A person's longing can make him do uncharacteristic things. If left unchecked, longing can bring even the most level-headed person to acts of insanity.

Everyone wants something. There isn't a person on this planet who could say there was nothing more he could want from life. It's basic human nature.

But how can I want something that I've never had? Why do I long for something that I've never even dreamed of? Try as I might, I don't even know what it is.

The open field flew beneath the transporter shuttle. Nothing more to see than grass and the occasional brush or tree. Yet Aeia couldn't look away. Anytime she tried, a tickle bothered the back of her mind, prodding her to remain alert to her surroundings.

She wasn't in dangerous situations often. She spent most of her time either in a locked room or in transit to another province—as was the case today. As a Void Jumper, she was always well-informed before heading into danger. She was far too valuable to be lost over something trivial.

Her position required very specific duties, and she had no life outside of work. Most people didn't even know of her kind's existence. Her skills went beyond what even the most energetic of imaginations could conjure up. It was how her superiors meant it to be, which is why she only interacted with the upper class, the noblemen.

Aeia pulled her cowl over her head, the cloth sliding easily over her short blue hair. The air was still and sterile within the transporter, and she longed to breathe fresh air. She longed for the breeze to brush her skin. But that was not possible.

She wore plain clothes, a brown hooded robe with a leather belt, which hid her frame so that at a glance, she figured she looked like a boy.

Not that it would matter. No one would know her name if mentioned. Aeia wasn't a noblewoman herself, neither was she a commoner. She didn't have a single coin to her name. No, Aeia was another class entirely, a being she considered to be far worse.

If she'd been given a choice, she would far rather be a peasant, half-starving on the street, than what she was now. The fine clothing and luxuries given to her were not nearly enough pay for what she was forced to do. In fact, she couldn't imagine there'd ever be enough pay. She wished that people like her didn't exist at all. The world would be a much better place without her kind, the Void Jumpers.

A seed of discomfort spouted deep inside at those thoughts, but she couldn't express it without risk, and she couldn't let her lifelong cover be exposed. She held this one secret, a secret she had managed to keep for years.

Aeia looked at her partner on this mission, a boy named Sen. He was her age. They'd trained together as far back as she could remember. But it had been years now since they'd a proper conversation. He was complete, his personality was locked away never to return.

She studied his face. Not a muscle moved despite his being fully awake and aware. Even if only from a side view, his eyes threatened to suck her in. There was nothing behind them. All his humanity had ebbed away. This was not the boy she'd once known. He was no more a human than the chair she sat on.

A Void Jumper like him was perfect in the minds of her superiors. A Jumper's power was dangerous, and someone like Sen would never think to rebel. Or even think at all.

Quietly, she slipped her feet out of her shoes and pressed them against the cold metal floor. Shivers traveled up her spine as the floor sapped all heat from her. The cold was uncomfortable, but that was why she loved it. It was terrible, but it was an easy, subtle way to remind herself that she was real. That her mind hadn't been stolen from her yet.

It was one small thing she could do that wouldn't get noticed. She did everything she could to retain her secret, even going as far as completely mimicking the others so that she would not stand out. So far that had worked, but she knew she would be found out eventually.

Why haven't I become complete yet?

Sen had become complete three years ago, and he was one of the last to go. Yet Aeia still retained herself, as if she had built an immunity to the mental refining that she was continually forced to undergo.

She turned back to the window, her breath fogging the glass. The outskirts of the city Feos started to appear below. The shuttle hovered not too far above the ground, close enough to give the illusion that it might scrape the tops of the farmhouses they glided over– farmhouses which grew in number the closer they got to civilization.

Aiea's eyes drank in the wide-open farmlands. *So peaceful out here.*

As if to contradict her, the shuttle passed a couple in the midst of an argument. They waved their arms wildly at each other near a broken cart.

So much aggression. You don't know how lucky you have it.

Aeia wished she could be like them—normal—with relatively little care about the world. She hadn't chosen this position, and she didn't want it. If she were given the opportunity to sacrifice all she had to live on some farm, she would take it in a heartbeat.

I can't afford to think like this. She sat back in her seat. *It's not like I can change who I am.*

Aeia looked downwards as the cityscape appeared below, watching in wonder as the people went about their daily lives.

She looked at a man who trudged along the side of the road. He bore no burden, yet he acted like he was carrying a boulder on his back. She looked at a few more, ordinary people who behaved in similar ways.

They aren't happy either, I guess. No one is in this world.

Why did that seem so wrong to her? It was the way things had always been, yet every day she looked out her window with hope for something different, for the world to somehow magically change overnight.

It was foolish, and foolishness got you killed.

Footsteps echoed as one of the crew walked past her seat. Aeia straightened up and immediately lost all emotion on her face, hid the deep sorrow she felt.

It worked, and she was indiscernible from the others. Another crewman walked by without a second glance, not noticing the one living soul among the walking corpses.

This was the mask she had to wear. And she hated it.

The crew prepared to disembark as the ship sank downward to land. She breathed slow breaths, not affording to take off her mask for even a moment. The hovercraft landed, and she stood in unison with Sen and followed him out into the open air. Outside the shuttle door, a crowd talked among themselves as they waited in front of a large stage.

The pungent aroma of sweat and dirt filled her nostrils. It was followed with the slightest bit of perfume from the few nobles in the audience. The deafening thunder caused by a thousand-people chattering among themselves pricked her ears. Everyone caring only for his own conversation, his own desires.

Another thing people shared.

She looked upon the crowd. A tint of blue covered them all, only disturbed by the occasional hat. But despite a great deal of effort, she couldn't find another person who wore a cowl. *These are supposed to blend us into the crowd?*

Aeia stepped gracefully down the final step, pulling back her hood as she did so. She took her position beside Sen next to the lucky noblemen she was assigned to.

Sir Allence was a simple man who owned no more than a few shops, hardly the bearer of a renowned family name.

He took a small, yet noticeable, step away from her as they started towards their seats.

Despite the reaction's commonality, it still stung a bit.

It's not like I'm not a human...

She focused on the mission at hand. She looked at each of the faces of the noblemen waiting in seats on the makeshift stage. None of them matched the description she had been given. Lord Hattin *would* show up. It was his rally, after all.

It should be an easy task. The nobles here are too far down the chain to know anything about Jumpers. I'll make this quick...

Aeia's chest tightened. *If the monthly refinements won't take my soul, this will.*

In no other mission had Aeia killed. She had been able to work around that. Only once had she kill someone by Jumping. It had been during her first trial run. And even when compared to everything else she'd done, it was the most horrific thing she'd ever experienced.

A shiver went up her spine as she remembered the loud 'snap' that echoed through her previous target's mind, the sound of consciousness breaking. That sound had been followed by the collapse of all the man's thought and function.

She'd vowed at the time that she would never do it again. And so far, she'd been successful. But now there were no other options. Her instructions were far too clear on what she had to do. No information retrieval, no incapacitation, just execution.

Maybe this was a test to see if she truly was complete. Maybe they had finally figured her out.

One too many excuses ... Now there can be none.

Her emotions bubbled up despite herself as she struggled against the impossible situation. She didn't *want* to kill anyone. *I hate this. I hate this life ...*

Aeia's mask of disregard wavered, drawing the attention of her noble escort. Her heart lurched as she struggled to regain control. Finally, emotion drained from her face, and the mask affixed again.

The Nobleman probably wouldn't say anything. Her reaction had been small, and most people feared her too much to say anything out of turn. He would probably just hope that she wouldn't turn on him after the mission was over.

Just do the job and go home.

She followed Sen as they took their seats near the middle of the large circle of city folk. Ahead, more Nobles stepped onto the stage. They sat in chairs that were prepared for them—their houses' insignia were etched into the wooden backrests. She read the names

Feu, Molna, Henshiir ... All local lords. Is this a town meeting?

She scanned the crowd, spotting the rare feathered hat or mantle. Most people wore little more than rags, although a few seemed to have chosen their nicest clothes for the event, despite their apparent lack of wealth.

Why would Lord Cer care about a town meeting? And why would my target even be here? She paused. *Unless he's going to ask them for support.*

She was sent to kill a man named Lord Hattin, who was an influential merchant whom everyone expected to join the Merchant's Board soon. He was very rich and shouldn't be anywhere near a simple town meeting.

What is going on here?

The mask slipped again, and she hoped no one spotted the new emotion. Fear.

Chapter Three

A low humming grew into a deafening roar, the source of the noise casting a shadow that covered the entire square. A massive ship hovered overhead, stopping just above the stage. Aeia glanced upward.

The ship bore no weapons—not a single ballista sat on its deck. It was nothing more than a trade vessel. Painted on its metal hull sat the increasingly famous insignia of house Hattin.

There you are.

Its bottom slid open, and a lone man dropped gracefully onto the stage. His rapid descent was slowed dramatically by the lifters attached to the sole of his boots and palms of his hands.

He was tall and surprisingly well built for a noble. Judging by a glance, she assumed that he'd had many years of labor in his youth before rising to his status. She scanned the crowd, noticing respect for the noble on the people's faces—for who he was, but more than that, for who'd he'd been.

Lord Hattin wore simple garb suited for someone much below his status. The trimmings that decorated even the least of nobles were nowhere to be found on his attire.

He must be trying to appeal to the commoners, get on their level. But what of the noble attendees?

His ship took to the sky, though not straying out of view. Even though the man's garb was simple, his craft told them all they needed to know of his magnificence.

Appealing to both classes, I see.

The duke strode up to the podium in a fashion that maintained his grace. "Thank you all for taking time to come here today. I know you lead busy lives, so I'll make this as quick as I can."

Aeia forced back a smirk. *I was right, he's going to ask them for something.*

"This great city was once a beacon to those throughout the kingdom. It was a city of life and hope. Even in the small village I was born in, I would hear of this city only in a good light."

The man spoke with confidence, but also with humility. His gestures were graceful and complimented his words and made her feel as if he were speaking to a friend.

"However, in recent years, that golden era has come to an end, and I'm sure you all have felt it as well." Hattin's face darkened, his striking features shadowed as he hid his face. He began to pace, his hands meeting behind his back.

"The great lords, as useful as they were in restoring order to our world, are slowly and inevitably shifting for the worse. The darkness that is washing over this land only goes to show this to be true."

He raised his arm, motioning towards fortress Cer in the distance. "Here we are, protected by the house of Cer, the house that has governed us for hundreds of years. Most of that time, they did a wonderful job. Scarcely did we hunger or go without a place to sleep. We never worried that our leaders would fight amongst each other over trivial matters. Or fight against other provinces unless under the most dire of circumstances."

Hattin paused and turned to the crowd. "But has that been the case these past fifteen years? Do you, the younger in the crowd, even remember the city I'm speaking of?"

He shook his head, feigning a disgusted spit. "No, the head of the house of Cer has made sure that you won't remember as long as he is in power. Before his reign, it would have been impossible to find so many homeless on the streets, to find so many families struggling to stay alive.

"Our city is set on a course for destruction, and even the wealthiest of families will not survive."

A handful of nobles, including her own escort, shuffled in their seats.

They really are worried.

"What has this to do with me? I'm a Nobleman myself, as you can see. But I too know these hardships. I have been without both food and home. And I tell you this: I would wish that on no man. But I alone do not have the power to change our fate. I need each one of you to lend me your strength."

He was publicly speaking about a rebellion?

It wasn't unprecedented. One had occurred even in her lifetime. Of course, it had failed, just as this one would.

"What strength?" A man called from the crowd. "He has the Bask. What can we do?"

Aeia could tell that the man had been sent, the man's shout staged. The crowd was completely enthralled with Hattin, and the outcry had been just a bit too sudden.

"You needn't worry about that. I have a plan to change that fate."

A muscle in her jaw twitched involuntarily. *He must either be very confident or very foolish. Lord Cer will hear everything he says today.*

Every single piece of Bask had been accounted for, she knew, and was in the hands of noblemen. Any Bask given had to be taken from someone else. How could Hattin expect to provide the people with strength when their source—the Bask—was beyond their reach?

Hattin cleared his throat. "Together, we can create a new world, one ruled by the people instead of by *tyrants*. No man should be bound as tight as we are. And so, I ask you join with me!"

The climax of the speech.

That was when she was ordered to end him. She lifted a small light that was designed to catch the attention of a speaker while not creating any visible mark on the target. She aimed it in his direction. As expected, Hattin looked to her subconsciously as he spoke.

They locked eyes.

Aeia's world grew dark, everything except Hattin's eyes fading away. The discomfort of the cheap seat in which she sat went numb, and her mind lost touch with her body's senses.

She focused harder while the final disconnects happened. Her body faded in the background. Her mind became free of the burden, she prepared to Void Jump---

An explosion from behind snapped her back, all her senses flooding in without restraint. Dizziness spun her, and she couldn't maintain her mental hold.

What was—?

Another explosion went off, closer to her this time. The concussion knocked her out of her seat, throwing her and her escort to the ground.

Pulse bombs!

She looked up, her suspicions confirmed. What used to be shuttles, which had carried her and the other important guests to the arena, were now were nothing more than piles of torn and twisted metal, destroyed by bursts of Bask energy.

Who set them off? Lord Cer himself sent me here! He wouldn't mess up a Jump assassination like that!

Right now, it didn't matter. She had to finish the mission.

Struggling to catch her breath, she climbed to her feet. Despite the attack, Lord Hattin still stood on the stage, wide-eyed from the sudden intrusion. With slow steps, he backed away from the crowds. His own ship still hovered above him. With one motion, it could be at his ready, but he didn't run, didn't flee.

Keeping face amidst this?

Either way, it was the perfect opportunity. Aeia pushed past the panicked masses. She made her way towards the outer edges of the square, an open path to the stage and her target.

Hattin was too overstimulated to be drawn in by her light a second time. She had to get within his view if she were to try another jump.

Free of the crowd, Aeia broke into a sprint. Her frail body strained at the sudden effort, but she ignored its complaints and charged forward.

Hattin glanced her way, though too quickly for her to start her Jump.

Suddenly, her momentum vanished and a force pulled her back. Her weight, little as it was, did not compete with the strength that redirected her.

Hands gripped her arms and pulled her into an alley. She tugged against whoever had her, and the grip released, sending her rolling. Her face hit the ground first, and pain shot through her cheek.

"Oh, sorry." An unfamiliar voice mumbled. "You're faster than you look. Almost missed you there."

She hopped to her feet, annoyance boiling up. Her vigor vanished as she looked at her assailant. She shrunk back, knowing she was no match for the mountain of the man who stood before her.

As small as Aeia was, the top of her head reached only to his chest. He wore a thick black cloak that covered most of his features. The gap in the hood revealed a mask that covered his face. It too was black and had a small white pattern that spiraled outward from the center.

A chill shot down her arms as she saw the eyes of the mask. Thick glass, impenetrable. Without being able to connect her gaze with his, she could not Jump. Aeia felt as powerless as a small child, and she had a feeling the man smiled behind that mask. He'd prepared for this, prepared to block her power. But how had he known she was coming, and what did he want with her?

Chapter Four

Aeia shuffled back a pace, her usual feeling of strength over others now gone. She compared her physique to her opponent's. She'd spent countless idle hours in a small room, not that working out would have changed her odds.

She was used to wearing an emotionless mask, however, and took this approach. Aeia didn't reward her attacker with a reaction as she looked him square on. If nothing else, she could *appear* a dangerous target.

The man lifted his hands. "I don't intend to harm you. In fact, quite the opposite."

"It looks like you're more worried about me hurting *you*," she noted, motioning towards his mask.

The man's raised hands swept outward. "Well, yes. My plan did involve catching a Jumper by surprise. I know how dangerous a surprised Jump can be to the target."

"Jumper's don't feel emotion," she said as plainly as she could muster.

"Ah." His voice was conversational, as if he hadn't just attacked her. As if they were chatting over tea. "For most Jumpers, yes.

But not you." Slowly he reached up, unlatched the mask, and removed it. He eyed it and then tucked it beneath his cloak.

He had a short beard. His skin was slightly wrinkled around his deep eyes. His lips were curled in a genuine smile, one that threatened to disarm even the most hostile of people.

"Is that better?"

She recognized him faintly, although where she had seen him before, she didn't know.

Be careful. He could be an inspector working for Lord Cer Testing her ability to complete a mission ...

A large rumbling echoed through the alleyway as Lord Hattin's ship took off into the sky. If this man was an inspector, she had already failed.

Aeia focused on his beard, not wanting a Jump to start just yet. "Who are you, and what do you want?"

"I am merely a whisper in the ears of those who stand for what's right. An invisible chain that binds many small groups together. But you can call me what I was once called, Eugho."

She recognized the name immediately. "You aren't...?"

He nodded. "I was known as Guard-Captain Eugho, yes."

She took a step back. This man had once been in control of the largest army in the world, the king's royal guard. Within it he was best known for utterly crushing the rebellion during the civil war. He is all but legend among the nobles.

"You're dead." Aeia stated.

"Yes, I am." He nodded, his strange smile solidly in place. "And it's actually quite convenient."

She remembered the day Eugho had died. She was close enough to hear the explosion. That event sent the entire kingdom into an uproar. The largest warship had crashed to the ground for no apparent reason is not something anyone could ignore.

A dozen questions popped into her mind. She tried to maintain the mask, but her curiosity overwhelmed her.

"What do you want with me?"

He looked over his shoulder, the chaos surrounding the recent event growing. The crowd darted in all directions, theirs included.

"Come with me, and I'll tell you."

I'm supposed to head straight to the nearest guard post in times like these. Not doing so could mean...

"I won't force you to come," Eugho said. "But are you happy? You aren't complete—I know that. I can see the mask you wear—it's quite similar to mine." He opened his cloak to show the mask again with a smirk. "Only I get to take mine off."

She ever so slightly furrowed her brows.

"There *is* a way out." Eugho prodded. "There always is."

Leaving with this man would mean death if she were caught. Or worse, her superiors finding out that her consciousness still existed and she was retrained to completion. Yet the man's words echoed through her mind. *There is a way out.*

"They'll catch me," she whispered. But she knew she'd either lose her life now—going with this man—or when she was finally found out. By then, who knew how many people she might have killed.

It was that truth, coupled with the tiniest amount of lingering hope, that caused her to slowly look up to the man. "I'll go."

His face softened, and he nodded respectfully before leading her down a dark alley, one that none of the others dared go down. Eugho took off his cloak and flipped it inside out. it now shone a light brown. He hung it more loosely, revealing his clothes underneath, common garb.

He moved as if he were out for an evening stroll. Aeia tried to replicate him, but her old habits of traveling were too deeply ingrained. She looked straight forward. Her feet hardly touched the ground as she glided down the street.

The further they got away from the bomb site the more people they saw who were out in the open. None looked at her for longer than a passing glance, but she expected them to recognize her and alert her handlers.

It's only a matter of time. She scanned the skies, waiting for the inevitable shuttle to swoop down and snatch her up, taking her back to her cell.

This is a terrible idea. Even with my heritage, I'll still likely be killed for running. The thought wouldn't leave her mind.

Her heartbeat quickened, and her throat tightened into a knot. She balled her fists at her sides and then released them, realizing her obvious tension would hinder her attempt at blending in. She focused on the road in front of her.

"Relax, all right?"

She glanced up.

Eugho smiled reassuringly. "They won't find you."

"How can you know? I'm dangerous, and they'll do anything to get me back—or have me killed."

"Despite his cruelty, Cer is as predictable as any other noble. He won't be finished searching the city for weeks. And in a few hours, we won't be in the city. Besides"—he patted her back— "he won't know why you left."

Aeia let out a sigh. Eugho was right. To Lord Cer, she was supposed to be as obedient as any other Jumper. He'll be expecting her to be lost in the chaos or killed during the attack.

She marveled at Eugho's optimism and forced a herself to stroll.

The man eyed her clumsy attempt at appearing normal, visibly holding back a chuckle. "Don't rush yourself. You have all the time in the world."

All the time in the world...

Could that really be true? Was she dreaming? Tomorrow, would she wake up back in the closet of a room at the fortress?

Aiea looked at each person as she walked by them, instinctively wanting to hide her face. She expected the people to be like those at the castle, glaring at her or looking away in fear. But oddly, not one person treated her like that. They were all wrapped up in their own lives. To them, she was just another face among the masses.

It was surreal and ... refreshing. For so long, people around her acted like she had a loaded crossbow pointed at them, just waiting for a reason to shoot. But even Eugho was treating her like ...

a person.

Excitement shot through her, and she couldn't hold back a whole-body squirm. Nobody noticed. Nobody even glanced her way.

But ... what do normal people do?

Looking around, she saw the commoners all moved with a purpose. They headed from one place to another and made no stops in between.

But can I ever really be like them? Am I ever going to be normal?

It had been nearly ten years since she was normal. Would she be able to revert? Or would she be stuck as an outsider for the rest of her life? It was better than being a Jumper, no doubt, but the idea scared her.

Another part of her stirred. Aeia had grown accustomed to being a Jumper. Not in the way of killing, or stealing information, but she couldn't imagine life without a mission looming in the future. She feared that she would grow restless and not able to enjoy a simple life.

"Eugho?" she said, simultaneously testing out the name. "What is that job you mentioned earlier? What would I be doing?"

"I phrased it poorly when I called it that. It's not so much a job as an invitation." He paused for a moment, bringing a hand up to stroke his chin. "Tell me, what do you know about the nobility?"

"That's not an easy question." She mulled for a moment. "I guess they're just people who gained power."

A flicker of something passed through his eyes. The side of his lip curled slightly. "What power specifically?"

She pondered for a few moments. "Bask?"

"Precisely!" He waved a finger through the air. "While nobles gain influence and social powers, the one thing that sets them on an entirely different level from commoners is the owning of Bask stones. If they have that, then their power is secure. The position cannot be taken from them, as it is the highest offense to steal the stones. And because of that, those without Bask rely on the generosity of those who have it."

She looked at the ground as she deciphered the meaning of his words. People are born needing Bask. They must charge themselves a few times a week to stay healthy, at least once a week to stay alive. The reliance on the stone was the one thing that nobles and commoners both have in common. The difference was, the nobles were the ones who owned the stones.

Aeia had never had any difficulty charging herself, since she worked for the nobles, but Bask starvation was becoming a great issue these days. The taxes commoners had to pay to get their weekly charges were going up, and many had difficulty paying. If you didn't pay, then you didn't get to charge.

The train of thought brought an idea to the forefront of her mind. Eugho bore an amused grin, raising his eyebrows as he waited for her to speak.

"Why are the taxes going up?"

"Most would think to line the pockets of those in charge. However, I think there's something more going on. Either way, if they have the Bask, no one can stop them. Anyone who tries to fight them won't last a week."

It was true. No rebellion had been successful in their entire history of six hundred years. The money it took to supply an army with constant Bask charges was humongous. If there were a rebellion, and if the rebels could get enough money to buy that much Bask, the money trail would lead the Guard Captain and his men straight to the rebel leaders, as had happened in the past.

That wasn't even considering that Bask itself was easy to find. The energy it radiated could be seen by a Hunstman from miles away. No one could hope to hide it for long.

"Now," Eugho interrupted her thoughts. "I still believe there is a way."

She wasn't so sure.

"Obviously, no commoner can hope to fight against the nobility. However, commoners aren't the only ones who don't like the system. There are some nobles who aren't happy with the way things are either."

Eugho motioned back the way they came. "Take Lord Hattin, for example. He worked his way up from the bottom. He's a rare case among nobles, one who's seen loved ones die from Bask starvation. He knows the way the noblemen behave is wrong, and he's trying to stop them in his own way."

She cocked her head sideways. "Do you work with him?"

His face darkened, and he shook his head. "We've met. He's a good man, but his way won't change anything. He thinks the system is fine under good leadership—*his* leadership. But what good will that do? How can we know his son won't be even more corrupt a leader than Lord Cer?"

Eugho shook his head. "Hattin's way will only be good for a couple generations at best. You can be sure that our descendants will find themselves in the same struggle that we're in today."

"Your plan will work better?"

He nodded. "I believe so. You see, if the nobility holds the Bask like a resource, there will always be greed. I believe no one man should be able to hold onto Bask. We need to make sure everyone is taken care of first, before anything else."

Aeia tipped her head, studying Eugho. He sounded noble, just like the stories she had heard about him. If he was honest, then his plan would gain nothing for himself personally. Would someone work so hard without hope for a reward?

"Can you imagine a world where no one has to worry about needing to charge with Bask?" Eugho continued. "Where none of the noblemen can steal the ability to survive from those too weak to stop them? Just think about how different the world would be if everyone had their own permanent Bask stone to charge themselves with."

It sounded too good to be true. No one did anything without the promise of something. Was Eugho really fighting only for the common people? What else did he want?

"If you want," Eugho said, "I'll let you hear my plan before you make your decision."

She stumbled, losing all composure. "You would trust me?"

She couldn't tell if he was manipulative or a fool. She could turn around and tell Lord Cer about Eugho's plan before he even had the chance to embark on it. Why would he trust someone he didn't even know?

Eugho didn't answer. He hooked his thumbs on his belt as he walked.

She narrowed her eyes. "What happens if I say no?"

He lifted his head, studying her, too. "I know some people. People who would be more than willing to take you in, get you started in life." He closed his eyes, rocking his head back and forth. "They're a bit old, but then again, you aren't exactly a child yourself."

Aeia stood straight. "Move in with someone? A permanent location? They'll find me."

"Trust me." Eugho looked her square in the eyes, an act of complete vulnerability to a Jumper. "You'd be safe, I'd make sure of that. You can live your life without worry."

A flutter appeared in her stomach, spreading. Could he really be suggesting what she thought he was?

Aeia's mind wandered back to the villages she had visited. They always felt so ... warm. Their people lived their lives with relatively little care beyond the next day's dinner. No stuffy manners or women with perfume caked on so thick that she could hardly breathe. Instead she would find wide open farm lands and simple meal cooked over a stone stove.

Her fantasy grew, as did her excitement. Her mind placed her in those villages. Somehow, she fit so *well* there.

But as if even the thought was forbidden, her temple itched. She reached up, feeling it. There wasn't anything visible, but below the skin sat her curse, one that could never be removed.

It reminded her what she was. It reminded her that no matter where she went, she wouldn't be able to make true connections with a new family. She couldn't even look someone in the eyes without great self-control. How would the villagers handle it? She knew how important trust was to people.

"I'm sorry that I can't help with your Void Link," Eugho noted, his face dark. "That's beyond what even I can do. No one outside of Cer fortress knows how the Void Jumpers work."

She shook her head and looked away. "I know. I'm used to it."

In truth, the knowledge of who she was—what she'd become—ate away at her. It wasn't natural. This was one of the biggest reasons Void Jumpers were conditioned to be emotionless—the lack of human connection was maddening.

"They know what you are, though. The couple who would take you in, they're fine with it."

Aeia looked back to him. Her brow furrowed as she thought about it all. Eugho gave her space to think as they journeyed on, making their way to the edge of the city.

The commercial buildings and signs soon faded, replaced with old buildings that would barely provide shelter from a storm. The people here looked just as worn, hardly looking up at them as they passed.

In the distance sat a beacon of life, a beautiful shuttle hidden at the end of an alleyway. It shimmered in the light, an oddity in this section of the city.

A noble's no doubt.

It did bear noble insignia, as all shuttles did these days. She didn't recognize it, so it had to either be from outside the province or from a house she hadn't had contact with.

The doors opened by a wave of a hand from Eugho. Before he stepped inside, he turned to face her.

"Where shall I take you? I will not lie—being with me will be dangerous from here on out. Whatever you do past this point is your choice, I will never order you to do anything you don't want to."

She pretended to think, though she had already made her choice. As much as she wanted the other life, the simple country life, she wanted more for Eugho's vision to come true. And maybe, someday, she would be able to look out her window and see something different.

"I'll hear what you have to say," Aeia sighed. "I'm coming with you."

Chapter Five

Myr strode down a long hallway, her long blue hair wafting from side to side with each step. She moved at a quicker pace than usual as she prepared herself to uncover the identity of whoever it was who would do something so bold.

That was supposed to be a peaceful meeting. A chance to learn more about Lord Hattin and his intentions.

Who would launch such an open attack? There had been many nobles there, some who were very influential. Not even someone as mad as Alonius Cer would risk such an attack.

But if it wasn't Cer, then who? Who had something to gain from that meeting's disruption?

The woman reached the end of the hallway where a large stone door awaited. Two men in full battle suits stood at each side. Neither hesitated in unlocking and opening the door once they saw who was coming.

Myr didn't even have to break stride as she entered the room, and a deep *thud* echoed as the door closed behind her.

Men and women filled the room, all pouring over various screens as they went about their work. One man tore himself away when he heard Myr enter the room. He stood to meet her.

"Captain, no serious injuries have been reported in Feos," Jak began. "The only damage were the four targeted shuttles. The blasts were relatively small."

Myr cocked her head to the side. *Odd.* "How many of our eyes were at the location?"

"Four, ma'am. All were able to return with their footage intact."

Myr nodded with a slight smile. "Excellent work, Jak."

He returned the nod and fell in stride beside her as she headed toward the back of the room.

"We just finished the reconstruction," he said, "but we haven't been able to pinpoint a suspect yet."

"Bombings are always difficult. The culprit was probably long gone by the time the explosives went off."

"Yes." His pause felt meaningful, and she waited for him to continue. Finally, he did. "This situation just seems *strange*. It was clearly meant to disrupt the meeting, and yet no one has taken claim for the attack. If it isn't a show of power by a Nobleman, then who would care enough to go through with it?"

Myr sighed. "My question exactly. I'll need to see it for myself."

Jak peeled off as they neared a door and shuffled to a terminal just to its side. Myr went straight through and entered a large chamber.

A strong sensation washed through her as the room came to life. The sound of echoing boots against metal floors changed to that of clacking against cobblestone as she headed towards the chamber's center.

One by one, portions of the room changed before her. A smooth wind blew across her face, bringing with it the smells of the inner city and its many inhabitants. The gray ceiling transformed to that of the wide-open and blue skies, only dotted with sparse clouds. The simulation of Feos became lifelike for Myr.

Next came the sound of a thousand-people squirming in their seats, followed by the loud and commanding voice of Lord Hattin as he gave his speech. The forms of the people creating these sounds soon followed, along with anything and everything that was in that courtyard earlier that very day. "This is currently five minutes before the attack," Jak's voice sounded in her ear. "The four shuttles attacked are … *these*."

A select four, out of the many shuttles at the foot of the event, changed color and became completely white.

Myr nodded. "Understood."

At this point the bombs would have already been planted. She turned towards the images of the crowd and walked among them. *Let's see if anyone is anticipating the attack.*

She scanned the faces, looking out for any signs of apprehension. At a meeting like this, people were worried about trouble, but there was a key difference between fear of danger and expectation of it. If she could find at least one person who seemed to be expecting it...

"Jak, help me out here. Does anyone look unusually scared to you?"

She walked through the rows, attempting to read as many people as she could.

"I only saw a couple when I went through on my screen. The lady *here*, and the man over *here* both caught my attention." Two people flashed white.

Myr raised a hand to halt the program as she moved to inspect the first woman. There *was* fear there, but it seemed to be coming from a man who was sitting in the row behind her. She was poor, her clothes too unkempt to be a disguise. Myr moved on to the man. He was a bit more promising, looked to be a young nobleman. At a glance, she could tell that the man was indeed afraid of *something*, but that something was a bit more immediate. He leaned to the side, as far away from his neighbor as he could. He struggled to keep a calm appearance, but the beads of sweat on his brow betrayed him.

But ... the person to his side was nothing more than a small girl. She had short, almost boyish hair, and was very frail.

That man is afraid of her?

the girl didn't look mature enough to be the man's wife, nor did she share enough features to be his daughter. Yet both wore the same noble insignia.

"Jak, got any idea who this man is?"

"Mar Allence, it says. A pretty small house. Just owns a couple of shops here in Feos. He seems to be the first of his family who has gained noble status."

Myr let out a disinterested grunt. "What about the girl?"

"Let's check the database here Her name is Alora Mari. Looks like both of her parents are deceased. A typical street orphan. She's likely employed by Sir Allence here."

Why don't I believe that ...? Myr looked closely at the girl before shaking her head. "Neither of these are our bombers."

She waved her hand, starting the simulation again. "How long until the explosions?"

"Twenty-eight seconds."

Myr jogged to the front and onto the stage where Hattin stood. She turned and faced the audience.

All right now. Give yourself away.

"Four." Jak counted down. "Three ... two ..."

All four of the shuttles exploded simultaneously. The shock wave threw nearly everyone to the ground.

Destructive, yet controlled. Myr raised a hand, halting the simulation.

The pulse bombs seemed to be carefully placed in such a way that no one would get caught in the initial bursts of energy. Meaning that whoever did this took great care to ensure that no one was hurt.

Already, that ruled out a lot of suspects. Hattin had enemies, of course. Every one of his status did. Yet none seemed to be people who would care about the lives of a few commoners. Maybe that was presumptuous, but her hunch was that this was not a grapple for political power. Whoever did this had a different goal in mind.

But that makes them so much more difficult to catch. I must figure out what they wanted.

Myr narrowed her eyes, lowering her hand to start the simulation again. *If damage or loss of life isn't what they sought, then that means that what happens directly after the explosion is what really counts.*

She searched the crowd, looking past the expected panicked reactions of all who were caught unaware. Quickly enough she spotted her first unusual reaction. More like a *pair* of people with unusual reactions.

One was the girl named Alora and the other a young boy. While everyone else rushed to escape the streets furthest away from the explosions, those two seemed to be moving toward the stage, the girl completely abandoning her Nobleman.

Myr jogged to her first. Something wasn't right.

The girl charged off to the side, toward the steps that led to the stage where Hattin still stood. The side of her disappeared as she ran, the girl running on the very edge of the recording's range. But the girl's goal was clear, so Myr stayed right next to her.

Alora circled around a frantic man, stepping outside of the recording completely. But Myr kept the pace and waited for the girl to re-enter once they neared the stage.

She never did.

Myr waited, watched the spot where Alora should have appeared moments ago. When the girl still didn't appear, Myr looked around for other possible entry points.

Where did she ...?

She had obviously been after Hattin. And at the speed she'd been going, nothing but an immediate change in direction would have kept her from re-entering the recording's range.

Did someone grab her? Attacked her? Did she decide to duck and roll to the ground at that exact second? How could the most important piece of information be *just* out of her reach? It couldn't be, the odds were impossible.

What is going on here?

Myr rubbed her forehead. She was being played, in all of this. Nothing made sense.

She turned around and looked for her other suspect. The boy was at the front of the stage, watching Hattin's ship go. He bore no expression, good or bad. He didn't have the look of someone who just failed his mission, whatever it could be, but he was the only suspect Myr had left.

"Jak, dig up anything you can about Alora Mari and that boy over there. Those two will be able to give us some answers."

"You think they're the bombers?"

"Honestly, no. But they had some goal in mind with Lord Hattin. And maybe if we can figure out what it was, we can find the real culprit's motives."

"Understood. Do you have anything else you want to see in here?"

Myr shook her head. "It's time we see the crime scene in person. We're going to Feos."

Chapter Six

A deep thump echoed through the forest, reverberating through the otherwise silent air that came from being so far from civilization. A long dagger embedded deep into the side of a tree. Alongside it was three others.

Aeia examined her result from eight yards away and frowned. Her fourth dagger sat outside the target she had carved, a mistake which would be costly in a dangerous situation.

She let out a disgruntled huff and trudged over to retrieve her weapons.

I'd thought throwing things would be an easier art to learn. She grabbed the hilt of a dagger, yanking it up and down until it wiggled free. *I should have taken up archery. Crossbows can practically shoot themselves these days.*

She cocked her head to the side, examining her shots.

All of them are a bit too far to the right. That's odd, I usually lean the other way.

Her now grown hair fell into her face, a strand somehow finding its way into her mouth. Aeia spat and brushed the hair back behind her ear.

At least her shots were deeper than before. Her new life was strengthening her far quicker than she would have thought. She could hardly believe that only a year ago, she'd spent all her time cooped up in a fortress, only let out for missions.

Eugho saved me from that.

She tugged on the last dagger, but the blade did not budge. She had to resort to the assistance of a second hand to pull it free and let out a grunt of surprise when it released immediately.

Aeia looked around and saw nothing but tall trees in every direction. She took the opportunity to straighten herself and paced back to where she'd been throwing from.

One more time. Any longer, Eugho might get worried.

She turned and faced her target again, carefully holding the blade of a dagger between her fingers. As with all metals, she felt a chilling sensation upon touching it. The tips of her fingers cooled. It wasn't as strong now as it was during her time in the fortress. She wasn't as charged with Bask now as she was back then.

She let out a breath, recalling the lessons Sestes had given her, before hurling the blade with a great deal of her strength. The blade whooshed through the air and landed with a satisfying thud in the tree trunk.

Aeia looked past her outstretched arm, smiling at her work.

Right in the center.

She prepared the next one, using the same tactic as before. She slowly released another breath and ...

"Aeia!"

She started at the call, her hand fumbling the dagger. With no desire to cut herself, she pulled back and let it fall to the ground.

After a hiss of annoyance, Aeia's dropped her arms to her sides and turned to face the newcomer.

"Was that *really* necessary?"

Eugho appeared from behind a tree, a wide grin on his face. "It was part of your training, of course! Being prepared for anything and all that."

Aeia glared and let out a huff. Though, were she completely honest, she would admit that she enjoyed the playful way he dealt with her. It made her feel normal, even if only a little. But she wouldn't let *him* know that.

She dropped the glare, mimicking his crossed arms and looking up with new interest. "Have they shown up yet? Did *he* show up?"

Eugho bobbed his head, a wide grin on his face. "They're all here, Jeffe included. He's not entirely convinced to join permanently, however. He wants to see how well we can conduct an operation like this."

"Like *this*?" Aeia tipped her head forward. "You could do today's mission by yourself if you wanted."

"Well, I'm glad you feel that way." He laughed. "But *I* may learn a thing or two from this man. Today will be interesting for sure."

He turned, waving her to his side. "Come on, I'll introduce you."

Aeia jogged up to his side, prodding him when she got close. "You really think he's special?"

"Absolutely. I contracted him once before, during the civil war. He was your age at the time. I gave him a target and only the name of which *city* he might be in. A day and a half later, Jeffe had tracked the man down and apprehended him, along with his ten guards."

Wow. "How did he do it?"

"Not sure." Eugho shrugged. "He can hunt, I know that much. But that doesn't explain it."

He's a Huntsman? The image of blindfolded men popped into her mind—the men who navigated on an artificial sense, instead of sight. A shiver traveled down her spine. To a Huntsman, her powers were useless. "Does that mean he's blind?"

"Not even a little."

Aeia cocked her head. Hunting was a heavy load on a person's mind. When combined with sight, it was often too great a strain. Which was why the skill was taught primarily to those who already lacked the sense of sight.

Eugho pulled his blindfold partly out of his pocket. "Hey, I can do it too. It's not entirely unheard of."

"Last time you did it you got a migraine. Does he get migraines?"

Eugho deflated slightly. "Not that I know of."

"Where did he learn all that? Is he a nobleman?"

"No, and it makes him quite unlike the others. It shouldn't be too much of an issue, I hope."

Eugho already had a few nobles on his team. She hadn't heard of most of them, but according to him, they were the best at what they did, which was usually not only running a business.

The team Eugho was creating was certainly not large, but according to him, they wouldn't need very many people to get started. In fact, he would always say that fewer is better, as they'd be a lot harder to found out.

Most rebellions started by creating an army first. But it was impossible to create an army in secret, and too soon, whispers of rebellion reached the Archduke's houses.

Eugho's plan was different, an interesting concept she hadn't seen tried before. They had similar goals as Lord Hattin and his following. Except Aeia trusted Eugho's ideals and abilities far more. He had no fluff talk like the others, and he certainly wasn't leading a mob of naive people to their deaths.

Nobody among Eugho's followers was naive. They were some of the most skilled people she had met. And that was worth much more than a mob of angry farmers.

Everyone is skilled except me.

She could void jump, but that was it. If Eugho was expecting anything else from her then he'd soon be disappointed. He'd even told her that she didn't have to Jump if she didn't want to.

If not for that, then why had he worked so hard getting her here? She'd tried quite a few things and failed at almost all of them. Throwing knives was about the only thing she could do semi-decently.

A sensation washed over her, a slight tickle in her stomach.

A Huntsman. That must be him.

He was probably somewhere nearby ... or nearby for a Huntsman, at least.

After a few more minutes of them walking she finally spotted him sitting in a tree. He was in his late twenties, which made him young compared to the other members of the team. He wore clothes typical for a Huntsman—wool pants and shirt with a leather coat thrown on top.

She waved out of courtesy but pulled her hand back when she noticed the cloth over his eyes.

Fool. He can't see you.

He tipped his head in her direction and offered a small nod. It startled her, and she felt even more embarrassed as she turned her focus ahead.

She saw Brunst next. He leaned against their ship, arms folded over his chest. He was a quiet man but gave his opinion when needed. He had apparently fought alongside Eugho in the Royal Guard and still had loyalties that went beyond rank or status.

Aeia was glad that he was on their side. He didn't look strong, as he was average size, but as a knight, he was far stronger than the average—no, any normal man.

Knights were augmented far beyond the rest of the soldiers, to the point where man and machine were nearly equal parts. It allowed them to surpass normal limitations, fight harder and longer than anyone else. She hated seeing men give up parts of their humanity to fight better, not when she had seen humanity taken away by force.

Then again, he looks so normal.

She examined him, looking for the signs of the augmentation.

There were only a few bits of evidence she could see. Rumors said that Knights' chests were made entirely of metal to protect their vitals during combat.

He must have noticed her staring at him. He looked up suddenly. Their eyes locked.

As usual the world started to go dark, a tunnel funneling directly and only to her target. Her body seemed to lose weight as her consciousness prepared to leave her.

She caught herself quickly and pulled back.

She fought against her Void Link as her mind threatened to leave her body. She hated it and quickly turned away, cursing under her breath.

Be more careful.

She could feel the man's glare burning into her through the corner of her eye. Unfortunately, he knew what she was. They all did.

It was the reason she wouldn't ever have lengthy conversations with any of them. Only Eugho and Meckea would ever see her as an actual person instead of a monster.

She glanced over to Sale who was working diligently on Brunst's hammer nearby.

If only I could be like him.

Sale didn't have any gifts other than his mind. But he was still one of the most valuable members of the team. Eugho had chosen him because he was clever and inventive. Everything good about him he'd acquired on his own.

She sighed and looked about the clearing. "Where are the rest?"

"I have some men on their way to help us today." Eugho said. "They're already informed of today's missions and will immediately move into position."

She leaned towards him a bit. "What about Meckea?"

Lady of the House of Shadows, as she was called by the underground of Feos. Aeia had trained under her for the first three months of her time with Eugho but hadn't seen her since. She was cordial, a much livelier person than she had expected of someone with her reputation.

"She'll meet us in Bisham. This isn't much of her expertise anyway. We should do just fine."

It was true. A shadow would never be this far from civilization. Their abilities stemmed from being able to fool Huntsmen into thinking the Shadow was someone else. A shadow could sneak in behind a nobleman into his own house and his guards wouldn't suspect a thing. But out in the forest like this their abilities would do nothing.

Eugho motioned to each member of the group to come forward. "A shuttle will be passing by here in an hour. Their cargo is someone of immense value. Someone we need for our mission. A man named Dust."

Sale perked up at the name. "Dust? Isn't he an outlaw?"

"Not just an outlaw. He led a large faction of the rebellion during the civil war."

"Sounds interesting," Brunst chimed in. His voice was a bit rough and had a slight electronic sound to it, a likely side effect of all the augmentations he'd been subjected to. "What's the plan?"

"Jeffe here will bring the shuttle to a halt with a Skybow. As a Huntsman, he'll be able to see it coming long before any of us could. You, me, and Aeia will handle the guards while Brunst breaks our man out." Eugho waited for objections before continuing. "My informant has told me that it is a small escort, only consisting of a single carriage. I don't think we'll have any trouble dealing with them."

We're only attacking one of the most powerful forces in the world. The outlaw Dust must be important for Eugho to attempt this.

Eugho gave a few more commands, then the group separated to their respective locations.

Aeia maneuvered through the forest, dashed across the road, and hopped into a tree for a better view. Strangely, she felt ready to fight again. It had been quite a while since her last battle. Excitement overwhelmed her nervousness.

She whipped out her weapon of choice, a long dueling dagger. It had a black hilt that matched her clothes. Its blade had carvings swirling up its length. She tested it, pouring a bit of her Bask energy into the weapon.

It lit up, and the carving filled with a blue light. It moved like a liquid, the metal thinned and stretched upwards to almost twice its original length. A weapon this well designed was very rare, and it would catch her targets off-guard. She only had to get it near enough.

A flash of light came out of nowhere, startling her. She fumbled the dagger and a sharp pain radiated from her hand. She glanced down to the long gash that now streaked across her palm. Aeia regained the hold on the hilt and wiped the blood on her tunic. She had no time to worry about that now.

Are we under attack?

She didn't hear any noise indicating combat. The flash itself had been completely silent. Turning toward where she'd seen the flash of light she quickly moved to a nearby clearing.

Aeia paused before entering the open area, and a figure caught her eye. A soft gasp escaped her lips as she eyed a young man, probably only a few years older than she, leaning against a tree. His head hung down, and she couldn't clearly make out his face.

"Who are you?" she called.

At the sound of her voice, the man sprang to his feet and turned toward her.

She let out a gasp. He looked different from any man she's ever seen. *He can't be from here. But if he's not from the Kingdom of Nont, where is he from?* His unfamiliar garments resembled that of a royal guardsman but without the King's insignia on it. What surprised her most was his hair. It was ... yellow?

She unintentionally locked eyes with the man then reeled back, preparing herself for the inevitable Jump because of her mind state. She hoped she'd be able to control it enough not to hurt him. But what should have been an instantaneous leap, took much longer. Her consciousness should have been gone by now, yet even while she stared nothing happened.

What? She looked deeper into the man's eyes, and her jaw dropped in surprise. *What is this?*

She didn't know how to react. She'd never ... she'd never been able to look at someone like this before. His eyes held a mix of worry and confusion, and she guessed her gaze did too.

How could this be happening?

She examined him curiously, focusing on the insignia on his dark suit.

That's not the uniform of any house I know. Could he be from the East? I haven't met many of the Barons or Dukes over there.

Her eyes stopped at his belt. A small contraption of sorts was strapped to his side. Too small to be a crossbow, yet it had a handle and trigger similar to one. Was it some sort of weapon? Did it shoot like a crossbow? But the arrows would be so small!

Aeia shook herself. *There isn't supposed to be anyone else out here. There aren't any towns for miles.*

She stood straight, crossing her arms. "What are you doing out here?"

He climbed to his feet, rubbing the back of his neck. "I'm lost, I think." His voice held a slight quiver. "Do you know where the other people from the lab are?"

Lab?

Aeia didn't budge. "I don't know of any *lab*. I have seen no others."

The stranger let out a sigh and turned in a small circle, taking in his surroundings.

Panic welled up, and Aeia reached behind and pulled out a dagger. "Stay there!"

The stranger immediately dropped back down, his hands raised. "Look. I don't want to hurt you, or anything like that. I just want to find out where the rest of the group is."

Could he be a noble himself?

He had to be. No one else would be able to wander from a charger for too long. Anyone not as prepared as her team would suffer Bask starvation.

Aeia didn't relax. "I don't know of any *group* around here. It's just me."

She continued to eye him as he let out another sigh and leaned against a tree. And, just for a moment, she felt sorry for him. But soon her better judgment nagged from the back of her mind. In all likelihood, this guy was part of a large gang trying to catch her off guard. Had someone discovered Eugho's plan? Was someone trying to distract her?

Convincing. She thought, proud at her deductive skills. *Almost had me.*

She motioned behind him. "If you have nothing else to say, why don't you head back to town?"

His eyes widened hopefully. "Town? Where is that?"

Aeia searched his face, not able to find a single crack in the man's disguise. He truly looked lost.

"That way." She pointed behind him again.

"Is it far?"

She shook her head. "Only a days' walk, if you're quick."

"A day?" He turned, mumbling something that she couldn't make out. "Could you take me there?"

"No."

She stole another look at his eyes. They were wide, pleading. "Please? I've never been here before."

Aeia's will wavered. "You got yourself out here, didn't you? You can get back."

"I guess you're right ... only I can't go back. I should have been teleported to a research facility in Sydney. Do you know where that is?"

Teleported?

This guy was spouting nonsense. As far as she knew there wasn't a place called 'Sydney.' Did he confuse the pronunciation of Seet?

That's the only thing I can think of, unless this guy is crazy.

He did look a bit crazy. He seemed to be in shock. As far as she could tell there was no one else in the forest.

Well, except for the Barrows. But they usually only move about at night.

Her mind wandered to the thought of the large beasts. While some are domesticated as mounts for war, most run wild through the forests of Nont. Their shoulders stand nearly as tall as a full-grown man when they are on all fours. They could easily overpower the unprepared.

She examined the man again. There were no tears in his clothes or bite marks on his flesh.

It doesn't look like he fought one. Maybe he just saw one and ran?

"You with me?" he asked.

She tried to get her mind back on track, unsuccessfully. "What?"

A grin of amusement crept over his face. "You don't know where Sydney is?"

She shook her head. "Never heard of the place."

His smile vanished. "Where are we then?"

He doesn't even know what province he's in?

"Vou."

The man only stared blankly.

"Vou ... in Nont," she clarified.

He shook his head, then lowered it to his hands.

A pang of sympathy shot through her. This seemed too great, too unbelievable, an act to make up.

And... something else tugged at her. Right now, she was getting the feeling that this person, whoever he was, was important. And more so, that he could be trusted.

While she didn't like the idea, and didn't want the added responsibility, taking him with her seemed the best option. And if he really was serious about being lost, it would be dangerous to leave him on his own in the woods.

"Fine," she stated, wondering if she'd soon regret it. "I'll help you out."

The odd man released a sigh of relief. "Thank you."

Thank you. Her heart warmed at the sound of it. It wasn't something she heard often.

Aeia cocked her head. "What's your name?"

He climbed to his feet. "Sorry, I've been rude. I'm Eric."

She offered a polite smile. "Aeia."

Eric returned the smile as he closed the distance between them. When he got to arm's length he held out his hand.

Aeia looked at it and blinked. *What does he expect me to do with that?*

Unsure what else to do, she bowed instead. An action Eric repeated.

"Now." Eric clapped his hands together. "Where was it that you said I was again?"

Amusement tugged at her lips. "The province of Vou controlled by Lord Gaelis, unified with the other five provinces under the crown Nont."

He stroked his chin thoughtfully. "I've never heard of it. What are the surrounding countries called?"

She blinked a few times. "Surrounding countries?"

"Well, yeah." Eric nodded. "Other than Nont, what's in this area?"

Other than Nont ...?

She shook her head. "I don't understand ... What else could there be?"

Eric paused, resumed stroking his chin. "Who's not ruled by the leader of Nont?"

"Um ... no one."

"You're sure? You're saying that there's only one government?"

"I wouldn't say *only* one. Each province has its own. But we all classify ourselves as under the crown of Nont."

Eric opened his mouth and closed it a moment later. He let out a large sigh and leaned against a tree once more. "I'm a lot more lost than I thought."

"I don't know what to tell you."

Eric furrowed his eyebrows. "In a different sense, I didn't think there was 'anyplace else' either. But that looks like where I've gone."

She cocked her head, preparing to inquire further, when the sound of humming in the distance interrupted her.

The prisoner!

Chapter Seven

Eric watched dumbfounded as the girl he'd just met charged into the trees.

"Wait!" he called, the last glimpse of her long blue hair trailing behind a tree.

She said she'd help me!

He started after her, then stopped himself. A humming buzzed through the air. A familiar yet somehow still foreign sound. What followed the sound was a vehicle. It hovered just above the treetops and a road, its propulsion engines aiming down and to the sides. The force they exerted bent the bows of the trees and scattered leaves in all directions.

The vehicle was large and was shaped like a sailing ship. Carrying it were a series of large propellers on each side. It looked deep, with plenty of space to carry cargo, a load of which bogged it down.

What is that thing?

It wasn't like any sort of plane he'd seen before. If it even was a plane. Without wings, it seemed a poor way of travel and would use a lot of power. Which country would make something like that?

Well, someone has to be driving it.

Eric started in that direction, heading towards a clearing while he waved his arms. He stepped out, a call forming in his lips—

A long thin projectile shot out from the other side of the clearing and slammed into one of the vehicle's propellers. The propeller blades met the thick steel of the bolt and broke off with a horrific *crack*.

The shout stuck in Eric's throat, turning into a gasp. He leaped behind a tree as shards of metal flew in every direction. A deep *thunk* echoed as one of the blades flew into his wooden barrier.

The vehicle roared, engines flaring as it tried to remain upright. The roar grew louder as it crashed downward.

Eric closed his eyes, waiting for the clash of metal against the ground, a sound which never came. Soon the roaring turned to a gentle hum again.

Eric crept around the tree to investigate. The machine had stopped completely. A collection of thrusters spouted a blue energy that held the vehicle a few feet off the ground.

What is *this place? What is that thing?*

Silhouettes flew into the clearing from the treetops on all sides, gliding down onto the damaged vehicle like a hawk onto its prey. They slowed unnaturally upon nearing the vehicle, barely making a thud as they covered the face and sides.

And still more people came into view, this time on foot as they set up what looked like large crossbows. None fired. They all waited as a show of force against the vehicle.

Eric lowered himself, hiding from view.

Is this a robbery?

He scanned the standoff. The attackers wore dark green garments, probably designed to hide their identities. Their locations were all perfectly spread out, leaving the vehicle no clear course of escape. It was preplanned, and not by some ordinary person by his guess.

What is this then? His mouth dropped. *Is Aeia part of this?*

She had been wearing the same color clothes as the attackers. Even though she'd been just a young woman, she'd stared at him emotionlessly, cold. She could very well be a soldier, or worse, a member of organized crime.

A rustle sounded to his side. A lone figure crouched in the bushes, pulling a mask over her head. The long blue hair was unmistakable.

Should he confront her and find out what's going on?

Was she dangerous?

She could very well kill him if he were to interfere with this heist.

He looked back to the standoff. Through the ship's windows, he saw movement, men rushing around in a panic.

This could get messy.

Eric gritted his teeth and jumped to the girl's side, squatting in the bushes.

Aeia started, losing her balance in her crouched position and nearly tipping.

"You!" She hissed. "What are you doing here?"

"That's what I'd like to know about you!"

Her brow furrowed into a glare. "It's dangerous! Go hide!"

Eric ignored the warning. "Are you going to kill the people inside?"

"No!" Her voice was too loud, and she winced at the volume. "*No.* They are holding someone very important."

A loud shrieking started, the earsplitting sound of metal tearing against metal. Eric looked back to the scene.

The men who had landed on the ship jammed long blades into the sides of it. The blades buzzed and tore like chainsaws, cleaving through the exterior with little effort.

"Who's in the wrong here?" Eric shouted above the noise. "Because that looks brutal."

"You know nothing about this." Aeia held a hand up to Eric's face. "Just *stay here, all right*? I need to go."

She darted out of the bushes, creeping towards the ship in a low crouch. Seemingly out of nowhere, a man shot out of a treetop and landed by her side, moving with her.

The screeching stopped, and the men perched on the ship pulled the blades free from the walls. They had carved large squares into the exterior, ready to be pulled out.

The people inside the ship did not give them that chance. All the squares burst out in unison. Men, in what looked to be full Kevlar armor, poured out from the openings. And all of them ... *all of them...* had blue hair just like Aeia. Eric couldn't spot one who had black, blonde, red, brown ... They all had that vibrant blue hair. As if it were natural.

The scene turned to chaos.

Bolts from the crossbows rained down on the defenders. The thin, lightweight bolts did little harm and barely pierced the soldiers' thick armor. The shots were nothing more than flesh wounds, but as Eric watched, each soldier who was hit paused mid-step, wavered, and fell to the ground.

Tranquilizers?

Eric released a small breath of relief. Maybe Aeia had told the truth.

The soldiers who'd managed to dodge the darts engaged the sword-wielders as they hopped off the ship's sides. A few seemed to notice the difference in purpose of Aeia and her escort and charged the two as they neared the vehicle.

Aeia's escort burst into action. He drew a long straight blade and struck a soldier's chest, knocking him to the ground. With one down he moved to the next, parrying away another attack. When the first regained his footing, Aeia's escort engaged both men at once, switching between opponents masterfully, eventually causing both to retreat as they struggled against his blows.

The escort snapped forward, engaging yet another soldier and striking his shoulder in a downward sweep with of the blade. With the strike, blue light flashed through the blade. It was quick, too fast to notice if you weren't looking at it directly, but with the flash the escort's blade changed shape entirely. It transformed from a straight blade into a curved blade, resembling a saber.

The weapon change, along with the escort's switching of stance, added a great deal of power to his attack. It tore his opponent's defenses, sundering the blade from the soldier's hand in the mighty sweep.

The escort whirled around again, lunging at another approaching soldier. Again, a blue light flashed through the blade, and the saber straightened and thinned until the blade was a rapier, which jabbed at the soldier's sword hand, separating gloved hand and hilt as the second weapon flew from the defender's grasp.

Both soldiers were rendered defenseless. The escort motioned to two of the assailants on the ship, who moved in to grapple and pin the soldiers to the ground.

A few more soldiers appeared, rocketing out of the ship like arrows as they drew their weapons. They aimed to land on top of Aeia but were caught by something mid-air. They tumbled to the side.

A new man had entered the clearing. He wielded a hammer that connected the head to the hilt with a long metal coil that now retracted back to a starting position.

Both soldiers hopped to their feet and pulled free their swords. The did not seem concerned by them and swung again with both hands this time.

The hammer head extended outwards like a powerful whip that caught both soldiers in a long sweep from the side and flung them across the field with little effort from the attacker.

Such strength ...

They rolled to a stop and climbed to their feet much slower this time.

"Knight!" one shouted between breaths.

"So, you know you're outmatched." The man held his hammer forward, and the two soldiers lowered themselves in response. Shortly after, they each got hit with a tranquilizer bolt and fell forward.

Aeia and her bodyguard moved in on the ship, their path again intercepted as a soldier emerged from the wreck. This time Aeia herself stepped forward. The two locked eyes for a few short moments, before the soldier wavered and collapsed to the side without a fight.

Shock echoed through the soldiers' ranks at the sight, the unknown threat stealing all their vigor in an instant. The attackers pressed in harder, apprehending soldier after soldier as their ranks crumbled.

The fight became one-sided. The soldiers were at the mercy of the attackers as they were pinned down one by one. Yet, not one of the attackers moved in for the kill.

What's their goal then?

Aeia and her bodyguard disappeared into the ship. A moment later, they re-emerged with a tall man in bright-colored clothes. All three hopped out of the wreck. The tall man's arms were tied behind his back. He had scars on nearly all exposed flesh—save a strip around his eyes. So, this was...

A prison break?

The archers swung their crossbows over their heads and onto their backs, moving in on the pinned soldiers. Each one swooped down and started administering some sort of drug to the prisoners. The soldiers quickly lost unconsciousness.

Eric narrowed his eyes. *But if this is a prison break, why are they going through such great lengths to win without killing?*

"Fall back!" The call came from Aeia's escort, who had an arm raised high in the air.

The attackers melted away from the scene. Eric ducked behind his tree as a few hustled by just a few feet away.

As quickly as they'd arrived, the attackers vanished, the last three being Aeia, her escort, and the prisoner. The young woman glided back to where Eric hid. His first reaction was to get up and talk to the girl, but he stopped himself.

He looked between the trio and the wreckage. Should he confront them? Would Aeia keep her promise? His heartbeat quickened as they approached. Who was he supposed to trust? The girl seemed nice, and they didn't kill anyone, but...

In a snap decision he hoped he wouldn't regret, Eric stood, exposing himself to the trio. A flash of blue light appeared before he'd even stood completely straight, a feeling of cold metal pressed against the side of his neck.

Eric froze, slowly looking up to meet the man's eyes. He could see them above the mask, a shining blue that burned like a flame. They pierced him, seeming to strip away all possibility of deception.

Eric was wrong. This was not a mere escort or bodyguard. In fact, the look of horror on the prisoner's face told Eric that this man was somehow infamous.

The man looked him up and down, his eyes narrowing when they met his gaze. "Who are you? What are you doing so far out in this forest?"

Eric opened his mouth but then stopped to think of the best way to explain himself.

"He's lost, Eugho," Aeia squeaked from behind.

The man, Eugho, held Eric's gaze, not turning to the girl as she spoke. "Lost? So far in the wilderness?"

"Yes," she said. "Lost and very confused. I think something's wrong with him."

Eric winced a bit, the words stinging more than the blade at his neck.

"So it would seem." Eugho paused for a few seconds. "So? What did you believe about him?"

Aeia blinked a few times. "I said that I believe he is lost, confused. I ... I said I would help him find the rest of his group. Or at least help him back to town."

"Good." The blade flashed again, returning to its original shape. Eugho slid it into its sheath and started up the path.

Eric and Aeia stood dumbfounded until Aeia grabbed Eric's arm, pulling him along.

Eric stumbled, clambering up to keep their pace. "Wait, you'll help me?" he called to the man.

Eugho nodded. "If that is what Aeia decided, then I see no reason not to."

Aeia looked back, pulling down her mask. "We aren't bad people, really."

Eric could only swallow. "I just saw you shoot a ship out of the sky."

"This man is important. We just rescued him."

Eugho stopped, and turned towards Eric. "But let's consider who is judging who. Why would a man would be *lost* so close to my operation? It would be wise for you think hard before judging those who *choose* to help you."

"Sorry." Eric gulped and pulled back from the enormous presence. The man's eyes burned into him a moment longer before he started back on his path.

"It's not an unwarranted concern," Aeia called. "I don't want people to think we're criminals."

The large man sighed. "To the world, we might as well be."

"Not once we save them." She turned to Eric. "That's what we're trying to do. The world needs a lot of help, and no one is stepping up to provide it."

"What's wrong with it?"

"Too many things to list." She shook her head. "But all of it leads back to the growing corruption within the nobility. They think nothing of the people they have been given care of, focusing only on their conflict with each other and the accumulation of power."

"Those soldiers back there." Eric motioned behind them. "They were the muscle of these 'nobles'?"

Aeia nodded. "The brutes following Lord Alonius Cer. I assure you, they would show a lot less restraint to us if the tables had been turned. We don't kill, and yet somehow *we're* the dangerous ones."

"If that's true, then I sure am glad it was you guys who found me first."

The girl smiled. "We're still the outlaws here."

Eric shrugged. He couldn't judge her, not yet. She was an outlaw, but that meant nothing, since he didn't know what the laws were. Where he came from, laws were mostly good, mostly written to keep people safe from harm. But this girl didn't seem the type to hurt people for no reason.

I haven't even heard of this country ... this Nont. It isn't a country on earth as far as I know. Does that mean that I...?

He looked to the girl bobbing just ahead of him, at her long, strangely blue hair, flowing in the breeze. It couldn't be dye, not unless *everyone* here added it daily. No, it seemed to be their natural hair color.

He looked from the towering trees to the quickly-darkening sky. It was comforting a bit to see stars above.

While everything else here seemed different, it was the one thing that remained...

He froze, pure dread dropping in his stomach.

A clearing in the tree line revealed a moon, but not his. It was too big, too reddish, and jagged instead of spherical.

I'm really not ...

What did this mean? The teleporter ... had it malfunctioned? No, that was out of the question. The odds of him appearing on a habitable planet was infinitesimal.

His mind struggled for an answer. From the corner of his eye he spotted Aeia, who was waiting, staring at him without an expression. "If you needed to stop, you should have asked. We're almost there."

He waved his hand, motioning her forward and following her down a path lined with brush.

How much should I tell them?

As soon as they cleared the bush, they found the rest of the masked group waiting for them.

There were only a handful of people, and they all looked at him as soon as he appeared. Most looked solid and strong. Like well-trained soldiers.

"Now, then." Aeia's large escort strode up to him. "What are you doing out here?"

"I'm trying to find my group in Sydney."

"Sydney?" he asked.

"The biggest city in Australia."

Eugho shook his head.

Not him too.

"He was talking like this when I met him," Aeia chimed in. "He's lost."

"So it would seem." Eugho turned to him. "Well, I've never heard of a Sydney. You're in Nont. But ... I'll try to help you find it, if I can."

"So, we're taking him with us?" A man stepped close to their leader. Eric recognized him as the one who'd swatted the soldiers aside with ease—the Knight. He was large, but somehow smaller than Eric would have expected for his strength. He didn't seem particularly large in muscle mass either, yet from the indent he made in ground he stood on, he must be very heavy.

"For now." The masked man looked around the forest. "I doubt he wants to be left out here."

"Is that wise?" the Knight asked. "We have no idea who he is."

"Exactly." The masked man waved a finger. "Look at him. His hair, his clothing ... I've traveled the kingdom, and I've seen nothing like it. I want to know where he came from."

That seemed to be enough for the man, who stepped back without a word.

The rest seemed hesitant, and so Eugho stepped closer to Eric. "You don't intend to compromise us, do you?"

Eric thought carefully. "I don't have any intentions aside from finding my group, sir."

The leader slowly reached up and pulled off his mask. "Then you're under my care until you do."

The rest of the group followed his lead, a level of tension dropping with each mask. None of them looked rugged, like Eric would expect of a group like this. They seemed the opposite. The clean-cut look only added to his curiosity about them.

They sure don't look like outlaws.

Everyone turned toward the forest. Eric hurried to keep up with them.

"I've seen a few of you before." The prisoner growled. "What business do any of you have in rescuing me?"

He didn't want to be rescued?

"Especially you." The prisoner nodded towards Eugho. "Last I checked, you were the one throwing me in there."

"Things are worse," Eugho said.

"Worse? Last time I was out, the whole Kingdom was about to fall apart."

"It has held on so far. But ..." Eugho relaxed his shoulders. "Things have changed, Dust. I don't regret what I did, but I know now that I couldn't change anything as the Guard-Captain."

"I could have told you that." Dust clenched his fists. "Ten years to figure it out for yourself, eh? Geralt had it right. And you helped him to his grave!"

Eric felt Aeia brush up against his side as she leaned in. "Those two were enemies." She whispered. "Dust was part of a rebellion. And Eugho arrested him after the war was over."

"I was trying to bring peace to the Kingdom." Eugho said to Dust. "Just as I am now. Like it or not, we're on the same side now."

"So, it's 'like it or not'? What's keeping me from heading off on my own?"

"Perhaps a kingdom full of *Wanted* signs? If you wish to head back to prison then so be it." Eugho waved an arm outward. "But I need your help. You eluded me for months. Not even Meckea could do that."

"Don't sat that name around me," the man named Dust said. "Cursed temptress … Do what you will. I won't promise I'll stay, but seeing *you* in hiding for once might just be amusing."

Chapter Eight

The sun was setting, and the forest grew cold very quickly. Eric shivered. His uniform wasn't designed for this type of weather. His face and hands were hit by the full force of the chill.

The vegetation was still green and filled with life. If not for the cold, he would assume they were in the middle of summer.

"So... what are you?"

Aeia's question drew his attention. She was close, and she studied his hair as she circled him.

"I'm a human."

"I've never seen human with yellow hair. Also, you dress strangely."

Eric winced. "*Well*, I don't really know any more than you do. Up until an hour ago I was the normal one. Where I come from this color hair is common."

She cocked her head to the side. "Yellow hair is normal there? Where are you from?"

"America."

Her brow furrowed. "Never heard of it. If you're not from one of the provinces, then you are very lost. You'll find nothing else unless you head out there." She pointed up into the sky.

That doesn't make any sense.

This world seemed like earth in so many ways. He hadn't seen many animals, but the few he had seemed familiar. Some birds, and he had even spotted an incredibly furry animal burrowing into the ground.

The place wasn't all that "alien." Aside from the blue-haired people and the jagged moon, he would have guessed that he had just landed on another continent.

They reached a clearing in the forest where a massive vehicle of sorts was parked. It looked very like a sail-ship back home, except it had a series of propellers like those he'd seen on the vehicle they'd attacked—although these propellers were larger. They were made entirely of metal and seemed advanced.

"Is it yours?"

Aeia nodded. "It's only a transport vessel, but we've made it work."

He examined the ship curiously. It didn't seem as efficient as, say, a plane. It looked far more suited to water. Wouldn't that large hull drag in the wind? And wouldn't the weight of the machine be too heavy for lift.

"That thing's huge ... Can it fly?"

"I don't see how useful it would be if it couldn't."

He couldn't help but grin. "So, you guys are some sort of sky-pirates?"

She tilted her head to the side. "Pirate?"

A snicker escaped his lips. "Don't worry about it."

Ahead, their leader walked towards the door, and it opened without any visible command from him.

Very advanced indeed.

She followed them inside.

Once the leader had ensured everyone was inside, he closed the door.

"All right." Aeia turned towards him. "Let me show you how we run around here."

She took a path separate from the rest of the group, which led further back into the ship.

"As you probably noticed, we did in fact attack a shuttle. A shuttle carrying convicts, no less. But I can assure you now that we are not bandits or criminals of any sorts. We don't mean to gain anything from the world, but to change it, make it better.

"Not all of us have a vendetta against those in charge—the nobility. It's not them we're after, but their leaders. Mostly one leader, a man named Alonius Cer. He steals from his subjects. He is a parasite that sucks the life out of his subjects, keeps us barely above starvation. And we intend to change that."

"Steal from the rich and give to the poor?"

She offered a blank look. "Not at all. Anything we give to the poor will be taken back. Alonius Cer needs to be removed from power."

Something caught his eye as they passed a room. He stopped and looked back to see a smooth, glowing blue orb the color of Aeia's hair resting in the middle of a machine in the wall.

"What's that?" He pointed to it.

She stopped in her tracks and slowly turned around. "You don't know?"

When Eric didn't say anything, she started to pace forward. "It's Bask, *Bask*. How could you not know what it is?"

He looked back again. It was strangely beautiful, but he was sure that he had never seen anything like it before.

"Um, what is it exactly?"

Aeia let out an awkward laugh at the apparent absurdity of the question. "It's everything!" she said, waving her arms flamboyantly. "Really, we need it for *everything*."

She pulled her dagger from her belt. "See this? It is powered by Bask." She then motioned to the lights, which flickered off, and back on. "Run by Bask. This ship, and everything in it, is run by Bask."

"I mean, we need it too! It's not like you can even go a week..." She seemed to realize something, her voice filling with concern. "How long has it been since you last charged?"

"Since I...?"

She grabbed his arm and all but pulled him through the hallway.

"No wonder your hair isn't blue! I should have known!"

They stopped at a small chamber. Aeia pulled a door open and shoved Eric inside.

"It's a wonder you aren't dead yet!"

She closed the chamber and pushed a button on the wall, and the room instantly filled with blue light—just like what had emanated off the crystal she'd called Bask.

He stood there in silence, waiting for something to happen.

I am just supposed to stand here?

She didn't seem to be expecting anything else. She watched him closely.

After a few minutes, the light dissipated and the normal room light turned on again. She stepped into the chamber with him, studying his face and hair closely.

"That's very odd..." She leaned in close, so close that her face was inches from his as she examined his eyes. "Nothing changed at all."

She was studying him as if he were a lab rat. But he was studying her differently. Blue hair, weird as that was, her small nose that complimented the rest of her features ... she was beautiful.

His thoughts went to all sorts of weird places, and his face burned. He cleared his throat, a cue completely ignored by the girl.

"I'm not sure what to say," he said. "I don't understand this any more than you do."

She was oblivious to his discomfort and quickly closed the gap "That's so strange. I've never heard of anything like this before."

"So, everyone has hair like yours?"

She blinked and backed up a step. "Yes. Everyone I've ever seen."

"Well, where I came from, the only people with blue hair did it on purpose. It was all blond, err, yellow. brown, red, black—"

"Black hair?" She looked to the ground, lost in thought, before slowly looking up with a perplexed expression. "That sounds terrible."

He laughed, mostly because she was completely serious.

She seemed confused by his outburst, waiting for him to calm down before motioning for him to follow again.

She led him through a series of doors, each opening just as they were starting to near them.

"How do you do that?"

She looked back quizzically, walking without hesitation as another door opened before her.

"The doors, I mean. Are they all automatic?"

"No. I'm opening them."

"How?"

She blinked again, seeming finally understanding the question. She tapped the temple on her head. "Implant. I can control doors like these with my mind."

Aeia pressed her hand on a console beside the next door, and the door opened. "You don't really need it. We can just call out to the technology when we encounter it. That's what most people do."

She reached and grabbed one of his arms and placed it against the console. "Do you feel anything?"

He closed his eyes, and focused. "What is it supposed to be like?"

"A connection. The machine will feel like another part of you. It can be controlled just as easily as a limb."

"I definitely don't feel anything like that." He winced. "I guess that means I can't open..."

She shook her head. "This is the way we control technology."

"Where I come from we use a lot of similar stuff. We couldn't control with our minds like that, though. We had to use our hands or sometimes a voice."

She turned to lead him on. "Sounds inefficient."

"Couldn't your way be dangerous though? I mean, couldn't technology be invented to take advantage of the connection to the mind?"

She froze a moment, then shrugged the question off. "Of course not. There are safeguards for things like that."

They entered a larger room, one which appeared to be a repurposed cargo bay. Its walls were covered with diverse types of equipment and technology. In the center of the room, two men sat at tables, each working on small devices.

"This is Sale's cave." Aeia waved her arm over the length of the room. "He's a master at handling just about anything having to do with technology."

"Not *anything*." The man—who Eric assume was Sale—looked up from his work. "I dabble in a lot of technology, but I specialize in force engines and metal manipulation. That said, here's your beacon back Aeia. Just hold your thumb to the front if you want to call for help. I Shadow-proofed it this time so Meckea can't get you in any more trouble."

Familiar words, yet their meanings went right over Eric's head.

Aeia accepted the Beacon from Sale and they both looked back to Eric. He's not from around here, Sale," Aeia noted. "He didn't even know what Bask was. Could you explain what you do plainly?"

The man's eyes narrowed slightly, and he tilted his head. But rather than questioning Eric, he stood holding a device and bearing the smile of a man about to show off something he was proud of.

"I don't mean to be condescending," Sale said, "but are you familiar with technology of *any* sort?"

Eric nodded. "I've seen similar stuff. But nothing that was powered by this 'Bask'."

"Good. Saves me some time then." Sale held up a small dagger. "This is about as basic as metal manipulation gets."

Without the slightest movement from the man, the device sprang to life. Blue lines of lights crawled up to the dagger's hilt, twisting around the blade in spirals. While it did so, the dagger stretched, becoming thinner and longer until it was twice the length it had been before.

It happened nearly instantaneously, and Eric couldn't help but step back. The action brought much amusement to the others.

"Nothing like this where you're from, I take it?"

Sale then flipped the dagger and held its hilt outward so Eric could hand it. As soon as he grasped it, however, the lines receded and the blade reformed to its original shape.

Eric noticed that the lines that the light traveled were carvings in the metal itself. "The carvings ... do they determine what the metal does?"

Sale nodded. "Good observation. Yes, the energy that Bask radiates effects many things in several ways. For metal, it causes it to change shape, allowing us to set pathways for the energy, thereby causing the metal to change in the way we desire."

Eric twirled it in his hands. "Very interesting..."

"It opens the door for all sorts of possibilities. Like our friend Brunst, the Knight. His body is enhanced with metals, and he can control them using a similar process, albeit far more advanced."

"That guy with the hammer?"

Sale laughed loudly. "That's him all right. If you saw him in action, you know the capabilities Bask allows us to have."

Bask does all of this?

It seemed so versatile. How could a single substance, no matter what it is, become such a crucial point to everything?

Sale plucked the dagger from Eric's hand. "I've got a bit more work to finish on this one, though, so if you'll pardon me."

With that, he went back to his table, resuming his work.

Aeia prodded Eric to move onwards, leaning in to speak once they were out of earshot of the man. "You probably wouldn't have guessed it, but Sale is actually the head of a rather large house. His work in technology has built him businesses in nearly every province. And due to the amount of Bask he owns, he has been granted the title of a nobleman."

"He's that important?" Eric looked backwards. "He definitely seemed smart. Reminded me of someone I know. But he acts superior."

Aeia glanced back, pleased. "It's a trait Eugho was looking for. Someone who can lead but isn't hard above work."

"That's a good policy. He must be a brilliant man, this Eugho."

"He's going to change the world."

Eric looked at the girl. She bore not a hint of doubt in her expression. He believed her. History showed that revolutionaries should never be underestimated.

"I would show you more, but we'll be having a meeting soon. Would you like to rest?"

As soon as it was mentioned, all the weariness he was pushing back crashed on him. He hadn't thought of it, but he had already worked a very long shift before all of this happened.

He laughed a bit and wavered. "That would be great."

"Good. I'll show you to where you'll be staying and make sure you get some food sent in as well."

"I really appreciate it, Aeia. I mean it. You've helped me more than you know."

Chapter Nine

Aeia couldn't help smiling as she headed to the meeting. The amount of appreciation Eric showed her warmed her heart. It felt good to know that she could help—not hurt—someone, even if they had only just met.

There was something about Eric, too. She knew that she should be more suspicious of him, but ever since they'd first met she'd felt ... at ease. He seemed to be someone she could trust.

No one else seemed threatened by him either. He was a mystery in both appearance and background, but not a threat. Hopefully Eugho felt the same and would let him stay for a while.

They had to keep him. Eric knew nothing about the world. Did that mean that they were adopting him? She giggled at the thought, considering that Eric looked older than she did.

He could always join our cause.

An optimistic thought ... perhaps too optimistic. But that would be the best possible solution in the end.

Lost in her thoughts, she approached the command deck sooner than expected. Aeia focused on the plethora of problems she had to deal with.

The door opened, unlocked by her specific signature. The seats around the table were filled. The rest of the group had already arrived and appeared to have started the meeting without her.

She bit her lip, a hint of anger seeping in despite the commonality of the event.

I was helping Eric. They should be interested in what I found out. The least they could do...

She sighed. No one had noticed her arrival, and she slid into a corner chair to listen.

The prisoner they'd rescued stood in the center of the room. Dust had changed into a simple outfit, probably one of Eugho's old sets.

"We went through a lot of trouble getting this man." Jeffe didn't even attempt to hide his annoyance. "Will you just tell us who he is?"

Eugho really shouldn't play around so much. Still, it made her happy. At least she hadn't missed out on anything too important.

"All right, all right." Eugho held up his hands. "This is Dust. He was a commander under Geralt during the war. He's the last Light stealer."

Dust is a Light stealer?

"*Light stealer.*" Dust scoffed. "Makes us sound like villains. Besides, the only one who was truly immune to the Bask energy was Geralt himself. The rest of us just tried to fight without it."

"Don't sell yourself short," Eugho cut in. "Your use of the Umbranium was brilliant."

"Dangerous, you mean." Dust noted. "It was a two-edged sword. We were able to hurt them slightly more than they hurt us."

A Light stealer. Aeia didn't think any of them had survived. Even though she'd only been a child, she could remember Geralt's execution vividly. It was shown for days on the news screens in each city. His death was an example of what happens when someone fights against the king.

"Besides, what do you care, Eugho?" Dust threw up his arms. "You're the one who hunted us down! And frankly I thought you'd died. I sure didn't cry during your funeral, either."

"I care," Eugho said. "I always have. Though at the time I didn't believe Geralt was the savior he was made out to be." Eugho narrowed his eyes and looked to the ceiling. "Actually, I still don't. My priority has always been the people of Nont. I just learned that I could never truly save them as long as I wore the title of Guard-Commander."

Dust nodded, a smug look on his face. "Ahh, changed sides once it suited you, I see."

Eugho shook his head. "No sides, not this time. This team will work for only one thing—a kingdom the people deserve, whether that ends up being controlled by the crown or by no one."

Dust narrowed his eyes. "Fine then. I'm assuming you already have a master plan?"

"I apologize, but I'd like to wait for the last member to show up. She's been held up a bit, but she's crucial to the operation. She'll meet us in Bisham."

Dust frowned. "Not Meckea, I hope."

"Meckea indeed. Like it or not, we'll need her if we're going to make this work."

"Humph." Dust grumbled. "You should have left me in that cage."

"Nonsense." Eugho waved off the man's irritation with a wave. "You're no ordinary man. You're more crucial to this kingdom than you know."

Dust blinked and closed his mouth. His brow still held a deep furrow.

Will he go through with it?

He had to. All of them wanted the same thing, whether they wanted to admit it or not. But with so many conflicting, and strong, opinions, could they really stay a team?

Sale coughed, a welcome break to the silence. "We're ready to depart."

Eugho nodded, his arms still crossed.

The ship came alive as all the cylinders powered up. The ship lurched slightly before slowly lifting off the ground. Once it got high enough, the propellers would take over, and the ship could move freely through the sky.

The engines' low hum filled the room—a sound that would continue throughout the voyage. It reminded Aeia that there was nothing for her to do for some time, and a yawn built up, escaping her mouth before she could stifle it.

Eugho noticed, the seriousness in his posture lifting visibly. "You can go ahead and retire for the night, Aeia."

Reluctantly, she nodded and slipped out of the tense air into the near-empty hallway.

The ship was large, bigger than they needed. It had been a cargo ship made for carrying substantial amounts of heavy materials, but they'd created it to be what they needed. She didn't mind the size.

It meant she got her own room, a luxury she hadn't had since she was a child.

She reached her personal space and was about to open the door when she reconsidered. She was a bit drowsy, but her mind was far too active for her to fall asleep so early. She needed time to meditate.

She headed up to the deck.

Cool air washed over her face as she poked her head out into the night. She inhaled the crisp scents of chilled vegetation that lay just below the ship. She would cherish the countryside. They'd be in the city soon, and she'd miss this solitude.

Aeia climbed out of the hatch. It was spacious out here and granted a clear view in every direction. Only a couple others were on the deck, and they would be too busy to bother her peace. *Especially not when I get in my spot.*

She crept past the crewmen and down to a lower part of the deck. There she would find a crevice, the perfect spot to sit and watch the world go by without any worry of interruption. Her greatest solitude.

Unfortunately, someone was sitting in her spot.

A pang of annoyance shot through her, and she nearly turned to stomp away. But she stopped herself when the individual's unusual clothes caught her attention.

"Eric? I thought you'd gone to sleep."

The man jumped and whirled around.

"Oh, sorry," she mumbled. "It's a good spot, I know. I wasn't expecting to see anyone either."

"I didn't hijack it from you, did I? It just seemed so secluded and ... comfortable."

She shook her head. "I give you permission to use it."

Eric grinned. "Thank goodness. I needed a place as good as this. Especially after what happened today."

"The battle? I thought it went cleanly. No one was hurt too badly."

He shook his head. "No, when ... never mind."

Aeia plopped down a few feet to his side.

"So, this is how you travel?" Eric asked.

"Like it?"

"It's smooth and quiet. Seems to move a lot better than I expected. We could have used these where I came from."

"Where you came from? Sydney?"

Eric chuckled. "No, I'm from Seattle. Sydney was where I was supposed to go to before I ended up here."

"Ended up ... In that flash of light. What was that?"

Eric scratched the back of his head. "It's classified, so I don't think I'm supposed to tell the details. Not that I know a lot of them, honestly."

Aeia felt a twinge of disappointment and tried to shake it away. "That makes sense. I was bound like that when I used to work for the Archduke."

"Guess some things are universal. Important people don't like to share their secrets."

No, they do not.

Aeia looked at her feet. She still struggled with choosing when to share what she knew and when not to. A life of not existing in the public eye constantly sat in her shadow.

"Where are we going, anyway?"

"My hometown, actually. We'll be staying there. It's called Feos."

"Your old stomping grounds, eh? Tell me about it."

Aeia blinked. "Um. It used to be a lovely place. It was one of the best places to move to whether you wanted to start a business or build a home. But that was a long time ago. Now you're lucky if you can even survive."

"Such a change ... What happened?

She let out a sigh. "Archduke Alonius Cer. He tore the city apart for no reason but personal gain. He no longer grants most people even the necessities to live. Anyone who cannot pay his enormous tax is either left to die in streets, or outside the city walls.

Eugho thinks it would be best to ... *remove* Alonius from power," Aeia said. "We don't have the manpower to fight constant battles. He wants to take care of the main issue."

"Makes sense. But what about the people who are hurting right now?"

Aeia slumped over the guard railing. "I don't know."

"I understand that feeling. You can only do so much."

"You're right. Our plan ... it probably won't help the people who need it right now. It will give us a better future overall, but..."

"Don't take what I said too seriously," Eric said. "I mean, I really don't know anything about this world."

Aeia shook herself. "You're fine. We can fix that. Your lack of knowledge I mean. We'll be landing in Feos tomorrow, and Meckea isn't supposed to show up until later ... I could show you around."

Eric smiled. "I would appreciate that."

Chapter Ten

Gray clouds covered the sky. It was a stark contrast to the liveliness of the city surrounding Eric and Aeia. Blues of all shades was the most prominent of the colors, as each person young or old had the strange hair coloring.

Eric struggled to keep up with Aeia's lithe body. She moved through the streets with an enviable ease.

She had convinced Eugho to let her take Eric into Feos once they had landed. She was now bent on giving him the full experience of the life she'd known, helping him understand her world.

Strange as it all was, he was content for now. He had no clue where he was or how he'd come here, but he was lucky to have been found by Aeia.

"We're getting close to the main streets."

Eric instinctively pulled his cloak further over his head to hide his blond hair. He wasn't sure how the law worked, and he had aided in the defeat of this kingdom's soldiers alongside bandits. For all he knew he was a wanted criminal who would get apprehended on sight.

He glanced at Aeia, who strode fearlessly. She made no effort to hide her appearance. The only thing she seemed to be hiding was that dagger she always carried with her.

"Does it matter if we're seen?" he asked.

"Maybe for you, but only because you'll be swarmed with people questioning your hair."

"What about those nobles you hate so much? Won't they know what you look like?"

"No. The only people who would know who I am are far too important to walk the streets. I'll be fine unless we run into a Huntsmen, and if that happens it won't matter what I wear. Besides"— she pointed to the crest on her shoulder— "no one will mess with a servant for house Alestal."

He guessed she believed her words would calm him, but tension still tightened in his gut. He'd left a world of crime a long time ago, and now he was traveling with outlaws working in the shadows.

Are they considered gangs in this world? They don't seem to fight anyone but the government. How do ordinary people see them?

Eric looked around. Though every single person had the same blue hair and eyes, they weren't all the same. Many had different intensities and shades to their hair. Aeia's hair was a very deep blue.

Most people wore clothing like Aeia's. It was made of wool and dyed assorted colors.

He'd been given a similar set of clothes. The trousers were loose and the thin shirt didn't seem nearly warm enough for the environment.

I've seen people wear weirder things in America.

Aeia slowed suddenly, matching his speed and leaning in close.

"Look closely," she whispered and nodded across the street. "What do you see?"

He followed her gaze. There were shops and kids walking along the streets. Nothing seemed to out of the ordinary. Except ... something was off. He couldn't quite place it. He noticed it as soon as they arrived in the city.

He looked at the gray streets and plain storefronts. What started to come to him was the strange lack of ... well, life. The city, while obviously full, was devoid of happiness.

"There's a very oppressive feeling." He scanned the area, but there didn't seem to be very many soldiers. Yet it felt as if there was a whole army stationed here, as if there were an invisible force keeping everyone in line. Eric turned to her. "What's causing it?"

She started to move again without a word.

He followed but hesitated when she went into the mouth of a dark alleyway. Aeia seemed capable, but she was still small.

"Aeia! Isn't that dangerous?"

She turned, staring at him sternly. There wasn't any hostility, but he knew not to question her now. He nodded and followed.

Soon he could tell that this was a lower-class part of the city. The smell hit him first, followed by the sights of filth and garbage. Then he saw the real problem. People, if you could call them that, lined the sides of the wall. Most didn't acknowledge him or Aeia. And those who did only gazed with eyes that had long since lost their life.

What is this?

Was there no one here to help these people? What was wrong with them?

Some didn't even look malnourished. Just …ill. Like they all shared some disease. Was that it? *Is there some sort of plague?*

Eric pulled his shirt above his mouth as subtly as he could and looked at Aeia. She kept moving, though, and he rushed to follow.

What worried him was her expression, which showed absolutely nothing. No compassion flowed from her eyes. No tenderness in her gaze. She cared, she *had* to care. This is what she was fighting against, wasn't it? Why else would she bring him here?

He spun in a circle and scanned everything in sight. All of it was breaking down, decaying. Everything was turning to dust.

Something is wrong in this world.

That thought kept recurring. It was as if the very earth, well, not earth, *ground* beneath his feet was plagued.

"Why are you showing me this?" he asked once they cleared the alleyway.

"I don't know," she said, her face still empty.

"Is this what you're fighting to stop?"

She nodded.

He understood. She wanted his help. But this wasn't his home. He didn't even know where he was. Not to mention that he hardly knew who she was. Worse yet ... could this world even be saved?

Aeia stopped. The slightest hope glimmered in her eyes, causing Eric's heart to quicken. "This isn't your fight. But you're different somehow. I don't understand it yet, but you aren't like us. You don't need Bask to survive, you aren't affected by my…"

He waited for her to continue, but she didn't. "Your what?"

She shook her head. "Never mind. I just think that because you don't have to follow the rules of the Kingdom that you … might be able to change them."

Eric lifted his hands as if to block her words. "I don't know what you expect of me. I can't change anything."

She locked eyes with him. Her face was now more active, the sudden seriousness took him aback.

"Somehow, I know you can."

That alone warmed his heart, and he felt almost unworthy of her trust.

"Look, I appreciate the trust you've placed in me, but this isn't my world. Maybe I should be spending time figuring out how to get out of this place ... get to where I belong."

The brightness in her eyes faded, making him regret his words.

"That doesn't mean I won't help." His words came quickly even thought his conscience warned him to shut up before he committed. "It just means, I guess, that I need more time and information before I commit."

He saw a flicker of hope in her eyes. "It was rude of me to ask so soon," she said. "I'm sorry."

"Don't be! I appreciate it, really. I've never had someone so eager to recruit me."

She flushed and looked down.

"Could you show me a part of the city that's a bit more ... lively?"

Her eyes widened and her mouth formed an O. She nodded, turned, and led him back toward the main street.

As they walked, he saw the more developed and stable parts of the city. It was larger than Seattle. Some of the buildings put skyscrapers where he came from to shame. They looked sturdier, too. They had open windows to let in the breeze.

A breeze washed over him and chilled him.

You'd think the people'd be bundled up in this weather. Eric pulled his coat tighter and breathed warm air onto his hands.

"You're cold?" Aeia's head cocked sideways.

"I'm not used to the weather here."

She raised an eyebrow. "Bisham is one of the warmest regions. It seems hot out today."

"I might need a warmer coat then." He feigned a laugh. "Not now, at least. But I can't imagine what your winters will be like."

"Cold."

He spotted a building that had a series of chambers like Aeia's Bask charger inside. These were guarded by soldiers, though different in appearance to the ones they'd fought yesterday.

He motioned to the building. "What's that place?"

"It's where commoners go to get their charge. Or try to, at least. It's run by the crown, to ensure that the common folk don't get forgotten by the nobility. But lately they've been increasing the price, making it harder for people to get charged."

"Why make it so difficult? Are they running out of Bask?"

She shook her head. "No, unlike other resources, Bask never runs out. There's no reason for the charging stations to be limited."

There's always a reason.

A flash of light drew his attention, pausing his steps. A large pillar close to the center of the city fired a thick blue beam into the sky, followed shortly by some sort of projectile that pierced through the clouds above.

Is it an attack? Eric prepared for a fight but a quick scan of the surrounding people's faces showed that he was the only one who was worried.

He caught up to Aeia, who'd continued in her even pace. "What was *that*?"

"What was what?"

He pointed to the pillar. "That thing! It just shot something into the sky!"

She blinked. "Oh, that's an Elso Tower. We used to have a lot of rocks that would fall from the sky. Those towers stand at the center of each major city and destroy anything that starts to fall towards us."

A chill travelled down Eric's arms as he remembered the meteorites that had filled the Seattle skyline. The meteorites that had set about the events that had led him here.

"Has it ever failed?"

She shook her head. "Not since they were built over three hundred years ago. We used to have lots of problems before then."

"Wow."

If only they'd had such technology on Earth. So much catastrophe could have been avoided. Billions of lives were at stake when he left. Were any still alive? He had no family left back on Earth, but the thought of his home being wiped out sickened him.

"Here we are."

They approached a little café. Back in Seattle, he'd assume it was a coffee shop, but he'd learned not to assume anything here. Aeia stepped off the sidewalk and into the fenced-off area and sat at a round table for two.

Eric raised an eyebrow. The restaurant seemed like a hole in the wall, and they'd passed much more appealing places. But then again, a local's recommendation usually meant more than flashy lights.

He took the seat across from her.

A young waitress approached their table. She looked a little older than Aeia. If years were counted here like they were on Earth, he'd guess her to be about twenty-five.

"And she's back!" The waitress glanced at Eric. "And with a *friend* no less! How was the delivery?"

"More of a pickup," Aeia corrected.

"Ahh, that's right. Let me get your usual." She turned to Eric. "And you?"

"He'll have the same," Aeia said. "He has to try it."

The girl laughed as she headed inside.

Aeia rocked back and forth on her seat, doing what could almost be called a dance as she waited for her food. For a girl who normally showed little emotion, it was refreshing to see her in a place she loved.

"You come here much?"

"Every time she's in the city!" The waitress returned to the table. "I get to hear all about her travels, though, so she's more than welcome."

"You own the place?"

"I do! Name's Tel. And *this*"—she placed a basket filled with bread in front of them— "is my own personal recipe."

In the basket were several small rolls, each one a varied color. It was like a rainbow of bread.

What confused him more was the smell. He couldn't begin to place it.

"What's it called?" he asked warily.

"Green bread!" The waitress chirped. "Well, it used to be green. The other colors were added later."

Aeia was already stuffing a piece in her mouth and *mm-mmm'ing* as she chewed.

"Well, I can't argue with *that*." Eric laughed and put the first one in his mouth.

The roll had a strong, tangy flavor like a lemon and just as sour. He scrunched his face, waiting for his mouth to adjust. Looking through his slits of eyes, he saw that Aeia was devouring them.

Tough girl.

He finished the blue roll, his mouth finally adjusting to the flavor. He felt much more confident when he grabbed a second.

His courage was quickly dashed after the first bite of a yellow roll. He might as well have bitten into a jalapeño. And with the rapid change in flavors, it burned even worse.

He coughed, struggling to keep the food in his mouth.

This earned him a hearty laugh from Tel. "That's the normal reaction from everyone but Alora here. I swear the girl doesn't have taste buds or something."

Alora?

"It's good." Aeia insisted. "It's something new every bite." She grabbed another roll and bit into it vigorously.

Eric smiled at her enthusiasm and tried to feign his own as he pushed aside the other colors for another blue one. He was able to finish it ... barely.

As soon as he finished, Aeia hopped to her feet and dropped some coins on the table as she led him away. She waved without turning when Tel called farewell.

"We're leaving so soon?" He jogged to catch up.

"You took a long time."

I did the best I could...

"The rest of the city will have to wait." She sighed. "The ship will be done recharging soon."

"A... shame." He coughed. After that, he was a bit worried about her idea of fun. He fell in step beside her. "So, why did Tel call you 'Alora'?"

"That's my name now. Aeia died sixteen years ago, when I was three."

"You ... died?"

She frowned. "It's a long story."

"I don't mean to prod. But I was just wondering because you introduced yourself as Aeia to me."

She didn't react. "It's what I still call myself. I don't tell everybody because there are still people out there who could figure out who I truly am. But you are different I know I can trust you."

But how?

If he were in her situation, he wouldn't trust himself. What had he done to deserve such confidence?

They walked along back roads quickly until they approached their destination.

As the ship was coming in view, he heard a rustling from above.

"Aeia. You're back."

Jeffe dropped to the ground a few paces ahead. He was wearing a long brown cloak that covered most of his features. Eric also saw he wore a blindfold, of sorts.

Aeia winced at the sight of the boy. "Eugho had you on watch?"

"Just precautionary. We don't want to be caught off-guard by a patrol, though wouldn't be too likely out here in the outskirts"

"I see," she said.

"What happened to that guy you had with you? I thought he was going to be staying with us for a while."

Aeia's eyebrows folded in confusion. "He's standing right next to me. Can't you see him?"

Well, he is blindfolded, Eric thought

The man lurched back and grabbed his blindfold, yanking it off. When he saw Eric, he jumped back.

Aeia seemed just as surprised.

"What is it?" Eric asked.

Aeia opened her mouth to answer but closed it again.

Jeffe stepped forward. "You don't have a signature, which is ridiculous of course. That would mean that you're dead, which is clearly not the case."

"Signature?" What in the world was this guy talking about?

"That's what we call it, but it's basically the one thing that separates you from everyone else. It's a foolproof method of telling one person from the next."

"Oh. Like a fingerprint?"

That earned him two bewildered stares.

Jeffe lifted his blindfold. "When I'm wearing this, I can see everyone within a mile... except you."

"That's ... discomforting" Eric admitted.

"Very." Jeffe whispered, his eyes narrowing to slits. "I've never met a *human* who had this trait."

Eric grinned. "Well, you wouldn't have seen them if you had, right?"

Jeffe scowled, spun, and sauntered away.

"He's always suspicious, but he'll give you the benefit of the doubt," Aeia said. "They all will. The kinds of people who will risk their lives to change the world with nothing to gain—they're unique people."

Eric wasn't so sure. How long would they stand his differences before they cast him away to face this world alone? But as he looked to Aeia, he knew he could trust her. "I can imagine."

"They're good people, Eric." She stepped in front of him. Her usual mask lifted, and her face turned serious. "If nothing else, always believe that."

"I'll trust them because you do.

"Good." She turned towards the door. "The tour will continue tomorrow. And then you'll understand why the team is so wary right now."

Chapter Eleven

A low rumble sounded through the skies from the dark clouds above. It hadn't rained all morning, but the lack of sunlight brought his mood down.

Aeia, the crew, rather the entire city was blanketed with depression today. They all acted as if they were at a funeral. But Eric hadn't noticed any change in anything he had witnessed so far in this world. He didn't know what was going on, and was worried about finding out.

He followed Aeia as they neared the main gates. The soldiers standing guard stared them down as they approached, but became disinterested when they saw the insignia on Aeia's cloak.

An icy wind buffeted Eric as he entered Feos, sending a shiver up his spine even with the layers of clothing.

It's a wonder people survive in these conditions in such loose clothing.

He'd grown up around ice and snow all his life, but he had a much lower tolerance for the cold than the people of this world. Aeia's short-sleeved shirt exposed her forearms, yet she didn't mind at all.

Eric pulled his cloak tighter. "You really aren't cold?"

She shook her head.

"I don't understand how that's possible! The wind chill here is insane."

"It is a bit windy."

Like everyone else, Aeia hardly spoke. The only thing she'd said all morning was "come with me."

Judging by what she'd said yesterday, he was worried. He couldn't imagine what could be worse than what he'd seen yesterday. Yet whatever it was, it dampened everyone's spirits. "Here." She motioned toward a warehouse. It bore a symbol on the wall that was identical to the one on the ship.

The door opened, revealing a warehouse that was packed full. She led him up a flight of open air stars onto a balcony that overhung the entrance and across from the loading doors on the back.

On the other side, she reached a panel, which became transparent when she settled in front of it on her knees.

"One-way view. No one will be able to see us from the other side," She explained.

He sat next to her. His finger tapped on his leg quickly.

For a few minutes, there was no movement outside the building. That morning's traffic was gone, and the city appeared vacant.

Finally, he saw the movement of a shuttle. It was identical to the shuttle Aeia's team had attacked a few days prior. it moved slowly just above the rooftops over the street.

Next, lines of fully-armed soldiers marched down in half-circles from the shuttles. Their faces were somber, and they bore the look of men who were intent on following orders despite disagreeing with them.

A large crowd followed the soldiers and shuttle as they funneled them through the streets and towards the main gates of the city. Sick, weak, the people staggered with floundering steps. Ever since Aeia had showed him those desperate souls yesterday, he hadn't been able to get them off his mind. Even worse than their frail bodies were the hopeless looks in their eyes.

"What is this?" he whispered in disbelief. "They're leaving?"

"They have to. They can't afford to be here any longer. Everyone who wishes to use a Bask charger needs to pay the tax. And if you can't pay ..."

There were hundreds of them, poor souls being marched away from their homes. Some stumbled and fell. Others pulled them up the best they could and they moved on. The ones that found no help were either prodded with metal rods until they did move or thrown into the back of one of the shuttles.

"Where do they go?"

Aeia rolled back, moving from sitting on her knees, to hugging them in front of her. "Into the wilderness, I suppose, to die. Lord Cer doesn't want their bodies crowding his city."

He couldn't understand how anybody could treat another human being with such callousness. People had struggled in America, but usually someone was willing to help the poor.

"It's barbaric!"

"It's how the world is, Eric. The great houses don't care for someone who doesn't make them money. To the Nobility, their deaths reduce the number of mouths to be fed. The number of people to be charged."

"But they're people! Doesn't that mean anything?"

At that, her face darkened. "Lord Cer doesn't care what you are, only if you can help him or not. And I can say that from experience."

He gritted his teeth at the sight of a child in the mix.

This has to stop.

As soon as he thought it, something shifted. A flame stirred in his chest. He knew he had to join the fight against this evil. Regardless of how he got here, or why, this abuse couldn't be ignored.

"This can't continue. No one deserves this. And I'd be a fool if I refused to help those who are trying to make a difference. I want to help."

She studied him, held his gaze. "Are you sure?"

Compassion and anger welled up within him. He'd never made a difference on Earth. He'd been just another face in the masses. Maybe this was his second chance.

The new flame in his chest burned brighter.

"I've never been so sure of anything."

* * *

Aeia entered the command deck. Eugho was talking with Sale, plans spread out in front of them on the table. She hesitated, and her heart sinking. She wanted to talk to Eugho alone. She dared to take a step forward to get his attention but paused, her legs not wanting to move any closer. Even after a year she still wasn't used to being part of a team, to have input on the decisions that affected her life. Her mind told her that Eugho wasn't like her past overseer's, if only her heart would listen.

Aeia, you've talked to him plenty of times. There's no reason to be scared.

She was just going to ask a favor... a big one, she'd admit. But a favor. It wasn't like Eugho had ever rejected her requests for no good reason.

Eugho noticed her and lifted his eyebrows. When she still didn't move, he motioned for her to follow and stepped away.

Once they were out of earshot of everyone else, he waited patiently.

And still, her heart nearly beat out of her chest.

What if he gets the wrong idea? I think Eric can be helpful.

She swallowed hard. "I was wondering about the guy we found in the forest..."

"Eric, yes."

Her vision became fuzzy, she squinted her eyes to compensate.

"I was thinking ... he might make a good addition to our team."

"Humph," Eugho grunted, a smirk crossed his face. "A man who can't be seen by Hunters? I'd say so."

"Oh!" She perked up. "You agree then?"

Eugho held up a hand. "Not so fast. We don't know about his past. I trust him, too, but we need to be careful. He'll stay with me for now. I'll get him up to speed in self-defense. The rest of what he should know about living here, I'll leave to you."

Aeia grasped her responsibility. She lived a dangerous life. Was she endangering him too much just because of her belief in him? Even though no one knew why he'd come to them—not even Eric—she believed he was there for a reason.

"I understand," she said. "Thank you, sir."

An amused smile crossed Eugho's face. "I thought I told you, I'm no commander here. Everyone is here by choice. Had you simply decided to bring Eric, I wouldn't have stopped you. I trust your intuition as much as my own."

"I know. But I respect your opinion. I asked because I wanted to."

Eugho let out a laugh. "You give me far too much credit! How I could surround myself with such fine people, I'll never know."

He led her back to the main resting area. A few people relaxed in chairs around the room. Eric was curled up near the fireplace at the back of the room. As soon as he saw them approaching, he hopped to his feet and faced Eugho.

"Calm down, lad. I just finished telling Aeia that I'm not the commander. We're here as a team."

Eric nodded and relaxed his stance.

"Now," Eugho continued. "Aeia told me you want to join our cause?"

"Yes, sir. I saw the round-up in Feos. People should never be treated like that. Back on Earth I joined the military so I could prevent such atrocities. And while my circumstances have ... changed, I intend to keep protecting those who can't protect themselves."

"Well said," Eugho said. "I've met more than a few soldiers with convictions like yours. All were men I'd recruit again." Eugho then let out a sigh. "You must realize though, this is no military. We work in the shadows, and there may be times where you'll feel more like a thief than a guard. Keep in mind that our end goal is to give strength back to the weak. Return the power that rightfully belongs to them."

Eric straightened his shoulders.

"Good, lad. And welcome to the team."

Relief flooded Aeia, and she released a breath she'd been holding.

"Thank you, sir," Eric said. "Where do I start?"

Eugho let out a laugh, patting him on the back hard. "Don't worry about that just yet. Everyone will have a part to play. For now, just sit tight."

With a polite bow, Eugho left them.

"That's no good." Eric sighed and turned to her. "I'd like to know what I'll be doing. What do you do here?"

She froze. The blood moving through her veins turned to ice.

Most people didn't know who—or rather what—she was. And those who were told of what she could do grew to hate her, even most members of the team.

Don't tell him. He'll react the same once he knows what you are.

"It's hard to explain what I do." She forced a smile before allowing the mask she wore so easily to return. "I'm ... complicated."

"Okay." He offered a warm smile. "Maybe you'll tell me someday."

She let out a silent breath of relief. They each took seats by the fire. "What did *you* do before all this, Eric?"

He looked up thoughtfully for a moment. "My life was pretty complicated too."

Fair enough.

"It really wasn't anything to be proud of. I fought every day. That's all I would do. By the time I learned the importance of helping people, it hardly mattered anymore. The one who needed it most was already gone. My mother held out so long for me. Far longer than any doctor said she would. But it still wasn't long enough for me to get over myself and visit her."

His face darkened with regret.

She knew better than anyone what it meant to do terrible things, to regret terrible things.

"I did horrible things." Her voice was a mere whisper. "I was only doing what I was told, but deep down, I knew I had a choice."

Eric smiled weakly and leaned back. "The past trails us, doesn't it? We can either accept it as a ghost or as a guide."

"Ghost or guide? What do you mean?"

"It's easy to let our past haunt us. But I choose to let it guide me, help me become a better person. The things I've done wrong have taught me what is truly important. Maybe we needed to discover our worst to learn how to become our best. I know I hurt people, and I regret that. But if I don't learn from it, then it was all for nothing."

Aeia frowned. "I wish I could have learned without making all those mistakes."

Eric chuckled. "Wouldn't that be nice?"

Aeia couldn't tear her eyes off him. He was so different that her. But she felt like she could tell him things, everything, and he'd understand her.

A masked figure moved in to the room from the side, landing right in front of her without a single sound.

Aeia jumped, pulled back, and grabbed the hilt of her dagger.

Before she had it free from its sheath, Eric leapt forward and positioned himself between her and the figure.

"Who's this you found, Aeia? He has good reflexes."

She recognized the voice and let out a loud groan. "Meckea! You should know better than to surprise me!"

Eric relaxed and stepped out of their way so the women could see each other.

"The fact that I shouldn't is what compels me to do so!" She pulled off her brown mask to reveal a wide grin. "Life's more interesting when you provoke danger."

She was taller than Aeia and had long hair that shined the deep blue that was only achievable by the extremely wealthy. And even though she had been wearing a full mask only seconds ago, her hair fell down the sides of her head with a perfection that Aeia couldn't achieve with hours of preparation.

Aeia scowled at the newcomer, annoyed more about her interruption than anything. "Do it for my sake then. You know I don't like Jumping when I don't have to!"

She waved her hand dismissively. "You never told me who your man is."

My man?

Aeia looked at Eric, who looked thoroughly confused. A pink flush rose his neck at the sight of Meckea.

It was understandable. Meckea was very popular among men. She was gorgeous, even in her traveling garb. It wasn't uncommon for some of the younger nobles to attempt to court her.

Meckea would never return anything more than a smile, too focused on her secret life to be distracted with things like romance.

"Aeia found me," Eric confessed. "I'd probably be frozen and starving by now if she hadn't."

"Yes." Aeia nodded. "He was sitting in the middle of the woods. He traveled there instantly ... or something. He's not from our world."

Meckea raised an eyebrow. "He's an alien?"

"I *am* an alien." Eric chuckled to himself. "Here I was thinking of all of you as aliens."

Meckea studied him carefully, her eyebrows furrowed in concentration. "He looks human, except for the hair. And his accent is odd. Sounds eastern... But you say you came from another world?"

Eric shrugged. "Maybe. There's no telling what happened. I never thought about the accent. It is rather strange that we're able to understand each other, isn't it?"

Aeia blinked. "Yeah, how do you know how to speak the King's Tongue?"

"I thought I was speaking English," Eric said. "This is how everyone talked back home too. Well, at least in America."

"An alien that speaks our language! How interesting." Meckea smiled widely again. "You found something intriguing, Aeia! We'll have to figure this one out."

The woman turned back to Eric. "I'm Meckea." She bowed gracefully before him. "Lady of House Alestal."

Eric let out a surprised huff and bowed. "Sorry, I didn't know."

"And he's a gentleman too!" She shot Aeia a sly glance and waved at him to stand. "Don't mind it. Not only am I not wearing anything suitable for a Duchess, but I would hardly expect aliens to know our customs. Anyway, I take it you'll be traveling with us?"

"I'm joining the team."

"Good! I look forward to working with you then."

With a small wave, she started towards the command deck.

Eric's gaze locked on her until she disappeared. Only then did he turn to Aeia. "She's a friend of yours?"

An unfamiliar emotion filled her stomach. She considered it. Jealousy. How ridiculous. "More of a co-worker, but she's one of the nicer ones. If you need something, then I'd suggest going to her first if I'm not here. Her presence here means I've got work to do."

She rose, straightened her collar, and turned to him. "The meeting's about to start for us leaders. I'll show you to your quarters?"

"Sounds good." He stretched. "Maybe tonight I'll get some rest."

Chapter Twelve

Aeia scanned the team. Even she was impressed with how many *legends* were in the room. Some of these people had been highly influential noblemen, soldiers, and even military officials. All of them bore the same contempt for the way things worked, contempt toward the nobles and the King who allowed such atrocities.

The nobles controlled the poor and didn't fear the commoners. The poor could do nothing but wish for a better world. Any action against the crown meant certain death.

But this group was different. Because they are nobles and leaders, they had certain privileges. They had the weapons, the connections, and most importantly, the ability to charge. That alone made them something to be feared. They couldn't be controlled.

"All of you have some idea of why we're here," Eugho started. "But I'll say it anyway—we are going to break this city and remake it as it should be."

Aeia straightened. *Such confidence.*

"That's a bold claim!" Meckea stated, though not displaying actual skepticism.

"It is. Alonius Cer is the most ruthless of the Archdukes. It will be no surprise to the locals when we start causing trouble. But we will still have trouble forming a rebellion with all the competition."

"You say that like someone else is going to start one," Dust said. He was cleaned up now and wore a combat suit with a symbol Aeia had only seen in history lessons. The mark of a Light stealer, one of the rebellion leaders that Geralt had trained himself.

Eugho nodded. "They have already. And rumor has it you would know its leader quite well. A man has appeared and gained quite a following in recent months. A man who claims to be Geralt returned."

Dust mocked with a laugh. "And who would be foolish enough to believe him?"

"People with nowhere else to turn."

Dust grumbled and crossed his arms.

Eugho held his arms out. "You all know as well as I that this is nothing but a scam. Geralt was killed in front of a large audience. But whoever this man is, he has connections with House Cer, so his 'rebellion' has yet to even draw a single raid from the Lord Cer's soldiers."

"How does this help us?" Jeffe leaned forward. "It's another scheme of some noble."

"It's a scheme fueled by the anger of hundreds, if not thousands, of angry men and women. Men and women, we can turn to fight for something other than revenge."

"Thousands or not," Dust said, "they won't have weapons strong enough to overtake one of the world's super powers. With those mechanical monstrosities he ironically calls 'Guardians,' Alonius is all but untouchable."

"Which is why we'll needing to bring in some help. There are only two forces that can match House Cer—Garlot Orlan and the Royal Guard."

Dust growled. "Another corrupt Archduke and lapdogs to the King who couldn't care less about what's happening to us."

"Yes, but those 'lapdogs', namely the one who leads them, still seek justice." Eugho paced the room. "Feos is turning into more of a garbage pit by the day. The laws of caretaking given to the Archdukes are constantly being broken. I believe that if we can show that Alonious is stealing Bask from everyone in the city, the Royal Guard will have no choice but to remove him from power until the King awakens."

"It's a possibility." Sale fiddled with some sort of small device in his hands. "But without the King to back her up, The Royal Guard-

Captain will be hesitant to start a full-blown *war*, which is the only thing that will come from a confrontation with Alonius Cer."

"Which is why we take the choice out of the Captain's hands," Eugho spoke. "There is one law that, even today, is still revered as the most important law for the noble houses to follow. Bask stones cannot be taken from one house and given to another without the approval of the Crown. It is the one law that prevents constant battles between the houses. If we were to offer indisputable evidence that House Cer is *stealing* Bask from the lesser houses in his control, the Guard will intervene immediately."

"Is he?" Sale swallowed hard. "I knew Alonius had gone mad, but *that*?"

"It's no coincidence that Bask starvation is higher than ever in Feos. Alonius is hoarding all the Bask he can get his hands on. Even at the cost of his own province's stability."

Jeffe leaned back. "Our plan is to take control of a faux rebellion and reveal the secrets of the most deranged mind in the kingdom? I don't see how this can go wrong."

"It's a risky plan," said Eugho. "Which is why I invited the only group of people capable of doing it."

Silence filled the room. Each member of the team was considered brilliant. If one were to refuse, the others would likely follow.

Should I say something to help Eugho?

She had decided months ago that she would put her faith in Eugho. The others may know that already, but wasn't she just as much a member of the team as them?

She cleared her throat. "If it wasn't you, Eugho, I wouldn't try it. I've heard of the type of leader you were when you were the Guard-Captain. During Geralt's rebellion, you won almost every battle you fought in. I will follow you."

Meckea leaned forward and put her hands over her knees. "Whelp, I'm convinced. Where do we start?"

A smile crossed Eugho's face, and he looked to the rest of the team.

"You're crazy," croaked Brunst. His decision to speak for the first time startled more than one. "I've been through worse."

"Crazy indeed." Sale nodded. "But I suppose you have to be if you actually intend to change anything."

Jeffe shrugged. "You proved yourself to me when you rescued Dust from the Guard. I'll keep my word. Abandoning this would leave a bad taste in my mouth."

All eyes fell to Dust. "Geralt was a great man. A man strong enough to confront the King himself. And even *he* couldn't win. But ... maybe strength alone isn't enough. I know how smart Eugho is. Every step I took, Eugho had already predicted it and set up a plan to prevent it. He knows how the Royal Guard and the Archdukes think. They aren't invincible, and they are losing the support of the people. Take away their control, and they are nothing but cowardly men and women. And without the King to intervene himself this time, I believe that this plan has a chance." He stood up, bowed to Eugho. "You have my support."

Aeia looked across the room. *Not a single voice of opposition ... amazing.*

"I'm honored." Eugho pulled his arms behind his back. "Let's get started."

His composure changed from that of a politician to one of a commander. Even though he claimed he wasn't in charge and everyone was equal on the team, all of them knew who they were following.

"For this plan to work," Eugho said, "what is said in this room stays within the team. If we succeed, no one will know this meeting ever happened."

Eugho motioned to Meckea, "That is why the task of investigating Lord Cer's Bask taxing will fall to those who can house an operation of Shadows in the direct eye of the public. Meckea, with the assistance of Aeia, will infiltrate the Trade Center of Feos. If they can find out who House Cer's allies are, we can expose them all in one sweep."

Jeffe leaned forward. "I was under the impression you wanted my expertise in gathering information."

"That I do." Eugho turned to the young man. "The House of Shadows can speak to the other Houses openly. I need you to stay in the underground where you are now. You perhaps hold the most important task. All of us will be focused on our aspects of the mission, we will be separated, inside the enemies ranks. I need you to keep us all aware of any unexpected movements. We can't afford to be surprised."

"The job of an informant? I could pass on one of mine to you. You hardly need me to see to this personally."

Eugho's face hardened, and he tipped his head forward. "You're underestimating Alonius Cer. He has manipulated every nobleman in Feos. There is not one who will speak against him. I suspect that by now even the underground is under his control. I do not need an informant. I need someone who the underground fears more than Alonius Cer."

The answer seemed to satisfy Jeffe, who leaned back into his seat.

Before meeting Eugho, Aeia had never even heard the name. How could a lone man be more terrifying than someone as cruel, resourceful, and manipulative as Alonius Cer?

Who is Jeffe?

She shook her head. It was probably just flattery, a way to get Jeffe to join their side. If he really *was* stronger, there was no way Eugho would make him aware of the mission.

Eugho turned to Dust. "You must return to the rebellion you left behind. Its reappearance cannot be chance, and I want to know the truth behind the man who leads it."

"A Geralt copycat?" Dust said. "Should be easy enough to unravel. There are many things that he wouldn't be able to know. One conversation will tear his persona apart."

"I can only hope it will be so simple. If you don't mind, though, I'd like to accompany you."

Dust furrowed his brow, but soon his expression turned to amusement. "You want to keep tabs on me?"

"More or less," Eugho admitted. "But it is also because I have no information to provide you about him. I'm no Huntsman, but I've been trying to learn their art. I can see what's going on around us."

"Ah, that would be good," Dust said. "I'd rather not walk into a trap."

A sly smirk crossed Eugho's face. "Neither would I. I already retrieved you from prison once. I admit your strengths as a Light stealer are very impressive, which is why I'd ask another thing of you as well. I'll fill you in on the details later."

Eugho let out a breath and stepped back to address the entire group. "Thanks to Sale, there are safe-houses stationed across the city. If anything goes awry, head to the nearest one and set off your beacon. And of course, anyone who sees a beacon going off should make it their priority to assist. Any objections to this, or to the plan as a whole?"

Aeia had none, and the idea that the help of so many were at the press of the button comforted her. She looked among the others, her team, and searched their faces for uncertainty.

Questions and concerns filled each person's eyes, but none lifted a voice against the plan.

At last. We can fight back.

* * *

Eric rolled to his side. The first light of morning shone into the room and across the silvery metal floor. Despite his weariness, he hadn't slept well. So much had happened in such a brief time. The past days had been unbelievable. *Was this all an elaborate dream?*

It wasn't. But what did that mean?

He sat on the side of his bed and looked at the combat suit that had been provided to him. A war. He had only been in this world a few days, and he found himself involved in a war. What was the purpose? As terrible as things were here, why was he supposed to help them? These weren't his people. With their blue hair, he wasn't entirely certain that these were his own species.

He could find his way without Aeia, or Eugho. Look for others from Earth. Surely he wasn't the only one whose teleportation went awry. Others went through the portal like he did.

But in those last moments of his time on Earth, he had felt something. A strong feeling as he'd directed the scientists towards the portal and their only chance of survival. When he rallied Nick to help him.

Purpose.

He'd had a mission then, just as he did now. That was it. *That was it!* Ignoring the fact that his mother was dying, fighting against anyone who looked at him the wrong way, cursing the father who had abandoned him as a child, all of it had left him with nothing.

But the few minutes helping others, the very last thing he did on Earth, had given him more satisfaction than his entire life before then. It didn't matter that he wasn't from here. It didn't matter that this wasn't a fight for his own land or people. Aeia needed his help. And if he could help, then he would know that his life meant something.

He hopped to his feet and grabbed the suit. The hesitation he had felt was gone. As he put on his suit, a sense of duty—much greater than his days of training in the Marine Corp. It was time to fight for a purpose. A reason beyond himself.

Eric gripped the handle to the door of his room. He pulled the door open and stepped into his new life.

Chapter Thirteen

A warm breeze ruffled Eric's hair as he stood alone in the alley. He smiled. This was the first time the weather had pleased him since he'd arrived in this world. Hopefully it would stay this way, at least for a little while longer.

He let out a contented sigh and brushed his hand through his hair, stopping himself just before he did it. He wouldn't want to mess up the blue dye before it completely dried, not after Eugho had gone through so much trouble.

I bet I look ridiculous.

Well, at least now he wouldn't be singled out. He hadn't gotten much attention during his walk here, so it had to be working.

Now if only the man I'm meeting would show up.

He leaned against the wall with his eyes closed. Any longer and he might just fall asleep.

A quiet clacking brought his attention to the ground, where a small metallic orb bounced against the pavement. He eyed it, watched as it began to glow blue. Energy surged out from within it, quickly filling the area with blue twirling light.

Eric raised an arm to protect himself from the explosion but felt nothing as the light danced around him.

"Eugho wasn't lying then." A voice came from behind.

Dust approached, looking Eric up and down as he neared. "Not even a slight reaction. You're just like... him."

Eric looked himself over, patting various parts of his body as he checked that everything was in place. "What *was* that thing?"

"A pulse bomb." The man twirled a second orb in his hand." That one was strong enough to kill a few men."

Eric gasped. "Kill? And you threw it at me?"

The man shrugged. "If you weren't as Eugho said, I didn't want to waste my time. But fortunately for you, he wasn't lying."

Lucky me.

"Anyway, I guess we haven't been properly introduced. My name is Dust, I was a leader during the civil war ten years ago." The man motioned for him to follow. "Were you here at that time?"

How much does Dust know? Eugho must have told Dust his story.

"I've only been in your world a few days."

"This will be interesting then. When I first met Geralt, he had been here for years. He was already a master at manipulating this world in his favor. That gift you have almost saved the world the last time it was used."

"Geralt? Who's Geralt?"

The man smiled and waved at a nearby wall. It shuddered then shifted inwards and to the side, creating a door. The door opened into a stone hallway. A glow of technology filled the air with light and a low hum as the two entered the building.

Screens came to life as they strode into a small room. The screens displayed surveillance footage from all over the city—or at least what looked to be the populated parts of town. Racks of weapons and gear filled the other walls, all in a perfect line.

"This all belonged to Geralt. He was a hero, a man who nearly brought down both the Archdukes and the King. He led the most successful rebellion that the world had ever seen. Many small groups that he led still remain all over the kingdom, waiting for their chance to strike again."

"Sounds like a great leader," Eric said.

"Actually, he wasn't." Dust shifted backwards and crossed his arms. "He preferred to work alone, which is why he had rooms like these hidden all over the city. The rebellion was led by a group of men trained by him, the Light stealers. That is what I am. We were trained to use the tactics and weapons he employed. And as such, we only allowed ourselves the bare minimum of Bask energy. The less we have coursing through us, the less it can be used against us."

"What do you mean?" Eric asked.

Dust walked to one of the weapon racks and pulled a sword free. It was small and black. Dust winced as he carried it, as if it were shocking him. "Geralt used weapons no one else could. Like you saw when the pulse bomb went off, not everything affects you the same way as they do us. Take this sword. It is made of a metal that repulses Bask energy. It cannot be manipulated as other metals can, and even being near it causes those filled with Bask to grow weaker."

Dust extended it toward Eric, who took it cautiously. It was surprisingly heavy, and he had to step forward to maintain his balance.

"Umbranium." Dust nodded towards it. "Don't know how Geralt found it. Never had heard of it before he arrived. But it will be your greatest ally in this fight. I use one, though it's mixed with a few other metals so I don't kill myself. That one is yours now."

Eric eyed it nervously and retrieved its sheath from the rack. "It sounds dangerous. I'll be careful with it."

"Not too careful. You'll use it more than a few times I'm sure. This fight *will* take lives. Geralt knew that better than anyone, and he didn't cower when he knew he'd lose his own."

Eric winced. "What happened to him?"

Dust's face turned dark, and he turned towards the screens. "I suppose I should show you. The entire world saw—an example of what happens when you challenge the King."

The screens went dark, and only the one in the center flickered back on. It shifted to a clear video of the wide area below a massive fortress. Two armies raged against each other, one was better equipped, but the other was larger in number.

The larger army must have been the rebellion. The armored were few, and most had makeshift protection over their clothes or none at all. Most had weapons of swords and crossbows, with a few scattered who seemed to be using common tools as weapons. What should have been a slaughter was instead a fierce battle as the determination and willpower of the rebels far exceeded that of the King's army.

Only so much could be done though. The King's army was equipped with highly advanced armor and weaponry. Sections on their arm-guards would unfold into small shields strong enough to deflect crossbow bolts. If needed, they could even leap through the air at heights far greater than any man should.

The rebels were steadily losing on every front, all except the very center, where they held their own, even against the greatest concentration of soldiers and war machines.

The camera moved in to that part of the battlefield, and Eric could see that the source of the rebellion's strength was a single man in crimson armor. He tore through the enemy's ranks. With each swing of his blade their weapons either failed or turned against themselves. Explosions of Bask energy ravaged the King's soldiers yet did nothing to the man in red.

The King's army shifted in a wave from the back, the wave continuing through the rebel army. Then, the King's army parted down the middle as a lone man strode forward.

He was tall, but his presence made him seem far larger than he was. His eyes burned like blue flames. His entire body shone of the Bask energy, visible waves emanating outward.

The King.

He didn't regard a single man as he moved through the masses. It wasn't out of pride or arrogance. He simply *was* greater than the others. He wasn't human—he couldn't be. Eric finally understood—he was the King, and that was all anyone needed to understand.

He stopped where the two armies met and looked down upon the Crimson Knight. "You are the one who has challenged my kingdom."

Geralt slowly raised his blade.

Despite what Eric had seen of the battle, he couldn't believe anyone would be brave enough to challenge the King. No matter the reputation, no matter what they could do ... how could anyone challenge something so absolute?

The King seemed surprised at the man's boldness and drew his own sword. "Very well."

The two blades met, a twisting whirlwind of energy as the umbranium fought against the Bask energy. However, the Umbranium did not react the same way as it had against the common soldiers. The King's energy fought back. Each wave that was repulsed turned back towards Geralt.

The clash repeated itself with each meeting of the two combatant's blades.

"Your magic is not unending, 'King'." Geralt broke free of the struggle and fell into a striking stance. "Most men fall within a few clashes of this blade. How long will you last?"

The King scowled and pulled back. "You forget where you are. This world, and everything in it, is filled with Bask energy. *My* energy."

A pulse of blue light exploded once again, coming outward from the King himself. Everything made of metal lurched outward before being pulled back towards the king. Even large vehicles dragged across the ground as they were pulled towards their master.

Geralt tried to attack but was stopped by a massive explosion of spinning metals.

Everything came apart, their many different forms and shapes bursting into small pieces and twisting in a whirlwind around the King. They reformed, without heat or skillful crafting, into large metal coils. And like a dozen metal serpents, they lunged forward.

Geralt retreated. He held his sword high and lashed out at the metal coils as they neared him. When he would land a direct hit, they would shatter apart and fall to the ground. It was no victory though. A mere a moment later, blue energy would pulsate through the pieces of metal once again, and the coils would regain their form.

As time passed, more machines and swords were dismantled by the King and turned into his weapon. Powerful as he was, Geralt was only one man against an unwavering foe. He couldn't keep up as the coils lashed out at him in quickening strikes. He was forced to turn from them to flee and toss pulse bombs, black daggers like his sword, *anything* to slow the onslaught of the King's coils.

A coil finally found its mark. It wrapped around one of Geralt's arms and lurched back, taking the man with him. Three more coils waited to wrap around his other limbs. They latched on, like serpents working as one. They pulled apart, until Geralt was stretched to his limit. Then they dragged the limp man back towards the waiting King.

"Now do you understand? You are not fighting only me, you are fighting the world." The King strode forward. He reached to pull Geralt's helmet free. It showed an old man, graying and wrinkled, without a single flake of blue on him.

Eric recognized him.

Nick!

Eric's stomach turned. He had seen Nick—the other security guard—only a few days ago waiting for him outside the portal. His face, so young and strong, was now replaced with a scarred veteran.

On the recording, Nick's voice sounded clear and strong. "I knew what I was fighting. Even if everything is against me, I will still fight."

"No. You will join the world."

The King wrapped his hand around Nick's throat. Bask energy surged from the King's fingers, pouring into the one man separate from the world. Nick fought it, struggled against the iron hold, but he was helpless. A single hair turned blue, followed by another. Soon, every hair turned the color of this world.

Nick's eyes were the last to go, his pupils becoming the crystal blue orbs that everyone else had.

"Welcome to my world," the King whispered. Every coil struck forward at once, impaling Nick in a dozen places.

It was too much. Eric's gut twisted. He couldn't help but lurch forward as he watched his old ally die.

Why? How was Nick here so long ago? Did the transporter send them all to this world at different times? And why had Nick been leading a war against the King?

Dust turned off the screen and stepped backwards. "The King killed many people's hope that day. He turned our hero into a man like everyone else. He had always been this untouchable warrior, a man who didn't follow our laws. He was—"

"A friend of mine," Eric whispered.

Dust whirled around.

"His name was Nick Barrier. He was in boot camp with me in the Marine Corp. Both of us were selected to protect a top-secret facility because of our talents ... He left my world the same way I did."

"How is that possible? He lived ... *died*, years before you even arrived here."

Eric shrugged. "I have no idea. He went through the transporter only a few moments before I did."

A few moments ... into years? If we were separated by that much. Then all the others ... How long have the people from Earth been in this world?

Dust leaned forward. "And you're certain of this?"

"I've spent years with that man. His face is unmistakable, down to the scar on his left cheek."

"That does explain why you both share the same immunities to Bask." Dust crossed his arms. "Does that mean that more can come from your world?"

The air caught in Eric's lungs as he remembered the calamity. "I was the last one through at the time. But I can't be sure if I'm the last one to arrive. Not anymore."

"Then the world needs you even more. We failed with Geralt—Nick. I won't let the same thing happen to you. I'm going to train you, teach you everything Nick learned and shared with me in his time here. You will lead the new generation of Light stealers."

Chapter Fourteen

The city was a welcome change to the wilderness. As much as she enjoyed nature, she felt at home among the buildings and people.

She felt more in her element here, especially having taken on the role of Meckea's steward. She knew how to not be noticed by the nobles, how to not make eye contact unless she meant to.

But there was one very important difference: she wasn't sent here to kill. Yes, Eugho had *asked* her if she would jump for him, but it was her choice. And if she did jump, it would merely be to extract information.

Her heart glowed at the thought. She missed jumping. She missed the power, using a skill that so few others had. Not that she disliked what she was doing with Eugho, of course, but jumping was a feeling that couldn't be replicated. It was her element, her expertise. Lately, she'd felt like a blacksmith in a lumber mill.

"We need to find someone who has seen the face of Lord Cer's Bask collector," Meckea reminded her as they neared their destination. "The nobleman we're about to visit makes the amount of business in Feos I conduct seem like a street shop! He'll know if anyone is acting odd."

She nodded, though she needed no reminding.

"We may not even see him today, but don't worry. This is only half an operation. We'll be coming here for business regularly."

The fact that Meckea, and even a few others on the team, were nobles who still carried on their trades had slipped her mind.

Aeia wasn't sacrificing much to be on this team. She'd hated her old life, and as a free woman, she had nowhere else to go. But Meckea was risking so much for this cause. Her entire house, which was not at all small, could be dismantled if she was discovered. Knowing Lord Cer's reputation, she risked much worse.

"Why are you here?" she finally asked.

Meckea turned. Her eyebrows slanted in a V.

"I mean, what made you join the rebellion? Why did you join with Eugho?"

"Why do you ask?"

"You have so much to lose."

Meckea smiled widely. "Why would a Lady of the house of Shadows care about lowly men and women?"

She nodded, lowering her gaze.

"Oh no, don't be embarrassed. It's a good question."

Emboldened, Aeia looked up again. "Then why?"

"Eugho." A wistful look crossed Meckea's face. "I'm doing this because I believe in him. Because I trust he's making the right choice."

That was it?

"Well, I do love him after all." She tilted her head towards Aeia playfully. "I know what kind of man he is, and I trust him."

Aeia looked at her feet. *She's doing it because she loves him? She's risking everything for that?*

"But what about your business?"

"I'm caring for them. We're handling everything as usual. But you're right. There would be great trouble if they knew what I was doing. Many, I think, wouldn't approve at all." "Aeia." Meckea said. "Have you ever loved someone?"

Love...?

It was an intense liking for someone, wasn't it? She had liked people in the past. Duke Dallen had been quite nice to her when she was under his care. He was one of her few overseers who made an effort to talk to her. And he always made sure that she was comfortable when he could.

She also enjoyed her time with Sen, before he became complete and lost everything that made him human. As a boy, he had a constant sparkle in his eye, foolishly anticipating his training to become a Void Jumper. They never got to play very much, but he did tell her stories of his life back at his family's estate and what he was going to do once he returned there.

But did she love either of them? Aeia rocked her head to the side and slumped against the wall of the shuttle.

You're supposed to know when you love someone, right? It should be obvious.

"I... I haven't loved anyone," she whispered.

Why were those words so hard to say? Why did she feel ashamed to not have felt something when she didn't even know what it felt like? It could be a terrible feeling that forces people to do things they normally wouldn't do.

Meckea's usual smug expression was gone, replaced with a parted mouth. "It will come. You will feel love, I'm sure of it."

Would she really? Should she even try to hope for it? Was it even worth hoping for?

The shuttle began to slow. Aeia pressed her feet against the floor to compensate for the decrease in velocity. She struggled to return her unemotional mask to its familiar place. Once again, she would be posing as a noble's handmaiden. Only this time it was with a good person, and for a worthy cause.

"You're all right," whispered Meckea. "You don't have to hide *all* of your emotion this time."

Aeia couldn't bring herself to relax now that her training was taking over. Meckea still eyed her. Aeia forced an awkward smile.

"Don't bother. The idea is to do what's easiest for you. Do what you need to. This visit won't matter too much. We aren't meeting with anyone *too* important today."

The shuttle stopped. Sestes, Meckea's chauffeur, hopped out and opened the side door for the two women. He was middle aged and had a kind face. A perfect front. Aeia knew the man personally, and he was one of the most skilled Shadows in all Nont. But looking at him now, she could be easily fooled that this was somehow a different kind of man.

Meckea stepped through the door, and Aeia followed. Ahead of her, Aeia stood with a grace expected of a handmaiden of a powerful noblewoman, a character she had played on more than one occasion. It was easy for her since while acting as a handmaiden she was merely meant to be available to a noblewoman for any of her needs. No one worth noting would give Aeia a second glance.

Taking a deep breath to settle her pounding heart, Aeia took Seste's hand and allowed him to help her down. The man was in his late fifties, though the gleam in his eye seemed to defy it. He had a short and well-trimmed beard that was a lighter shade of blue, as many servants limited their Bask intake for the sake of modesty. Aeia paused beside Meckea.

The man bowed before the two. "I'll await your return, Lady Alestal."

"I may be a while." Meckea took his hand and patted it. "Please try and get some rest."

The man bowed again and returned to the shuttle.

Meckea turned towards the building they had stopped at. "Ah, and there they are."

Aeia followed her gaze and her mask crumbled in surprise before she resurrected it. *Of all the nobles ... Him?*

Lord Hattin strode up to them. Each arm swept upward at his side as he showcased his estate. "Welcome to my home, my lady!"

Aeia couldn't be mistaken, Lord Hattin was infamous for his manners. No other noble would welcome a fellow Lady in such a casual manner. It was fit for a commoner's invitation of supper to a fellow worker, not between two very influential merchants. He should have bowed and led Meckea without highlighting his achievements. A proper nobleman doesn't need to tell what is apparent.

Aeia hoped that her hair would mask her face. A pointless gesture, as the man would have no idea who she was or how close he'd been to death at their last meeting.

She swallowed emotion that threatened to choke her. She'd never had to be around one of her targets before. Her missions had always been completed, her face wiped from her victim's memory. Only her superiors and a few powerful noblemen should ever recognize her.

"Thank you, Lord Hattin. I am delighted to be here," Meckea purred.

Hattin laughed. "If only it were for a happier reason! I would have enjoyed your presence here quite some time ago."

"Oh, I'm sure you would have." A smirk crossed Meckea's face. "Though I mean no offense, Feos is not a city I like to visit. Its master is as good a host as a wild barrow."

"Oh, it's not so bad. A fed barrow can be surprisingly tame." Hattin laughed at his own joke.

"Fed or not, there are many other things I would prefer spending my time with than a barrow. A ravenous one serves best returning to dust, wouldn't you agree?"

Hattin blinked. "The words of a Shadow if I ever heard them." His eyes wandered up the noblewoman's figure. "And with all the grace of a woman. Yes, I can see why you're good at what you do, Lady of Shadows."

Meckea scowled and cocked her head. "With respect, you *don't*. A Shadow that could be understood in greetings would not last her first night. It is our job to be anything we need to be, to ensure the murder never gets linked back to us, to remove a house and its lord from the playing field. But enough about that. A man as careful as you will probably get to meet one someday."

Hattin shifted as all his arrogance melted away. He turned and faced Aeia. "Forgive my manners, I haven't yet learned the name of your handmaiden."

"Forgive me," Meckea said. "This is Alora. She is assisting me in my visit here, in *all* regards. She needs this information as much as I do, if not more. Her skills are far beyond what even I can accomplish."

The man studied her more curiously now. Aeia had to fight hard to keep herself from shrinking back. His gaze was serious, and she feared the telltale look of recognition that could cross it.

"One so young caught up in all this? A true shame if I ever saw one." He shook his head and turned towards the manor. "Well, come inside. The courtyard is no place for the discussions we'll need to have today."

Lord Hattin led them up the cobblestone walkway leading to his manor. On each side of the walkway were small trees, each carefully maintained to bear the same amount of foliage. The decorations were simple but showed a dedication to detail that was lacking in other estates Aeia had visited.

The manor was built more like a massive cottage than a grand mansion and would seem to be a lower-class building if not for its size.

That was only at first glance, however. As they neared, Aeia noticed that each wooden support was masterfully carved with complex designs. Aeia marveled at the pillars.

"You like those?" Hattin asked.

Aeia started and glanced up. Lord Hattin looked at her expectantly, puffed a bit with pride.

Aeia regained her composure. "They're lovely."

I've become too relaxed! Like this, I'll spoil the mission and get us all---

"I'm glad! Not many of my guests take the time to look around, a shame since I spent so much time carving those."

He did that? An itch appeared in her mind, it prodded her to ask further. *It's foolish. I don't need to know more, but ...*

She looked to Meckea, who already seemed to know what she was thinking. She nodded, and Aeia picked up her pace slightly. "I thought you were a merchant."

"Indeed I am." Lord Hattin nodded. "But that wasn't always the case. I grew up the son of a carpenter. Woodwork is my way to remember my roots, so that I won't become like the average nobleman."

"A woodworker became a member of the merchant's board. How did you do that?"

"I've always kept a close eye on the trade. My father often mused that I spent more time learning the economy of carpentry than doing it. I was well-trained, more than most. I let my tongue loose while I was putting in trimming for a local merchant. Guess I impressed him, because he took me as an apprentice, and... well, you've seen the rest."

"Quite the story," Meckea said. "It puts to shame people like me who were born into success."

"Ah, I wouldn't say that." Lord Hattin waved a hand dismissively. "You've had to learn from childhood how to talk to those miserable nobles. I'm far less refined. Impressing the head of a House is not something I can often do. Honestly, I'm just lucky I've always been able to make an offer better than they could refuse. I don't envy the theatrics you need for your own show. I was given a document once. It listed off all the things nobles are supposed to do when talking to each other. Ridiculous nonsense if you ask me."

They reached the door, and Lord Hattin opened it for them, waving them in with a bow.

"Thank you." Meckea tipped her head forward, accepting the gesture. "And I'm sorry. I may have been a bit harsh towards you."

Lord Hattin chuckled. "It's nothing I won't shake off. And *I* should have regarded you in a manner more fit for the esteemed noblewoman you are."

"Plenty do already. Besides, neither of us is here to further our business. I think more casual conversation could be in order?"

"Done." Hattin clapped his hands. "By the King, that's a wonderful thing to hear."

Both deflated as if they'd released a long-held breath. Hattin waved them to a small wooden table and matching chairs. "You wanted information on someone of the merchant board, if I understood correctly."

"As you know, Lord Cer has been taxing nobles of their Bask stones to keep them at bay. The stones he takes are passing through the port—we know that much. Where it goes after that is a mystery. All the ships controlled directly by Lord Cer are clean. He's using someone else to move it for him."

Lord Hattin nodded slowly. "I can see why you'd start with the main traders in Feos then. I must say, I'm surprised; it is all but agreed among us traders that Feos is a lost cause. I don't know why anyone would ally themselves with its crazed leader."

Aeia glanced up to the ceiling. "Maybe they're getting a portion of the Bask he collects? They could be planning to leave Feos once the economy collapses."

The two stared at her. And only then did she realize what she had done. "Sorry. My tongue is too loose today."

Hattin waved her words away. "It was good insight! While a merchant would have to be mad to try and get the better of Lord Cer, the alternative in working for him out of loyalty is even harder to believe."

Meckea shot Aeia a smile and turned back to Hattin. "If that were true, it may be beneficial to start investigating the nobles who could easily move out of Feos should the time arise. Are there any houses that come to mind?"

Hattin leaned back in his chair and put a hand over his chin. "Just about all of us have moved our businesses out of Feos. Although... Lord Vant, the younger of course, has all but abandoned the city as of late. He hardly gave any warning signs—just started to pack up and leave."

"That doesn't sound like someone allying themselves with House Cer," Meckea mused. "However, that could mean he has already has already been visited by whoever is collecting the Bask for Lord Cer. He might be trying to escape before he loses everything."

"You may want to have a *chat* with him first," Hattin agreed. "Anyone who does substantial amounts of trade in Feos could be working with Alonius, but Elit Vant might just have a better idea of who."

"We shall, then." Meckea rose. "Thank you for your time, Lord Hattin."

He leaned forward. "Leaving already? We don't have to be all business! You are more than welcome to stay for dinner."

"I appreciate the invitation. However, we have a great deal of work to do, as I'm sure you can imagine."

Defeated, Lord Hattin rose and led the way to the door. "Of course. Good luck on your quest."

"Thank you." Meckea bowed before departing. "I'll soon contact you with my findings."

Chapter Fifteen

Eric trailed behind the two former revolutionary leaders Eugho and Dust as they traversed the outer city.

Tall buildings surrounded them. Unlike what he'd seen in the inner city, these buildings were devoid of life and population. Old paint appeared in patches on the walls. Some were crumbling, revealing rotting wood and dilapidated stone. And those were the stable ones. Many were entirely caved in. A few buildings had come down completely, their debris lying in heaps.

They passed one of the few buildings still standing. The orange glow of fire shone out of the broken windows like a dim lamp. Eric raised himself onto his toes, spying in one of the windows to discover the source.

A group of at least twenty people crowded the makeshift fire pit, huddling together for warmth.

As he sucked in a breath, a layer of dust filled his nostrils, and he sneezed.

Dust spends all his time out here? Well, at least the name makes sense now.

Eric clutched the hilt of his crossbow. He missed his gun, but it seemed to draw too much curiosity whenever he brought it with him.

The style of the crossbow was similar enough that he should get the hang of it quickly. He'd demonstrated his aim well enough earlier that Eugho had given him one to carry. His military training was useful for something.

The crossbow was small, built for self-defense. Dust carried one three times the size of Eric's, stating it was strong enough to puncture walls. The bolts fired from it were big. Dust only had enough room for four. "Calm, Eric." Eugho moved his hand away from the hilt. "We won't find trouble out here. Most who live here are too weak to fight, even if their looks make you think otherwise. The only thing we're worried about is whoever might reside in Dust's old hideouts."

Eric nodded and relaxed.

I guess it would be foolish for anyone to attempt to mug three armed men.

"What happened here anyway?" Eric asked.

"These are the parts of the city that could not survive Alonius's rule. Stripped of their life, they return to dust once more." Dust grazed the side of a wall as they passed. The brick gave away to the light touch, crumbling to the ground.

"Bask powers more than just humans," Eugho added. "It gives life to all things. Without it, the world dies. You will find any place on this world outside of the Kingdom to be in a similar state. Some believe that Bask was once everywhere before it was gathered by the humans. And we were wrong for harvesting such a vital part of nature."

"Some also believe that Bask itself is alive." A hearty laugh rumbled from Dust. "It's a source of energy. One we need to live, just like food. Are they going to tell us that *eating* is wrong?"

"Can food power our ships?" Eugho asked. "Or your crossbow? While I agree with you to an extent, Bask is different."

Dust shrugged. "In the end, all that matters is that everyone gets a fair shot at it."

Eugho nodded. "That we can both agree on."

Dust raised an arm, and they all stopped. He crouched down, his eyes traveling all corners of the street. Eric and Eugho copied his action, and the three of them pressed against the crumbling wall of an old brick building.

"Something's not right." Dust whispered. "I can't tell what, but something's changed since I've been here last."

The sound of feet falling on stone echoed through the alleys, with the occasional scrape of a leg lazily lifted. Not many feet, no more than two men, approached their location.

Their mumbles grew louder as they came closer. A chat between two friends. "I *still* can't believe you actually drank it!" One exclaimed. "I thought for sure we'd be getting an unwanted view of your supper after that show."

The other laughed heartily. "Liquor is liquor! And it was free!"

"You bumbling barrow!" A loud clank of metal meeting stone walls sounded, along with the scraping of stumbling feet. "It's *all* free. Perks of the storm!"

"Oh yeah. Still gettin' used to that."

Eric pressed hard against the wall as the two men came into view. They passed in front of the alleyway Eric and his comrades were hiding in. Both wore slightly rusted armor. One's armor hung loosely, ratting as he walked, while the other's clung tight around his gut.

The stench they gave off trailed after them—odors of sweat and alcohol.

They didn't notice the party at all, half stumbling as they seemed to wander without aim. As soon as their footsteps could no longer be heard, Dust rose, scratching the back of his head.

"Looks like the first sight of your rebels, Eugho. Those were a pair of recruits if I ever saw them."

Eugho rose as well. "Recruited by a 'Storm' it seems. I'm unfamiliar with that? Have you heard of it?"

Dust shook his head. "And a beer tab doesn't sound like anything my old commanders would set up. Besides, only Geralt and the Light stealers actually knew about the hideouts in this part of the city."

Eugho leaned back. "You're the last one to fit that description."

Dust nodded. "Looks like that wasn't actually the case. Someone is holed up around here, and our old hideout is the only place you could stay."

"Beer tab ..." Eric repeated, cocking his head to the side. "Someone would have to be pretty rich to just give away drinks like that, wouldn't they?"

"They would indeed." Eugho frowned. "And that is not a good sign. The one who controls the coin now controls the men. But who?"

Dust stroked his jaw. "None of the Light stealers had more than a few coins to their name. Everything went to funding the war." He moved a hand to his forehead. "Not only is one alive ... But he's sold himself out to some nobleman?"

Eugho pulled out a cloth wrapping to cover his eyes. "We can only speculate until we get a closer look."

Sight without eyes. What would that even be like? Eric marveled at the thought.

"What do you intend to find?" Dust questioned.

"If there is a nobleman involved, they could very well have someone on watch." He nodded at the two men. "Lead the way."

They crept into the narrow street. The trio crouched slightly, placing each foot carefully in front of the other. They made virtually no sound as they moved, the only noise was the sound of the wind pushing dust through the streets and against buildings.

"There are men down those two alleys, lots of them." Eugho motioned to the openings on the opposite side of the street. "Only inside the building, no guards. And ... a Huntsman!" He hissed. "Nearly missed it, but he's definitely there."

Dust grimaced. "We can't see anything from this far away."

"We know enough. A nobleman is funding this rebel faction."

"A noble in my hideout!" Dust turned and spat on the ground. "I want to know *who*. Forget what I said about being wary. We should pay the man a visit."

"I'd rather our presence didn't get exposed so quickly." Eugho growled. "I hardly think he'll welcome us, whoever he is."

"Got a better plan?"

"Let me look," Eric said. "Those 'Huntsmen' can't see me, right?"

Eugho scowled, then nodded. "I can't see you right now, and neither could Jeffe. And if *he* couldn't, then a nobleman's hired Huntsman sure can't."

"Should be simple then." Eric dropped to a crouch. "I know a thing or two about laying low."

Dust's brow furrowed. "Is sending a rookie alone a good idea? He's talented, sure, but I haven't had time to work with him."

"We don't have options." Eugho said. "Not unless we want to get Meckea's shadows involved. But it could take weeks for them to have a successful infiltration."

"Time is already against us." Dust sighed. "If you think it's fine, then I won't object."

"Just get a look around. Listen for names, and listen for anybody who calls themselves Geralt," Eugho explained. "Don't get in too deep. I don't want you to get caught."

Eric nodded and moved across the street. From there, he easily spotted the two alleyways in question. The tiling of both was much more worn then the rest of the street. He moved to the side of one entrance, grasping the hilt of his sword as he peeked around the corner.

The alley narrowed to a heavy wooden door. Just like Eugho had said, there were no guards posted. Though Eric couldn't count that as a blessing, because it meant he'd have to go in further. He made his way towards the door, stopping just in front of it. *What happens if I get caught?*

This world was still so foreign to him, he couldn't even begin to guess the implications. Would the men in here be like a gang back home?

He tugged on the door, and it creaked open. Before him, a deep staircase led down into complete darkness. It would seem crypt-like if not for the faint sounds of shouting and laughter.

Eric crept downwards, testing each wooden step for sound before he put his full weight on it. It was sturdy, and he was able to move without risk of detection.

The warm firelight grew in intensity as Eric neared the bottom step. The staircase opened to his right into a very large room. He looked around the corner to see a mass of people. They moved about without much purpose, mingling and enjoying themselves as if it were some sort of party.

Most of them wore clothes like Eric's, so he should blend in. Still, he kept behind his cover as he scanned the room.

On the far side of the room the tone was less jovial. A table had been set up, and a well-dressed man sat behind it. He conversed with a few men at the front and seemed to be filling out various papers for them.

Is that recruitment?

An idea flashed through Eric's mind. Should he join their ranks? He and the others could learn little by sneaking around the hideout, but if he joined, he'd be able to uncover the truth.

Eric stepped into the light with feigned confidence. Few looked his direction. Those who did turned away as if he didn't matter. Good. With his dyed hair and familiar clothing, he fit in.

He approached the table just as two men were leaving. The man looked up to him with a smile. "Welcome. I'm glad you decided to come see us today."

"What *is* this, exactly? I mean, I've heard the rumors."

"And they are correct." The man nodded. "This is the Storm, the new face of the rebellion."

"Good, then I'm in the right place. I want to join your cause."

An amused smirk crossed the man's face, and he looked past Eric to the festivities behind him. "Many do."

Eric straightened his shoulders. "There is a time to celebrate and time to fight. I'll celebrate when are cause is won. For now, I just want to help the city."

"Then you and I will get along." The man rose and bowed. "My name is Vestan. I command this hideout under Storm leadership."

Eric returned the gesture. "I'm Eric. I have much to learn."

"We will change that. But first..." A look of concern crossed the man's face, and he leaned forward. "We don't have much, but do you need to charge? Your eyes are hardly blue."

Nervousness began to rise, despite Eric's trying to control it. "I'm fine. I have my own resources."

The man studied Eric's face, unsure, but soon relented and backed away. "If you say so. Now, we're about wrapped up for today, and I need to speak to the crowd before they get too drunk. I'll fill out your information later. You can take this."

The man dropped a small wooden token into Eric's hand. It was painted black with a yellow lightning bolt down the middle.

"That will allow you to enter the commons of any Storm hideout, though I wouldn't wear it on your clothes. Soldiers are not too fond of us." Vestan offered another small bow and headed around the table to the front of the room. "Attention! All beer taps are closing for the night. Conserve your strength. Training starts tomorrow afternoon, as we only have two weeks until our assault against Lord Bealing. Today's recruits will *not* take part in that battle unless they show exceptional skills in the next few days. Be safe, we need every man in the coming days."

Somehow the words pierced the drunken haze of the men, and the festivities started to die down. Eric took this as his chance to leave before he got locked in.

* * *

Eric tried to ignore the disapproving glare from Dust. After he'd returned to them and reported what all that had happened, they all but dragged him to the safe house. The building was tiny, but well hidden beneath the floor of an abandoned warehouse. Shelves covered three walls of the main room, each filled with supplies. The last wall was covered in weapons of all types, and a small rack of weapons designed for training. Aside from a few metal chairs there weren't any furnishings at all.

"That was foolish, Eric." Dust shook his head. "You had no idea how they gathered their recruits! You could have easily been captured, maybe even killed for trespassing!" The man's voice rang through the small safe house. The walls and doors were thick to prevent any prying ears from hearing their words, but Eric couldn't believe that anything could dampen Dust's voice.

"They used a Huntsman, didn't they?" Eric countered. "They wouldn't expect an unwanted person showing. I look like the others, and if I act like I belong, then most will think I do."

Dust scowled. "Most!"

"I agree with Eric." Eugho's face scrunched as he tried to recover from the noise of Dust's shouting. "A man on the inside will help us greatly with information. Besides, he did far better than 'paying them a visit,' as you put it."

"I know how those boys think, Eugho. I still believe I could get them on my side without much trouble. Eric hasn't been here a month!"

"Regardless." Eugho gestured towards Eric with a smile. "He did well! No matter the risks he took, he succeeded. A leader as yourself should be able to appreciate that."

"I do. And if he's going to be the new Geralt, then that is a good trait to have."

Eric winced. In the face of all the wonders he has seen he felt … normal. And yet Dust constantly compared him to Nick.

How could he convince this guy he wouldn't be able to do what Nick had? "I'm not going to be—"

"What did you find out?" Dust asked.

Eric let out a breath. "A lot. They seemed far too casual with it all. They plan to attack someone named Lord Bealing in two weeks. And they shared that information with all of the newest recruits as well."

"I know the man." Eugho stroked his chin. "He used to own a great many plantations outside the city. Last I heard he was shutting down almost all of them."

"A weak target is good for building moral." Dust shook his head. "It's effective in gaining popularity, but it's a cowardly move that wastes both time and energy. Who is leading the attack?"

"A man named Vestan," Eric said. "Or at least he was the one commanding the hideout."

Dust turned to spit on the floor. "He was one of my boys! He knows better than this!" The anger on his face soon melted away, and he slumped into one of the metal chairs. "He can't be blamed. Ten years without a leader, and I'd do the same thing."

"This hasn't been a kind time," Eugho agreed. "Hopefully the rebels haven't strayed too far. But we'll only know when we see how they act in battle."

"Aye." Dust turned to face him again. "Eric, we're going to be busy these next weeks with training. I can't have you dying in that fight."

Eric tensed. "Are you saying you want me to fight in that battle? Against a businessman and his security or something? I thought I'd be collecting information."

A smirk crossed Dust's face, and he strode across the room to remove two training swords from a rack. "You joined the Storm. Running from fights won't build their trust in you, that's for sure."

"It's not about running from a fight. It's about who I must kill. Besides, Vestan says only the exceptional new recruits will have to fight."

Dust tossed one of the practice swords to Eric and motioned towards the door. "We'll make you exceptional then!"

Chapter Sixteen

The chatter of hundreds of people filled Aeia's ears. Enraptured in their own conversations, they took little notice of her as she trailed Meckea through the crowds of the Vou business festival. She felt a bit of discomfort in the dress she wore but Meckea insisted that she retain her femininity.

At least she wasn't the only handmaiden. Two others were beside her, though Aeia didn't know if they were true handmaids or Shadows themselves. She mimicked their movements and gestures with ease, and her experience made her feel at home in the task.

She allowed herself a few casual glances at the scenery, as the other handmaidens did. The world was strange to her whenever she left Feos, especially when she was in the presence of nobles and nobles alone.

There was no depression here. Or rather, the depression was hidden very well. The gathering hall was decorated with many vibrant and varying colors.

It was a festival, yes organized so that various Houses could form partnerships with each other. As a result, the decorations were designed to show off the uniqueness and wealth of the different houses.

To her, it all looked the same.

She had to admit, this place offered the perfect opportunity to talk to Elit Vant. Meckea's house had some standing, and he should be thrilled to get her attention. Even more so since she was stationed outside of Lord Cer's influence and wouldn't be linked to any troubles he might have gotten into.

Vant wouldn't be alone in that thought, as many Houses tried to call Meckea over to their displays. They were all turned down with elegance and yet chilling coldness that was unique to Meckea. Aeia wasn't sure she'd ever seen so many hopes dashed in a single day.

Some partnerships might have even been beneficial, and yet Meckea disregarded them completely in place of the mission.

What did Eugho ever do to gain so much loyalty?

They passed the larger booths at the front and made their way to where the lesser houses resided. Here, no one gave much more than a lingering glance. They already accepted that their business wouldn't be nearly large enough for Meckea's consideration, and mostly talked amongst themselves.

It was here where they found Elit Vant. He had a pretty impressive display of what his house could offer. And the lord himself looked collected and focused, despite what Hattin had said about him fleeing the city. His young face was hidden by a short beard, a failed attempt to hide his youth so that he could gain more authority.

He looked up with astonishment when Meckea stopped at his table and quickly rose to offer a bow. "Lady Alestal! It is an honor."

Meckea smiled and returned the bow. "Likewise, Lord Vant."

The man launched into his prepared presentation. He was a salesman, tried and true. Aeia couldn't help but be impressed with how much his small house seemed to offer. He spoke of being able to guarantee that his specialized cargo shuttles would be able to move products far faster than a large ship. And the Meckea could receive goods from another city in a matter of hours.

Meckea was another story. She listened but lifted her hand to stop him when his presentation became more specific about the business opportunities.

"Forgive me, but that isn't why I came to see you."

The man's countenance dropped, and he clasped his hands behind his back.

"Don't get me wrong," she said. "I see no reason why we can't do business with each other in the future. If you do well in your new location, I will consider partnering with your house before it meets my normal requirements."

The man's eyes widened, and he started to speak, but Meckea continued. "However, I would like to ask a favor of you. Could we talk somewhere private?"

Elit nodded and motioned for the four of them to follow.

He led them to a door with a sign bearing House Vant's insignia. It opened to a small room with a lavish table and chairs set. There were even some chairs against the far wall, set up for servants like Aeia.

Elit moved to the side and waved for them to sit.

"Thank you. I'll try to be quick, so that you don't lose out on partnerships with others."

Meckea shifted in her seat, and acted as if she was nervous. "It's really only a question. You see, I have someone I wish to do business with in Feos, but I've been hearing some odd things from there. I learned that your house is evacuating and … well, I wanted to know why."

At the mention of Feos, Elit's face darkened and his hands clenched his pantlegs. He avoided eye contact with her.

"It's a … feeling, mostly," Elit said. "I don't trust Lord Cer."

Meckea shifted forward on her seat. "Forgive me, but … is that the only reason? I agree about Lord Cer, but you left rather quickly."

Elit cleared his throat. "I look to my future, and I don't think my future is in Feos."

Meckea nodded. "Thank you. And I'm sorry I probed so much." She turned back to her handmaidens. "Alora, will you take my coat for me? It's getting warm in here."

Aeia moved forward at her signal and stood. When she came behind Meckea, she jerked her head upwards. This caught Elit's attention, and they locked eyes.

The world started to fall from around her. Everything except her and Elit faded away. She let go of her body, allowed her mind to fly free from its restraints.

She pierced the man's gaze and moved beyond into the world of darkness between minds. The world known as the Void.

Chapter Seventeen

A loud *clack* echoed throughout the empty safe house as two wooden swords met each other at full force. The sound was repeated again and again.

Eric stepped back, his warm breath sending a small cloud of fog into the air. His hands ached, from both the cold and from the vibrations from fighting with the practice swords. So far, his movements had kept all but his hands warm, but as his energy began to wane, he could feel the chill of the icy night seeping into him.

He fought back a shiver and held his stance as Dust moved in once more. It was a side swipe, slowed only slightly so that Eric could have time to analyze and prepare for the attack. He lifted his elbows, so Dust's strike would meet the side of his blade, but his stiff muscles moved far to clumsily, and the attack slid past Eric's defense and connected with his side.

The blow was absorbed almost completely by the protection he wore, and Eric felt not much more than a pat. He let out a quick breath and took a step back.

"Something wrong, Eric?" Dust lowered his sword. "That attack was nothing new."

"S-sorry." A shiver ran through him. "It's cold."

"Ah, right." Dust walked out of the ring and placed his weapon on a rack. "I'll bring a heater in the morning."

Eric put his weapon away and removed his armor, quickly replacing it with his coat. "How do you people handle this cold?" He eyed Dust's clothing, which was thin and loose.

Dust lifted an uncovered hand and eyed it. "Geralt used to complain about that too. Bask helps us with a lot of things. I've wondered if it helps us with warmth. There had to be some reason for people to start using it in the first place."

Eric rubbed his hands together and followed Geralt out of the room. "You mean you didn't always need it?"

Dust shrugged. "Nobody knows for sure, but there are tales. The kingdom of Nont hasn't been around forever. And some believe that Bask hasn't either. For all we know we could have been just like you in the past."

"We are alike in just about every other way. And what happened with Nick, what the King did to him..."

"He looked like one of us before he died." Dust's voice was grave. "I thought a lot about that. It's a shame—there is very little history prior to the founding of the kingdom. The world the King has built is the only world the people know. There is nothing else."

"I can see why there would be so many people fighting to restore it then." Eric threw a thumb over his shoulder. "Back on Earth, if a country fell to the point of no return, there was always the option to simply move somewhere else. If things were getting as bad as they are here, you would see an influx of refugees crossing the surrounding borders."

"That happens among the provinces, but only the fit can make the journey between them. Those who get expunged from the city—those without access to Bask—have no choice but to wait for their deaths outside the walls. Even if they were to make it to another city, most nobles aren't exactly charitable."

Dust motioned to the sparring arena. "That's why I'm training you, Eric. You're going to face off against a nobleman tomorrow. Lord Bealing won't show any mercy. And if the rebels lose, you have to escape with your life."

Eric thought of his practice weapon. "I don't think I'm ready to use a sword in real combat."

"You have talent. But confidence only comes in time. For now, you need something to complement your blade." Dust unwrapped a cloth, which revealed a crossbow.

"The crossbow is the perfect complement to the sword. At medium range, it can kill a man and can puncture body armor. When used properly, it is capable of taking down a knight."

Eric hoisted the weapon. It was heavy, but when he lifted it to aim through the sights, it formed perfectly to his body. It didn't feel unlike a rifle, although the bow at the front made it much wider. It didn't seem as efficient as the weapons back on Earth, but it was at least like a rifle. And he was good with a rifle.

Eric fired at one of the targets past the sparring arena. The crossbow bolt flew much faster than he'd expected. It rocketed past the target and into the stone wall behind.

Dust pulled a small lever on the crossbow. A new bolt slid from a compartment below. It rolled up the side and placed itself at the top of the crossbow. Then, blue light streamed through a set of gears and cranked the bow until it was at a full firing position.

"One and a half seconds, that's how long you have between shots. The tide of battle can change in that short of a time, so use the time to plan your next shot."

Eric fired again. This time, the bolt sunk deep into the target. It was off-center, but still within a ring.

Dust nodded his approval as Eric loaded his next shot.

Eric glowed as he aimed his next shot. Now *this* was a weapon he could use. He'd shot many different weapons as a Marine, and he could feel his training resurfacing. At least one part of Earth was still alive in him, and that part would serve him well in battle.

He fired again, and this time, he pierced the target through the center with a satisfying *thud*. He started to smile as a new target rose from the floor and rolled quickly towards him on a moving pad.

It gained fast as Eric reloaded, and he crouched down to line up his shot so it was ready as soon as the crossbow was. He fired again and hit the target close to the center. It stopped as soon as it was hit and went into reverse.

"You can see how important that time is now. Always be on the lookout for new threats."

Eric nodded and rose. "How much ammo does this thing carry?"

"Six bolts in its backup, and one on top. With an extra backup on your side that makes a total of thirteen. It's not many, which is why you need your sword with you as well. Even if you only intend to use it as a last resort."

"A mixture of both... I'll try to keep that in mind."

Eric couldn't suppress a shiver. This time it wasn't from the cold. He was about to enter a battle in which he truly didn't belong to a side.

He swallowed and looked at Dust. "Where will I be aiming? The chest, head?"

"Neither, not this time. I don't know how battles were fought on your world, but here it is all about lack of casualties. All a nobleman's manpower is hired, and they won't sacrifice everything to protect their master. That means that all you need to do is break their will to fight."

"Sounds too easy. Any man can be dangerous."

"While this is true, many don't have very much loyalty towards their master, especially when dealing with a man like Lord Bealing. I'm not saying to lower your guard but to know what battle you're actually fighting."

"I understand." Eric pulled the crossbow up for another shot. "That's the type of battle I'd rather fight."

Chapter Eighteen

Nothing. Aeia was floating in nothingness.

The jump had been successful—she'd made it into her target's mind. And as usual she was left floating in a seemingly infinite void.

She knew this wasn't what it seemed. The man's mind, and all his secrets, were just below the surface.

This is why she was called a Void Jumper. For when the first Jumpers tried it, they thought that this was all there was. It was only in recent times when they started discovering the tricks on how to do it right.

She pushed deeper into the void, thrusting her consciousness farther inside.

It threatened to swallow her, bring her to a point where she could not return. And as usual, her instincts screamed at her to pull out to safety. It was a true fear. Many Void Jumpers have been lost in another person's mind. Their body left an empty vessel. It was a risk she had to take with every Jump she performed.

But just when it seemed she would be lost forever, she reached a wall.

There you are.

She pushed through it. It felt like she was moving through water. And then, she reached the surface.

Colors and shapes came from nowhere, twirling around her like a tornado. She was trained to know how to handle this and started piecing together the meanings behind all of them.

Emotions. She knew. *Fear, anger, happiness, love...*

She ignored them all, rejecting any influence they sought to put on her, and kept moving. Next, she saw her objective. Memories.

She moved into the section and found herself in an expansive field.

The field was no ordinary one, however, the grass continually changed colors, and there was no sky, only darkness.

Strange as it was, it seemed very familiar to her. Almost every person's memory section was the same, and she imagined hers was as well.

Keep moving. He doesn't know you're here yet.

She pushed just a bit more into the memories, the action causing an earthquake in the area. Stone walls rose out of the ground. At first, they seemed random, but quickly they formed castle.

This vision wasn't the host, it was her. This vision was the one she was trained to use when infiltrating a person's memories. It allowed her own mind to bypass the host's defenses very efficiently.

By creating a physical place, the host would be tricked into playing along. Its walls would be passable by her when she moved through the castle, and its innate defenses would appear as other physical things in the area, usually soldiers.

As expected, it worked perfectly. The host would eventually catch on, but for now she could move freely and find his memories with ease.

She made herself a bod, a replica of herself but with certain additions. In here she could make herself faster and stronger than she was in the real world.

She was still limited by how much she could do. Any abnormal movements in the mind would attract attention.

In theory, she should be able to make herself strong enough to simply tear apart the castle to find what she wanted, but the effects on the host were terrible, as the walls were merely symbols for the host's actual mind. She didn't want to destroy him, and tearing his mind apart may do that, and it would often cause the mind to react violently, which would put her in danger as well.

Instead she would search quietly, secretly. That had always been her way of doing that, and it was the safest, albeit slowest. She could make herself strong and fast, but also follow the rules of the castle.

A feeling just like wind blew over her body as the host's mind made the place more *real*. Other feelings and sound also came in. Each time it was the same, yet it still amazed her how much the subconscious payed attention to details like this, all spurred by her creation of the castle.

She crouched down, preparing herself, then bolted forward. Her new-found speed made the trip, which would be equated to a ten minutes' walk in the real world, pass in seconds.

The massive gate loomed before her. She wouldn't go through it. The host's mind looked there to protect itself. It focused more acutely there than any other part of the castle, just waiting for someone to come knocking.

Instead, she surged forward, doing a short jump to build momentum. She crouched as she landed, before propelling herself upwards. The action threw her high above the walls, and down towards the roof in a large arch.

She landed in the parapets with a roll, her imaginary body not feeling any pain when the action could have broken bones or even killed her real one.

The area shook slightly, indicating that even an action that small had attracted the host's attention. But for now, he would only give her a passing glance. He wouldn't start investigating until later.

Now, she could search freely.

The castle always gave her an ominous feeling at first. Right now, she was alone. There were no images of people yet. And due to having just passed through the void, she felt like the only person in the universe.

This was good. People meant trouble.

She moved through a long hallway and spotted the first door.

If her castle worked properly, then the host would fill it neatly with its most important memories. All she had to do was figure out which sections were filled with what.

Opening the first door, she was hit with a gust of wind, and with it a wave of scents.

She recognized them as coming from a forest, probably sometime in the spring. Not quite like the forest near Feos, but somewhere near it, she was sure.

She saw the swirling colors of emotion.

Pink, attraction. Light green, eagerness. A date with someone, or at least flirting.

She shut the door quietly and continued down the path.

Very strong ... These memories are recent. Hopefully the ones I'm looking for will be as well.

That alone gave her a good idea of where she was. The castle was her mind's creation, and therefore she would figure out its layout quickly. She could move between the sections to find the things she wanted.

She headed into what should hopefully be a more serious section, one that was often filled with a person's work. In this case, it would be filled with the man's most important meetings with other nobles.

She slowed her pace. Even if the host didn't know she was here yet, she could encounter his most important and heavily protected secrets.

Getting spotted by the host's mind was a sure way to get trapped, but it also showed her which rooms to look in. So actually, such self-protection caused them more harm than good if they were being infiltrated by a more professional Jumper.

She pulled a door open to check her position.

This time she was met with a smoky smell and a slight mustiness to the air. Also mixed in were the smells of people, men specifically. *Their* smell was unmistakable.

She saw the colors of respect, duty, and a hint of apprehension.

A meeting with superiors.

This could be important. She stepped inside, felt the warm, stuffy atmosphere of a meeting room. She moved closer to hear the conversation better.

"The southern provinces are getting too close."

Aeia didn't recognize the voice. It didn't belong to the host. "I've been hearing many disturbing things from my Shadows stationed there, things that suggest Orlan may be stockpiling weapons, preparing for a war."

A flicker of blue flashed through the room. The host's fear.

Interesting.

Another sensation tickled her slightly. The host was beginning to realize she was there. Not too suspicious yet, but there might be a guard lurking about soon.

She wanted to press forward and see the man he was talking to, but doing so would recall the memory too much and show the host where she was.

"Elit, I want you to start building relationships with some of the houses in Orlan's territory. Find out the severity of these rumors."

An orange light grew—pride, and a hint of how important this meeting was to the host, and how deep she was into his memories.

That was all she needed to know, and she backed out of the room.

Getting close.

Now she would search for a more hidden room in the area, one more protected. At least, that was what the host thought it was.

When making the castle, she'd intentionally built hallways that lead nowhere. In doing so the mind would instinctively create its own hallways, ones it thought were hidden. There it would place the most valuable things.

She went to the first one, a hidden doorway that opened with the pulling of a wall torch. It didn't have to be elaborate, in fact she could have just made a wall that you could walk through, but to her, this was more interesting.

The door slid open showing an extremely long hallway filled with doors, as expected. Fortunately, the host had stuck to her pre-designed layout. Unfortunately, the host had applied locks to each of the doors.

She let out an annoyed sigh, moving towards the door at the far end of the hallway. She spotted a guard patrolling the door farthest away.

Not too big an issue.

She changed her body completely and shrunk to the form of a flying bug.

This way, she'd be able to get past the guard easily. She would be seen, yes, but it would cause drastically less commotion than if she still looked like a person.

That was one of her own tricks. Most Jumpers would simply kill the guards before being seen. Effective, yes. But just like breaking walls, it could have a harmful effect on the host's mind and she would rather do as slight damage as possible. The effects of a mind attack were horrifying.

She fluttered past the guard, only getting a slight glance, and waited for him to turn into a different hallway. As soon as he did. She returned to her normal form to move the rest of the distance.

She reached the end, picking one of the doors that seemed most important. It was padlocked, much like the others.

There weren't any key holes—they weren't supposed to be opened by anyone but the host. She had no choice but to give herself a burst of strength. She did so and crushed the lock in her hand.

That'll get me noticed—got to be quick.

She opened the door and was met with the smell of wet wood and the obvious stench of the inner city. Nervousness, suspense, and fear swirled in the air. This was to be a secret meeting.

Moving in she felt the crisp, cool air of night time and heard footsteps above, followed shortly by a thump of someone dropping onto a wooden floor.

"Elit." The demanding voice was one she recognized from the last room.

"Danton!" he called in a whisper. "What's wrong? Why did you summon me?"

Danton? She only knew one man by that name, and he wouldn't be in a place like this.

"It's Alonius. He's gone completely mad. I can no longer escape this wretched city. But you, *you* can still escape."

Elit shook his head. "You're not making any sense. What is Alonius doing?"

"He's taking it all, Elit. Every piece of Bask is being stolen, *taxed.*" The word was spat like a curse. "I'm giving him everything he asks for, yet he always comes back for more. It won't be long until he takes all I have. And then I won't be of any use to him."

"He can't do that. You can't let him! Why aren't you fighting back?" Elit stepped forward and grabbed the man by the shoulders. He was close for Aeia to make out his face.

Marquess Danton Vant. She narrowed her eyes. *Alonius targeted him? His own border protector?*

"You don't understand," Danton said. "You can't fight Alonius Cer. He has weapons, weapons you'll never see coming. They'll kill you without leaving a trace of evidence. Armies mean nothing if you don't even know what you're fighting."

Void Jumpers. The Marquess knows of them? That will be troublesome. She shook herself. It wasn't important yet. Elit knows nothing, but Danton Vant does. He would have to be her next target.

The memory faded as Aeia backed out of the room. A bit too late, it seemed, as the clanging of armor sounded through the halls.

Here we go.

Turning, she saw that the guards were all equipped with swords. A strong indication that they considered her foreign, and that they wanted her out *now*.

I don't blame them.

She gave herself a boost of speed and strength and dashed towards the guards.

The first one thrust a sword at her, and she ducked it. In the same motion, she lifted the man over her shoulder with ease and tossed him aside as carefully as she could, making sure no harm would come to him.

She didn't stop as she ran, dodging and maneuvering past the guards, not stopping long enough for them to mount a worthwhile resistance.

Got to get out.

She knew full well that if she could make herself strong and fast, then the host could do the same. If he figured it out, that was.

The host could do much worse than she could. Right now, his mind was held back by its idea of reality, something she knew didn't matter in this place.

*But if it did figure things out...*She was merely the guest, exploiting the powers that the mind already had. She had no control over the mind itself. Every guard could become as powerful as she is.

That was why she had to be careful about who to jump into. If the person was trained in mental protection, then even the greatest Jumpers wouldn't stand a chance.

That was not the case this time. She made it past the guards with little trouble, leaping past them faster than they could react. But even with her rush, there was one more thing she had to do before leaving.

With the layout she had created, it was always conveniently placed near her preferred exit point.

She came to the room that controlled the host's consciousness and recent memory.

Wiping someone's memory was extremely complicated. As one would expect, it had been attempted many times, however the other Void Jumpers have never gotten it quite right.

For one thing, memories were categorized in many ways. One could try and erase the memory of a specific event, but the host would notice the gap and figure out where you are quickly and one can't just erase all of someone's memories—that would get the jumper hunted down like an animal by the host's baser instincts.

But there was one way. One can erase memories if they're very current, causing someone to forget up to the last half hour.

She collapsed the recent memory storage, which would unravel the images, sounds, sights, and smells in a way the mind would not be able to piece back together.

This effect was tough on the conscious mind but mostly harmless. The host would fall unconscious but would wake up with no ill effects in only a few minutes.

As soon as his eyes closed, the connection would be severed, so Aeia didn't waste any time in pulling her mind out of Elit's.

She reentered the Void.

* * *

The world rushed back as Aeia returned to her body. The scene was exactly as she had left it, as only a few moments had passed for everyone else.

Elit's eyes rolled back into his head, and he fell forward. He wasn't harmed. The worst that would happen would be a few minutes of confusion as he tried to remember how he had come here. All memories in the past half hour would be lost, including all the interactions he'd had with them.

"He won't be out for long," Aeia whispered.

Meckea nodded and stood. "Did you find what we needed?"

"All he had to offer. He hasn't met the Bask collector, but he knew someone who has."

"Efficient work." She smiled. "Let's get back to Eugho then."

Chapter Nineteen

A low, continuous thumping rocked the nighttime streets. The few houses and stores still open closed their entrances to the noise. They were not the targets, but the anger that emanated from the rebel group struck fear into anyone within earshot.

Eric trailed the group as they jogged down the street. He couldn't bring himself to move further into it. He could feel their emotions, and they wanted nothing less than blood tonight.

So much hate.

After seeing the way Lord Cer treated those who couldn't afford to charge themselves, Eric could understand the men's anger. But he dreaded of what the night was going to show him.

He looked beyond the group. Lord Bealing's manor was in view. They were approaching rapidly. Not a single light shown in the building. It looked abandoned.

Impossible. The rebels wouldn't risk such an open attack if they knew no one was there, right?

The dread in his stomach grew. Something wasn't right, and he was surer of that with every step.

Is it just me?

He hadn't been in a battle for quite some time. Was this his fear of the conflict? No, fighting had always come naturally to him.

What is it, then?

They neared the manor. There was no movement inside. Surely someone had heard them coming.

He scanned the building. Seemed the place had been abandoned and they'd come for nothing, or the Nobleman was inside waiting.

"Vestan!" Eric called and approached the commander.

The man looked over his shoulder but didn't stop.

"This feels like a trap! We can't just barge in!"

Vestan looked at the building. He must have pieced it together immediately. He slowed to a stop.

The ragtag soldiers continued and burst through the front door in their fury. They all stopped in the center of the first room.

The fools!

Eric ran up to them and pulled himself to the front. "Get back! It's a trap and they'll ..."

He looked up. Guards appeared from behind overturned tables in a half circle at the balcony of the twin staircases in front. They bore crossbows aimed at the rebels.

Eric darted to the side as bolts rained down on them. Behind him, shrill cries were cut short as the ill-trained soldiers struggled in vain to reach cover.

"Split up and return fire!" Vestan called.

Eric hugged the wall and pulled out his own crossbow. The floor had been cleared out of all furnishings, so he had nowhere to take cover as he fired his first shot at the enemy.

We'll get massacred if we don't change something!

Eric called out to the soldiers behind him and started towards the stairs. Men were waiting at the top, but he wasn't any better off on the ground floor. The sound of footsteps from behind indicated that at least a few men were willing to risk the exposure with him.

Eric fired a few shots at the enemies above, but they ducked behind their cover, and his bolts stabbed harmlessly into the wall behind them.

He held his air, waiting for them to reappear. Instead, a lone orb flew over their barricade and bounced down the stairs toward Eric and the rebels.

Eric dove toward it, throwing his body over it as he pinned it to the ground.

It went off, blue light twisting out from under him, but he felt nothing.

He rose and looked backwards. None of the men had been hit by the blast. Their faces were frozen in shock.

"Go!" Eric pushed all implications of his actions to the back of his mind as he ran up the stairs.

The enemies peeked over their barriers. They pulled back in panic as Eric and his men crashed over the barriers and fell upon them. Eric pulled his sword free and plunged it on his first target with enough force to penetrate the man's armor.

The loud clangs of metal against metal sounded as the rebels washed over the noble's men, turning the bolt massacre into a fair sword fight. And even with the rebels' casualties, they still greatly outnumbered the nobleman's soldiers.

Eric pulled his blade from his victim's shoulder. Rebels washed over the barrier behind him attacking the guards with sickening roars. No mercy—pure rage. The guards were ordinary men who worked for the noble, and yet they were treated as if they themselves were stealing Bask from the poor.

Eric covered the mouth of the man he had stabbed and he put a finger to his lips. Slowly, the man realized what was at stake and lay back to feign death.

The rest of the guard were not so lucky. They seemed to be running out of ammo, and with their position comprised, they had little hope of defending themselves against the mass of men. Soldier after soldier fell, each carved by a dozen furious swords.

Eric tried to ignore the carnage and looked for Vestan. He found him at the front of the group. He seemed to be ignoring what had happened, his gaze focused directly ahead.

He offered Eric a weak smile. "Good work. I saw you lead that charge. You ended the battle before too many of us were injured."

"It looks like we've … won."

"Not yet. We still haven't found Lord Bealing. These men won't be satisfied until we do."

Eric swallowed hard and followed Vestan as they continued to the next door.

The rest of the manor was nearly empty, stripped bare of anything of value. *Were we not the first ones to attack this place?*

There were no signs of life until they reached a single door, which was sealed shut with boards.

"Barricaded himself in!" Vestan announced. "Bring out the Pulse Cannon!"

A man appeared from the group. He lugged with him a large cylindrical weapon that had both amount and trigger attached. The man ran to the front and dropped to one knee a few yards in front of the door.

"Firing!" he shouted, as the mouth of the cannon began to glow.

An invisible force burst from the mouth, seen only by the effects it caused on things around it. There was no recoil against the gunner, but the door blew backwards.

Instantly, the men charged, despite the Vestan's shouts for them to stop. They didn't get far before they stilled.

Eric moved forward to see that there were half a dozen men hidden behind various covers, all with their crossbows pointed at the rebels.

"You'll come no further!" a lone man shouted from the back of the room. "Leave now or I'll tell them to fire!"

The rebels in front were hesitant to charge with weapons pointed directly at them, and the ones in the rear, the ones who couldn't see the threat, tried to push the group forward.

"Pull back you fools!" Vestan called from behind. "Do you want to be killed?"

Reluctantly, the group receded into the hallway, parting to either side of the door.

Vestan shouted to his soldiers. "Those with shields will lead this charge, like we practiced. Protection squad to the front and take your places."

Men left the mob from random places, lining up before Vestan and readying themselves.

"The rest of us will follow. Those with bolts left over will return fire!"

The men looked at each other, nodding as they took their places. They moved in what almost resembled an actual line as they approached the door.

"No!" Lord Bealing called again. "Leave! ... Fire, men, fire!"

Bolts from both sides flew through the room. They battered shields and overturned furniture as the two groups came closer to each other. A few times one would find its mark, and one of the attackers would pull back into the mob.

But before the attacking forces could be broken in any significant way, the rebels reached the nobleman and his guards. And the balcony's carnage was about to repeat itself as the rebels neared the terrified men.

Eric pushed past the rebel group and rushed at Lord Bealing. The nobleman raised an arm in defense, but Eric instead stopped short and turned to face the mob.

"Enough!"

The rebels halted, confused at the one man who didn't share in their bloodlust.

"Are you all animals? Is this how you want to shape the kingdom? By becoming the monsters ... No, becoming *worse* than the monsters you're fighting?"

"He enslaved us!" a man shouted. "He'd kill us just as easy!"

"I thought that is why we were fighting. To end all of this. If we fight like monsters, then the world we create won't be any better than the one we seek to destroy."

The crowd became confused. Many wanted to rush, but with their allies unsure, their blades were stayed. Murmuring grew and slowly became more aggressive.

Eric was the only thing standing between a group of men who had suffered many injustices and their revenge. Somehow, he still stood strong. Another man joined him.

"I agree with him." Vestan held a hand to his hilt. "Geralt never killed without reason." He gestured behind Eric to Lord Bealing. "Our enemy is defenseless. And..." He turned to Lord Bealing and addressed him as much as the men. "He is more than happy to donate some Bask to our cause, isn't he?"

Wide-eyed and confused, Lord Bealing nodded.

"Then I see no reason for us to continue fighting. Do you?" He narrowed his eyes and stared down every last of his men.

Slowly, they relented. The majority backed up while a few rebels selected by Vestan moved forward to capture the terrified nobleman and his guards.

Eric let out a sigh of relief and sheathed his own sword. *I need to stop doing stuff like this.*

* * *

The rebels calmed down completely after a night's rest in their hideout. They settled back into their drinking and eating with little regard to the nobleman they had in their captivity.

"I can't thank you enough!" Vestan glowed as he approached Eric in the main hall of the hideout. "I had just about given up on these men. I thought they were going to become savages no matter what I did. This *drinking* and *slaughtering* ... Geralt's rebellion was a noble cause. Not an outlet for inner monsters."

"I hope you don't expect me to do that again. I wouldn't dare stand in their way a second time."

"I'm not sure you'll have to. Once all the adrenaline wore off, the men were much more open to your way. A few apologized to me for their behavior."

"Really?"

"These men aren't the beasts you saw yesterday. They joined to fight for more than revenge and free resources." Vestan closed the gap between them and held out a green cloak. "They just need someone to show them that."

Eric looked down at the cloak, identical to Vestan's, and the responsibility it represented. "I can't accept this. I have no experience as a leader."

"Leading is about a lot more than experience." Vestan didn't lower his arm. "And I haven't met another man I'd want at my back more."

Still, Eric hesitated. He was only here for information about the Storm's leader, so taking it would be a lie.

This would be the best way to find out what he needed to know.

It still felt wrong. He'd earned this man's trust. How could he have Vestan's back if it couldn't be his top priority? *But I* do *have a top priority. If I must lie to achieve it ...*

He accepted the cloak and nodded. "I'll do what I can."

Chapter Twenty

Aeia sat cross-legged on a chair as she waited for everyone to arrive. One by one, members of Eugho's group entered the command hall, just like they had when Eugho had first proposed his idea.

She let out a sigh of relief as all the other leaders arrived. She wasn't entirely surprised, but wars often took the greatest of people with them. One small mistake would kill even the most experienced.

Another face appeared soon after the last of the leaders had entered. Eric entered the room with Dust. Or, at least the man looked like Eric.

He had changed a lot in these few weeks. He'd lost some of the perpetual shock in his expression. He looked more focused and moved with more certainty than before. His unusual clothes had been replaced with those a commoner would wear, enhanced with a sash around his shoulders.

Eric caught her gaze as he passed and offered a small smile. Aeia blinked, still surprised by the way she was never forcibly drawn into his eyes, and smiled back. *At least that part of him hasn't changed.*

But why was he here? Had Eugho accepted him into the group that much already? She turned to her leader, the man climbing to his feet at the arrival of the final two.

"I'm glad you all made it. I know this meeting may have been a bit of a disruption, but communication is integral to our success, and we have to be sure our actions won't collide with another's."

He held out a palm toward Eric. "Eric here has successfully infiltrated the rebel group Storm and has already started to move up in the ranks."

"How does that help us?" Brunst asked. "Dust should be taking control of the group anyway."

"It's not that simple," Jeffe interjected. "The Storm is being controlled by someone important, someone with great resources. We can't expose ourselves."

Dust cleared his throat. "We think a nobleman is controlling the group. And the quickest way to learn his identity is through the Storm itself."

Eric is doing that? But that was so dangerous.

He seemed calm, sure of himself. That didn't make her feel any better. She'd talked him into joining them. What if something terrible happened to him? This wasn't even his fight.

Eugho rose from his seat and stepped forward. "We can't afford to have a second adversary in this battle. Combating Lord Cer is an enormous task. Having the Storm turn on us would ensure our loss."

"What does this man have to gain?" Meckea asked. "If we know that, then my Shadows can assist in unmasking him."

"That is the question, isn't it?" Eugho waved a hand. "Jeffe, what happens to a nobleman's estate after an attack from the Storm?"

Jeffe shook his head. "I haven't considered that. I have been … preoccupied."

He reached into his coat and pulled out a small device. After a few moments, it connected to the main screen in the room, and the image of a lone woman appeared.

Aeia didn't recognize her, but the commotion in the room meant that she was in the minority.

"Myr ..." Eugho shook his head. "Where did you see her?"

Myr? Aeia cocked her head. That was the name you'd call a street urchin, specifically a girl who had no home or family. That lady looked nothing of the kind.

"I found her in the outskirts of the city. She has set up a hidden base and has been visiting the city regularly for some time."

"Another adversary in Feos!" Brunst shook his head. "The mission is turning for the worse."

Eugho pointed a stern finger in his direction. "Myr is *not* our enemy. I'd say in this war she will become our greatest ally. But for now, we should be even more careful about covering our tracks. If she gets wind of us she *will* discover us. *All* of us."

"She sounds impressive," Eric said. "Who is she?"

Meckea laughed. "Eugho's daughter."

Eugho whirled in her direction. "I raised her, but I share no blood with her." He let out a sigh, and turned back to Eric. "She took my place as Captain of the Royal Guard. In the King's absence, she commands the largest army in the kingdom."

"Why haven't I seen her face?" Aeia asked. "I have even seen the recording of the ceremony where you received you title, Eugho, and that was long before my time."

"The King is still absent. He hasn't been active since she's been captain. Most of the archdukes don't respect her authority because of that, and they haven't allowed her influence inside their cities. Her soldiers are another matter however. Anyone who fights beside her knows she is more than worthy."

"She certainly doesn't have the support of Lord Cer," Jeffe agreed. "She has undergone every precaution to ensure he doesn't know she's in town. It will be some time before she takes action."

Eugho rubbed the stubble on his chin. "We don't have any time to waste, then. Meckea, what have you discovered of the Bask collector?"

The woman looked to Aeia with a teasing smile.

Aeia shifted in her seat and then looked in Eugho's direction. "Elit Vant never encountered the man organizing the Bask taxing. He was warned to leave the city by his brother, Danton Vant. Danton looked to be at his end, believing that he was too far gone to be saved."

"Danton Vant? That doesn't make any sense. He guards the eastern border. Not only does he keep the crown at bay, but he keeps the Archduke Garlot Orlan at bay as well. Are you sure it was him?"

Aeia nodded. "I have no doubt. He has likely been stripped of his Bask stores."

Eugho closed his eyes. "We don't have a choice then. You should interrogate Danton immediately. Meckea, are you free to be a Shadow?"

She thought, and then shook her head. "No, but Sestes is! He should be able to get Aeia in without much trouble, especially if the Marquess is weakened."

"Good." Eugho opened his eyes, a look of determination growing on his face. "The two of them will infiltrate his base tomorrow."

Eugho turned to Jeffe. "As dangerous as it sounds, we need to trust that Myr will not act yet. I need you looking into the acts of the Storm. Or rather, who cleans up after they leave." He walked back to the front of the room and gestured to the whole group. "The rest of you know your duties. As usual, report anything unexpected. It will only get more dangerous, and we all need to stay alert."

The group began to disperse. Eric started towards Aeia, but she grabbed his arm before he could speak and walked with him as they exited the room. Outside, she pulled on his cloak.

He looked amused. "Where are we going?"

She led him to the top deck of the ship and to the secluded spot they'd both found so comfortable.

"Here ..." Eric whispered. "What's the matter, Aeia?"

Eric sat beside her. "You're a spy inside the Storm."

"It turned out that way."

A frown cracked her still face. "You don't have to do that. It's dangerous."

"Coming from someone about to sneak into a fortress," Eric said with a snicker. "My job seems safe compared to that."

"My life can only be spent working to save this world. You ... you aren't one of us."

Eric rested his elbows on his knees. "You asked me to join your cause."

Aeia twitched. "I never expected you to ... You're a true member of the team. Your mission is one of the most dangerous. If the Storm found out what you were doing, they'd kill you."

"No doubt." He leaned back onto his hands and looked upwards to the jagged moon. "But you can't tell me I'm not part of this world. I have no home, and my actions affect this world, not my own. Because of you I have the power to change things for the better here."

He rolled his head towards her and smiled. "I could die fighting alongside you. But I could have just as easily died in that forest, alone, never having done anything of worth in my life. Don't think I have a burden because of you. Know that I was saved."

Aeia wrapped her arms around her legs. "I wanted you to stay with me for selfish reasons."

"What? I hardly think—"

Aeia rolled to her knees and placed her face a few inches from his. She looked into his eyes, and felt nothing. "You're the only one. The only one who doesn't remind me of my curse."

Eric's face turned red. "W-what do you mean?"

Aeia let out a breath. "It's a secret I've had to carry. I am not a human like everyone else. I'm a design, a tool created by Lord Cer to bypass the laws of this world, so that he can achieve things no man should be able to."

Eric furrowed his brows. "What are you talking about?"

"I am not going to interrogate Danton Vant tomorrow. I am going to bypass all normal forms of communication and take his secrets straight from his mind. With my power, I can do the same to anyone I meet. And most of my life, I was a tool used to find the weaknesses of Lord Cer's enemies. And help him kill them in the ways they would never expect."

Eric's eyes had grown wider as she talked. But he hadn't moved from his spot. "You can do that?"

She nodded. "It's not always voluntary when I do this. If I look anyone in the eyes, the process begins. It's dangerous to even be near me."

Aeia waited for Eric to retreat. Perhaps it would be for the best. Maybe he would give up the fight and look out for himself, as he should. She didn't tell him the truth about herself when she convinced him to join her. Not about her abilities, nor her heritage.

Even if he hates me ... he needs the truth now.

Eric didn't move. His face didn't twist with disgust or curl in anger at her deception. He offered a slight smile. The only emotion she could read was compassion.

"I'm sorry, Aeia. That sounds like a burden no one should have to carry."

She could barely draw in her breath. *I told him all that. And he's worried about ... me?*

The faces of all who knew her secret flashed through her mind. Her caretakers, the guards posted at her station, even the looks Eugho tried so hard to hide. They all feared her, and with good reason. She was a weapon, a tool that violated everything a person *is*.

Then why?

Eric rubbed the back of his neck. "I'm also sorry for anything you might have seen in my mind. As you may know now, I was not a kind person in the past."

She shook her head. "No! You're the only one I can't do it with. Your eyes, I look in them and nothing happens. I've never met *anyone* like that. I've never been able to ... As long as I can remember ..."

She wiped dampness from her cheeks. Crying was a sensation she hadn't felt in so long.

Eric pulled out a small cloth from his pocket and wiped the tears from her face. "I had no idea. I take so much for granted, but I can't imagine not being able to look someone in the eyes. You must feel so lonely."

His cloth didn't help, as the tears weren't stopping. "I'm separate from this world too. I'm not like them, and I can never be. So, when I found you, I didn't want to let you go. Because I might never meet someone like you again. I'm selfish."

"I don't think that's selfish. People need each other. We aren't meant to be alone. The fact that you feel this way means that you're not as different as you think you are."

I'm ... not?

Eric looked off the balcony. "Looks like I can't afford to die now, not if you need me to stick around. Changes my plans up a bit. I'll have to play a bit safer."

Aeia kept her eyes fixed on Eric. "You're the only one who hasn't become afraid of me when they found out what I am."

Eric shook his head. "I have no reason to be scared, even if you could invade my mind. I trust you."

Her next heartbeat was far more powerful than the last. It shook her being, the embodiment of everything Eric had given to her. She didn't know what she had done to deserve it. But she knew then that she could never lose it.

Her skin started to feel warm. And it grew hotter the more she looked at Eric. Unable to handle what was rising in her, she turned away from him.

Tears, and now this? What's happening to me?

Chapter Twenty-one

A beam of sunlight hit Eric's face, waking him. It was an unusual way for him to wake. None of his rooms had windows.

Where am I?

He rose to a sitting position, his body stiff from a night slept on wood. What greeted him was the humble view of the surrounding cityscape. He remembered now. Aeia had not said a word the rest of the night, and they had never retired to their rooms.

His entire body was cold and stiff except for his arm. His arm was warm, and he looked over to see Aeia at his side. She was facing away from him, curled in a protective ball. Eric gently rocked her shoulder.

She rolled on her back to look at him with sleepy eyes. "Eric? Where are we?"

"On the deck." He smiled teasingly and poked her. "You kept us out here all night."

She wiped the dried tears from her eyes. "Sorry. I unloaded a lot onto you."

Compassion shot through his heart, and he reached out to help her up. "You needed to."

"I can carry it alone. I have for a long time."

"You've kept that burden far too long. It's too much for one person to bear."

She slowly accepted the hand, though her face flushed as she did.

"Well, you don't need to anymore." He hoisted her up with ease. "I'm not asking for your permission, by the way. You're just going to learn to tolerate me."

She smiled a truly genuine smile, unlike anything he'd seen from her before. It was the kind of smile that made all the loss, all the risks worthwhile.

"See? I'm selfish too. I spent all night talking to you just to work out a smile."

Aeia turned red and pushed past him onto the main section of the deck. Eric couldn't help laughing as he jogged to her side. "What time are you leaving for the mission?"

"We don't move in until nightfall, but I need to speak with Sestes before then. I haven't run an actual mission with him yet. We need to understand each other."

"Ahh, that's too bad. I don't have to report to the Storm until this evening. So I'd hoped we would have time to waste before then."

"I don't have to go immediately."

A flicker warmed Eric's chest. "Then we can go get some of that bread you like so much. It's a short trip from here, isn't it?"

"You didn't like green bread," she said, feigning coldness.

He smiled. "You could tell?"

"Why would you want to go back there?"

"You like it. I could have handled it a second time."

Aeia stopped and looked down. "Why are you so different from us?"

Eric passed her and turned to face her. "Us aliens aren't obsessed with rocks."

Aeia shook her head. "That's not what I mean. You're different because you aren't filled with Bask. But it's more than that. You look at things differently than we do. You trust when others wouldn't. Show compassion instead of disgust. So many things."

"We aren't that different. People from my world act just like those from this one sometimes." He leaned back against a wall and flicked at his shirt sleeve. "But ... this is something my parents taught me."

"What do you mean?"

Eric sighed, wishing he hadn't brought it up. "Well, they believed that there was always someone watching us. An all-powerful being who loved us more than we could imagine. It was because of that belief that they tried to show the same kindness to others."

Aeia's eyes widened, and she leaned closer. "There's someone like that in your world? Someone like the King?"

Eric shook his head. "They believed that He was much greater, that he created the universe and everything in it."

Aeia's eyebrows furrowed. "You keep saying 'believe,' as if they don't know."

"You can't see God like you can see the King. They can't prove to others that he exists. Well, other than the witness of what he does."

Aeia rested her face on her hand. After a few moments, she looked back up. "Do you believe he exists?"

He looked up to the golden morning sky. "It's hard to say. I used to, back when my parents were still … I stopped looking for him in adulthood. At one point I considered myself a devout follower, but with all that's happened, I don't know what to think. No one on my world knew this world even existed. How could that tie in to our beliefs?"

"I *wish* I could believe in something like that," Aeia whispered. "If the way you are is what he is like, then this world needs him."

Eric nodded solemnly. "I wish I could believe, too. The very idea that God saved so many people on my world from problems they couldn't face alone—it changes life into something different."

"A world of love." Aeia cooed. "Thank you for telling me. Even if it's just a thought, it's something I haven't imagined before. If only I could see it come true."

"A world of love."

Eric stiffened. That phrase had been in his mind for so long. His mother talked about it so often, it had long since lost its meaning. Aeia said it in the same way, a way that he'd forgotten—with desire, with awe.

But your world is gone now, Mom. Where is the love in that?

Anger bubbled up inside of him, and he struggled to keep it hidden from Aeia. *She doesn't need the dream broken yet. Not if it helps her.*

Why was he thinking like that? He had believed, stopped only by his own negligence. Why did the very thought of God make him mad?

Eric hopped to his feet and started towards the entrance back into the ship. A moment later he heard the patter of Aeia's feet as she tried to catch up to him. "I'm sorry. I shouldn't have asked so much about your home."

He shook his head. "It's gone now. It doesn't matter."

Eric felt an arm wrap around his own. It tugged backwards with a force greater than he would have expected from someone so much smaller than he. He turned to face her.

She was scowling at him. "Don't lie to me, Eric. I know when you are."

"I'm just thinking about my past life."

That seemed to be enough for her, so she pulled on his sleeve to urge him forward again.

"Sometimes I wish I could hide what I'm feeling like you do, Aeia. I might be able to get away with something for once."

A mischievous grin touched her lips, and she looked at him through the corner of her eye. "It can be useful."

They moved down the companionway to the lower deck. Most of the team was already gone, save a lone man in black who leaned against the wall in the corner. Eric didn't recognize him, but Aeia did. She stepped between Eric and the man and bowed.

"Sorry." She looked back over her shoulder. "He is here, so I have to go."

With a twinge of disappointment in his gut, Eric nodded.

It's for the best. I should focus on preparing for this evening anyway. The thought didn't help, but a few rounds with Dust might.

He turned toward the door and pulled it open. He allowed himself one last wave at Aeia before he departed.

A world of love, huh?

Right now, he couldn't imagine one without war.

*　*　*

Eric jogged with Vestan as they navigated the dark city streets. This time, the Storm moved orderly, not like they had in the other raid. There was no sense of anger, no wild stomping that made them sound like a pack of beasts.

He had wondered how much his words had gotten through to them a week ago, but already he could see a difference in how they acted. He still worried how they would behave once they reached the manor, but at least they weren't riling themselves up beforehand.

The group slowed at the edge of the nobleman's land. Eric stepped in front of the group. "Remember, we're here to capture the manor. Don't kill anyone unless you absolutely *have* to."

The men nodded. Their eyes were wide, and each small sound pulled their full attention. Without the bloodlust, fear of battle had begun to set in. Eric had seen it before, back on Earth.

It was a much more dramatic change than he'd expected. The group had gone too far in the other direction, from anger to fear.

Eric tightened his fists. *They can't fight like this.*

He reached to his side and drew his sword. "See this? This tool isn't what you have been using it for. Weapons are not made for killing, for revenge. Men use them for that, but with those motives, men can never use them to their full potential."

Eric looked across the eyes of the men, pausing just slightly as he passed them. "Why did you join the rebellion? Each one of you have a reason, or you wouldn't risk your life fighting. Maybe it *is* revenge, or at least that's what you believe. But *I* believe that you chose to fight because you have something worth protecting. Am I wrong?"

The men stayed silent.

"Think about that, then. Whatever it is you want to protect. Don't let your anger guide you, but instead be motivated by the desire to protect the people you love. That will make you far more powerful."

The edge of fear remained, but the men looked more certain of what they were doing than before.

There will always be fear. But if it doesn't control them...

"Let's take this manor then." Vestan nodded his approval to Eric. "One step closer to taking back Feos."

Eric turned back towards the manor. He moved forward, quickly yet quietly. The rebels trailed him. They made noise, but far less than they had before Eric started training them. As they were, the limited guard shouldn't notice them too early.

The acrid odor of metal filled Eric's nostrils, accompanied with the faint clanking from the factory in the distance. His feet left the grass, with only dirt and stone ahead. The nobleman's manor, and everything surrounding it, was designed for his convoys' ease of travel. It was efficient yet left the whole area without many signs of life, replaced with empty buildings and stone pathways.

Eric glanced among the men. A few winced at the scenery, he guesses at memories of years spent working for this man. From what he had been told, Lord Herou would trap his workers, make them completely dependent on him for survival. With that accomplished, their working or living conditions no longer mattered to him. They would work on building cargo ships every day without breaks. In its height, the sheer amount the enslaved workers would produce made Lord Herou the leading supplier of ships in Feos.

Now the place was mostly desolate. There was nobody to be seen all the way to the manor, with the its condition just as bad. The odor of metal was awful and got worse as they neared the manor house.

Why would you build your house so close to your factories?

A call sounded from a balcony. A lone man rushed back into the house upon seeing their arrival. Commotion arose in the household, lights blinking on in every room as they rushed to the building's defense.

"Prepare yourselves!' Eric called as he unmounted his crossbow.

The rebels burst through the door with little effort, the building designed as more of a home than Lord Bealing's had been. As they entered the building, men poured into the central common room from various doors. The men had swords drawn as they charged but were pierced with crossbow bolts before they made it very far.

A few more men armed with crossbows emerged on their left, and that side's group turned their shields in their direction as they created a wall for the rest of the group. The right side positioned themselves above the left's shoulders and returned fire under their protection.

It worked flawlessly, each side protected the other as they moved down the center of the building. Lord Herou's defense didn't stand a chance, and the rebels reached the inner parts of the house in a matter of minutes.

A worthwhile defense was standing ready as they came closer to the lord's office. These men had time to retrieve their full armor and weapons.

Eric halted the group and eyed the opposition. They held their weapons out in front, unable to keep them stable as their bodies quaked violently. They wouldn't be much of an opponent, and his rebels could likely take them without a single casualty on their side.

But. Eric started to step forward. *They don't need any casualties on their side either.*

They gripped their weapons tighter and yanked them in Eric's direction. None fired, as Eric suspected. All waited for him to make the first move.

"Where is Lord Herou? If we can talk this out, we won't need to attack you."

They seemed loyal, but the thought of fighting the rebels seemed too much. A man in front patted the man next to him, and the two pulled back into the room behind them, leaving only ten guards behind to face off against the rebels.

The standoff only lasted only a few more moments before movement appeared at the door once again. A lone arm waved out. "If I come out, will you shoot?"

Eric smiled. "Only if you shoot first."

Cautiously, the man moved into the open. Eric had to admire his bravery, which was more than Bealing had displayed.

"My wife and kids are here," the man said. "Please, just take me if you have to. Leave them."

Eric waved the thought away. "It doesn't have to be like that. The lives of the people here are on you. If you cooperate, then no one else will be harmed."

Herou blinked and opened his mouth to say something. Nothing came out, and he closed it again.

"I'll get down to it then." Eric pointed out a nearby window. "Those factories must either close, or their workers get the wages they deserve. It doesn't seem like you can afford that, so I want them shut down within the week."

"I, uhh..." the man started to speak. "That is how I support myself... What shall I do?"

The words shook the rebels. Angry murmurs started to rise, only silenced by a harsh look from Eric. He turned back to the nobleman. "There will be work for you within the rebellion. Your safety and that of your family will be assured as long as you remain with us. You will be no different from the rest of us, however, as your assets will be acquired by the Storm."

A flash of anger crossed the man's face, but it quickly vanished when he looked at the threat before him. Soon, he let out a breath and looked down. "Very well."

His guards placed the weapons on the floor in front. The rebels instantly moved in to retrieve them.

"Good choice," Vestan nodded. "From here we can—"

A light flashed past the window, accompanied by the soft humming of a shuttle. Eric ran to the window and peered out.

Two large shuttles were hovering above the manor. They hardly made a sound, unlike the usual roaring of shuttle engines.

"The royal guard!" Vestan exclaimed. "What did you do, Herou?"

The nobleman waved his hands in front wildly. "No, no! I didn't call anyone! I didn't have time to!"

"It doesn't matter how they came to know." Eric started toward the exit. "Leave a few people here to watch them, but we'll want most of our men at the front doors."

By the time the Storm had reached the entrance, the shuttles had landed and emptied. They looked prepared, yet passive. It was a gut reaction, but Eric believed they wouldn't fire unless his men fired first.

He would bet his own life on this first as he stepped into the open air alone. No shots were fired, and his rebels quickly took his sides with their weapons drawn.

The opposing soldiers were in full combat armor and carried weapons far more advanced than the crude devices the rebels carried. They were spaced evenly and would be able to bring down many rebels before Eric's men could retaliate. Even with their numbers, Eric couldn't see them winning this fight.

One woman stepped forward. Her armor was indistinguishable from the rest, save a small sash that wrapped around her shoulders. She stood in complete confidence.

Myr. Eric remembered from the photo. *Let's hope Eugho's right about her.*

"Which one of you is the commander here?" she called, her eyes scanning their ranks.

Eric stepped forward. "I am one of them."

"Tell them to lower their weapons. No one else needs to die tonight."

He gave the order. One by one, the rebels placed their weapons on the ground. Once they had finished, Eric turned back to the soldiers. "We haven't killed anyone. That's not why we came."

The woman narrowed her eyes. "We'll see the truth in that statement." She motioned forward, and one of her men pulled ran inside. "Assuming you aren't lying, why did you come here, if not for blood?"

"Forced surrender. We want to change the city, but we don't need to be murderers to do that. The nobles we fight surrender their assets and give their word to cease their actions against the commoners."

"You force a promise? What makes you think they'll uphold it?"

Eric looked back at the manor. It was ill maintained, only a portion of the damage was his fault. "Things are bad, and even the noblemen are desperate."

Myr studied Eric closely. Her gaze was only interrupted when she looked up to a figure appearing in the window above.

Eric turned to look.

Her soldier shouted, "They're all alive, Captain. Wounded, but alive. Lord Herou is unharmed."

"Huh" She nodded at her man, then met Eric's eyes again. "When did the Storm start operating like this? Not long ago you were leaving piles of corpses in your wake."

"It's a new vision."

Myr watched them for a few moments longer, and then she waved for her men to lower their weapons as well. "Since Lord Herou was not harmed, this is not a matter for me to handle. It's under the Archduke's jurisdiction. He should be here shortly."

Panicked murmuring rose among the rebels. A few bent to retrieve their weapons, stopped only by Eric's open order. He addressed Myr. "He'll kill us all. You know that, don't you?"

A smirk crossed the woman's face, and she stepped to the side. Her men created an opening in their line for the rebels. "Yes. Which is why I would advise you to leave before he arrives."

Eric nodded and started forward. He was interrupted by a shout from inside the manor. Lord Herou and everyone else inside poured out of the building. "Take us with you, please! If Lord Cer is coming here, then we're all dead!"

"You are a respected nobleman, Lord Herou." Myr stepped forward. "What would he gain in harming you?"

He shot a nervous glance her way but ignored the question. He moved closer to Eric, his eyes pleading for help.

He's serious? But why?

The man's reasons for fleeing didn't matter right now. "I said I'd give you protection, and I will. I suggest you keep up."

* * *

Myr bowed slightly, arms still crossed. "Borias Shaw."

The man scowled and closed the distance between them. "Captain Myr. What is going on here?"

"A rebel attack. I came to intervene."

Borias looked around the scene. "And where are the prisoners? Or did all of them escape your men?"

"No one was killed. The Lord of the house himself wasn't harmed. I couldn't hold them."

Borias moved closer and looked her square in the eye. "They attacked a nobleman! And you let that slide by?"

Myr raised an eyebrow and rested her hand on the hilt of her blade. Borias's eyes moved with her hand, and he took a step back. "I have no obligations in this matter. This is the Archduke's problem. You should be grateful that I stopped the fighting before anyone was seriously hurt."

"Lord Cer won't be happy about this. He's done you a kindness allowing you to pursue your pointless endeavors in his city. One would expect a token of appreciation."

"I don't care how the Archduke feels. All that matters to me are the people of this city—something your master would do well to take into consideration." Myr waved and called for her men to fall back. When they were moving, she turned back to Borias. "We'll be leaving for the night. There's no one left here anyway. Turns out Lord Herou trusted the rebels more than your Archduke."

Myr turned away, forcing back the smirk. She would face consequences later for tonight's actions, but the last thing this city needed was a massacre of innocents.

Chapter Twenty-two

Aeia slowed her decent with the lifters on her arms and landed on the wall with barely a sound. Sestes landed beside her.

She lowered to the stone and looked each way down the wall. Not a single Huntsman in sight, and the men who did man the stations were barely equipped at all. She spotted one man who wore casual clothes. The dagger at his side looked out of place at best.

What would they hope to do against a real threat?

Danton Vant had fallen farther than she thought. It seemed impossible. The image of the strong and proud commander was burned into her mind. He was a man she looked to as a hero as a child, a great guardian of Feos.

She let out a sigh at the pitiful band of soldiers and rolled over the wall to the other side. She landed gracefully in the Huntsman's field, though it had no Huntsman to back up the name, and dashed toward the fortress.

Up ahead, light streamed across the grass as one of the side windows lit up. A man wandered around inside, unaware to their approach.

Sestes jumped forward, propelled by his pack. He leaped up and into the room in a single bound. Aeia heard a thud as the he met the other man. The two rolled against the floor fighting, and she followed with her own leap, landing on the window sill.

Sestes was crouched above the unconscious man. He pulled a small dart free. He looked her direction and nodded. "Sedative. I understand your aversion to killing."

Aeia smiled, though it was hidden by her mask. "Please don't use it on the Marquess. An unconscious mind is dangerous to be in."

Sestes nodded and moved toward the hallway. He looked each direction and gave her a quick motion before moving into the darkness.

Aeia followed as closely as she could, difficult as it was to keep with the man's larger strides. But despite his size, Sestes maneuvered the hallways with an incredible lithe. She nearly stumbled at sharper turns, and she resorted to quick acceleration to regain her place at the Shadow's side.

One particularly noisy slide caused Sestes to glance back and slow his pace. Aeia flushed slightly and shook her head. She couldn't believe she was being so easily outmaneuvered by such an older man.

She willed herself to move better but couldn't focus properly on her movements as she traversed the dark hallways. Her lack of experience showed, and worry began to flicker in her chest.

A door opened and a young man entered the hallway. Aeia reached for her sedative dart, and she stooped into a crouch before she sprung back in the man's direction.

He was preoccupied, and he only noticed her as she was nearly upon him. He shouted and raised an arm. She thrust an elbow at his throat, which cut his cry short. She then stabbed her sedative into the man's side. She moved around to his backside, quickly pulling him into a hold as his body started to go limp.

She let him down softly and looked up to Sestes. A smirk grew across his face, and he nodded at her.

Aeia returned his nod and started forward again. From then on, any interactions were handled by Sestes. While apparently trained, the guards had no armor or mediocre weapons and stood little chance against the Shadow.

It wasn't long until they reached the back of the fortress, where the hallway ended at an open doorway into a room. Three men were inside. One worked on at a desk while the other two lounged at his sides.

Aeia blinked. Was that really the man she saw in Elit's memory? His eyes were sunken, and he barely held himself upright as he worked. He looked older than she knew him to be—in his mid-thirties. His dark blue hair had turned nearly white, and wrinkles lined his eyes.

What little doubt she still had was gone. Alonius was taking everything from everyone. Not even the noblemen survived his city.

Sestes looked her direction and paused as he waited for her signal. Aeia took in a deep breath and focused her mind.

She nodded.

Sestes lurched forward, immediately throwing a dart at Danton's first bodyguard. It hit him in the exposed part of his neck, and the sedative immediately took effect. Sestes lunged at the second guard, who was unsheathing his weapon, and the two met blades.

Danton Vant rose and bellowed out a call for assistance as he reached for his own weapon. Aeia moved forward and she pulled back her hood so that the top of her face was revealed. It caught the man's attention, he turned to the new attacker, and their eyes met.

* * *

Lights of many colors glided through the air, each carrying with it their own emotion. They twirled around Aeia, passing over without causing her to lose speed. She was undetected, an invisible presence in Marquess Vant's Mind.

She began forward, each step careful and light. As before, walls of stone rose from the ground, and the castle took shape.

Aeia worked slower this time. A man of this status could very well have training on how to defend against a Void Jumper. The mind is a dangerous place, and a trained one could overwhelm her.

Or worse, trap her.

The host's mind started to fill the castle. This much could not be trained to ignore. All the Marquess's secrets were vulnerable, especially the ones he didn't want to come to light, as those would have taken the most effort in hiding.

Aeia curled into a ball at the base of the stone wall, her body taking a new shape. She shrunk and twisted as small wings erupted from her back, her skin replaced with a hard exoskeleton as she transformed completely into a small roach.

She took flight.

It was a much slower ascension than the jump she had performed before, but far less noisy. She was able to peer into the windows of the castle without worry about being found as she looked for signs of training.

There was nothing unusual. Only a few guards lumbered about aimlessly.

That's strange. I was sure—

A low rumble began to sound, drawing louder from every direction. At first an earthquake, it slowly became more rhythmic, a constant *thump*.

Then, they appeared.

Soldiers in full armor materialized out of nothing. They marched through the castle and searched for its creator.

Aeia winced and went flat as a patrol went past. *So many... How am I supposed to get past them all?*

She flew around to the top of the castle, where there weren't as many guards. Here she might be able to enter undetected, at least for a short while. She flew through an open doorway and evaded a passing guard.

Calm. Keep calm.

As long as her mind wasn't too active she wouldn't be found. It would be slow, so she'd have to trust Sestes to take care of her body.

The guard stopped as she passed and looked her direction. Aeia ignored it, not wanting to give off her presence. But the guard continued to look at her.

Forward, only forward.

Footsteps sounded behind her as the guard changed directions. It followed her, the mind already suspicious of her form.

How? I haven't made any mistakes.

Another pair of steps joined the first as a second guard tailed her. She looked back in time to see a third appearing as well, and they gained speed.

She was out of time. Any longer in this form, and she would be caught. She took a deep breath, mentally preparing herself. And then burst forward with everything she had.

Her form changed back to her own body, and she bolted down the hallways as fast as her mind could move. Faster than she ever had before.

Calls of alarm rang out that resonated through the castle, the host's mind both startled and angered at the intrusion.

The halls started to fill with the soldiers as they all converged on her position. She kept alert to where they were and stayed ahead of them.

Metal crashed against stone with deafening clangs and scrapes as the mass of guards tore after Aiea. Even at her speed, flailing hands grappled just behind her, she could feel the movement of air as they nearly brushed her back.

At every turn, they hounded her. No quick change in direction or unexpected passageway hindered them for long. And the few times she *did* manage to lose one group, another was already rounding the corner.

Two groups of soldiers appeared in each direction. She couldn't evade them both, and neither had any gap in their ranks she could squeeze through.

Aeia halted her mind, her projected body coming to an immediate and complete stop. She waited for the guards in front of her to come close and then burst into action.

She transferred all her focus into strength, and swatted the first guard who reached her side. He crashed all the way through the wall, an injury that caused a ripple effect through all the guards.

It was the chance she needed. She grabbed the next closest soldier and pulled herself up and over his head. In the same movement, she placed both feet on his back and jumped forward with all her strength.

The crashing of bodies echoed through the halls, loud enough to satisfy her with the damage she'd done without stopping to look back.

Now, where is that memor—

More soldiers appeared before her, and she had to take a detour through a side door.

This is impossible!

Marquess Vant was too quick, too informed. His mind was commanded with the efficiency he used with his own men. And this was *his* domain. Not only was this his mind, but the castle Aeia has been trained to create only seemed to work against her. She had her own twists in the building, but the Marquess had figured them out.

Aeia glanced out a window as she passed. The swirling darkness of the void was closing. She was losing her opportunity. If she didn't leave soon the connection would fade, and she'd lose her chance at escape.

But the mission.

She gritted her teeth. This was her only job. The one thing she could do to help Eugho. To fail here would put everything he had done for her to waste.

What other option did she have? She had two choices now—execute or escape. If only she wasn't limited to a castle, a Marquess's specialty. Just about anywhere else she would be able to find some way to slip through their ranks, run down an alleyway in a city or hide in a bush.

But she couldn't. A castle was the only way... wasn't it?

Wait. Was the castle the only way? It was all she was trained to do, since it made for efficiently finding information. But was she limited to that? Was she limited *at all*?

This—a shock-wave rocked the fortress—*is not working!*

The castle shook violently. A crack shot through the ceiling above them as the entire structure split in two. As each piece of stone fell, it dissolved just before hitting the ground.

The castle was gone in moments, becoming nothing as quickly as it had risen from the ground. The guards had no clue how to handle the situation and struggled to regroup into their formations. Aeia would not give them that chance.

New, smaller structures started to rise out of the ground. They appeared in vast numbers, separating the soldiers as they scattered. Clothing shops, restaurants, even a Bask Charging Facility. She thought she was building things at random, yet Aeia found that her own mind was creating a replica of Feos before her eyes.

It was easy, and the Marquess didn't know how to react, his mind lost her position as it tried to figure out what was happening. Why hadn't she been taught this? She could have completed missions in the past so much easier.

Because they didn't want us to think. If a person retained their mind with this much power, they could do almost anything. It was dangerous, an unacceptable outcome. It was... free thought.

With new vigor Aeia took to the sky as a bird. She flew over the city unnoticed as the guards struggled to gain their bearings.

Now... She scanned the cityscape. *Where would a Marquess hide something important?*

She shook her head. That wasn't the right question. Where would the Marquess have met with Lord Cer's Bask collector?

She turned her gaze to the Marquess's manor. *Would it be so simple?*

Alonius Cer was not known to be timid. It would be very like him to send his representative straight to the lesser Lord's estates. There would be a great many memories stored in a place like that, but in the state in which the taxing had left the Marquess, it could be on the forefront of his mind.

She flew toward the building. this was the most defined and detailed of all the buildings in this imagined city. It was a focus of the Marquess, and he seemed to be filling in his own knowledge of the place. That was good—it meant a lot would be stored within.

Aeia wouldn't go through the front door, which would leave her to navigate through the flood of memories. Instead she headed straight toward the Marquess's office, where the Bask collector would most likely be brought.

She fluttered at the window and tapped it open with quick pecks from her beak. As soon as she did, the room filled with life.

Colors of blue and red—fear and anger—escaped. Soon after, apprehension followed as the door to the office opened with a click.

A lone man strode into the room. He was dressed in a crimson combat suit that completely covered his features.

"What do you want now? I gave the Bask you asked for!" The Marquess stood tall. But it was a farce, the whirlwind of color betrayed his feelings.

"The Archduke requires more." The man's voice was deep, almost inhuman.

The Marquess rose from his seat, fists clenched as he glared. "More? What could he *possibly* be doing with so much? I gave him enough to power a warship! You're asking far more than is allowed by an Archduke!"

"It is not your concern. You are to comply, and that is all you need to know."

Red, anger, filled the room, only tempered by a small amount of sadness in blue. "And if I don't? Will you send your street Barrows after me? Like I'm some sort of merchant who can't defend himself? You forget my allegiances. I was commissioned by the King!"

The crimson soldier seemed unfazed and turned towards the exit. "Bring two shipments in three days' time to the port."

The door closed with a thud as the soldier left. All traces of blue vanished to the red, and Danton roared with rage as he swept his arm across his desk, clearing it in a single swish.

Three days, three days ...

Aeia fluttered further into the room, eyes darting as she looked for a calendar. There was none in sight, and the documents on the floor were blurred with unimportance.

But once she was fully inside, she heard a new sound. A quiet *tac tac* of dripping water. It was overcast outside, raining.

This memory was nearly as clear as the present. Which meant it had occurred recently.

It rained two days ago. That must have been when this meeting happened. Which meant the marquess will take the shipment tomorrow!

Aeia flew back out the window, the memory fading and the cloudy sky turning back into the dark void. Guards were arriving at the manor, loading bolts into their crossbows. But they were too slow. Aeia was already traversing back into the void and out of the Marquess's mind.

Chapter Twenty-three

Eric tramped down the staircase leading into the hideout. It was odd being so relaxed in a hostile base, and he often had to remind himself of his intentions. He had to find out who oversaw the Storm.

The life of the hideout greeted him once more. The rebels seemed more enthusiastic about their training, and they didn't look as if they'd been drinking nearly as much. If not for the familiar faces, it would almost seem a different group of men.

He looked for Vestan and spotted him leaning against a wall near the bar. His face was dark, the one sour expression in the building. A twinge of worry stuck Eric as he approached.

Without a word, Vestan motioned for him to follow him into the head office. When they were inside, Vestan closed the door behind them and stepped off to the side.

"I'm happy to finally meet you, Eric. Tales of your accomplishments have been traveling through the Storm in considerable number."

A figure appeared from the shadows. It was a man covered from head to toe in crimson armor. It looked very like the armor Eric had seen Nick wear during the civil war against the King, at least at first glance. This man carried himself differently than the rest, as if he were ready to lash out towards anyone without warning. Nick had been a beacon of hope. This man was a coiled viper.

Eric did his best to mask his apprehension and offered a polite bow. "I do what I can. You are…?

"I am Geralt, the leader of the Storm." Obviously, this wasn't Nick. His old friend would recognize him on the spot, despite the costume. This had to be an imposter. A part of him had hoped that Nick was somehow still alive, that he wouldn't be the only man from Earth here.

I am alone here.

"It's good to finally meet you," Eric said. "You've done so much for the kingdom. But I thought you were lost."

The man nodded and started pacing, his arms behind his back. "I will not lie. The man who bore this name before me is gone, killed by the King for all to see. But that does not mean that Geralt has died."

"I don't understand."

"Geralt was not the man's true name. This armor, and the ambition that comes with it, is what the name represents. The need for change did not die with Nick."

You knew him.

"And this world does need change," the new Geralt said. "Which is why I came tonight." He looked down as he paced, as if counting each footstep. "Both Lord Bealing, Duke Herou. You left them alive when you had them at your mercy."

"They had nothing left. They didn't need to die."

Geralt's gaze snapped towards him. He halted inches from Eric. "They *do*. I did not revive the rebellion to *scare* the noblemen away. I came to remove them. They have lost their chance in this world. They are a stain, nothing more, and they need to be wiped out."

Eric held his ground. "You can't found a new kingdom on corpses."

The man backed away. "You overestimate us. We are the enemy of the entire kingdom. We cannot afford to leave enemies alive."

Vestan took a step forward. "Bealing and Herou will never challenge us, commander. Lord Herou is within this building, hiding from the Archduke."

Geralt turned his head toward Vestan. "You are hiding someone from the Archduke? He will look hard to find him, and you have him in one of *our* hideouts!"

Geralt sighed and covered his face. "The Archduke of this city has tools beyond belief. He will use those dukes' survival to find us, Vestan. We may already be dead."

Vestan shook his head. "I don't believe that, and neither should you."

Geralt turned towards the door. "Vestan, go check the front."

Murmuring from the training area was growing. Eric hadn't noticed before, but now he heard shouts, chaos. Vestan opened the door to see all the men near the entrance to the base had gathered around a single point, moving like a giant blob toward them.

The mob parted and revealed Dust as he strode toward them. He already walked as if he were the one in charge.

"Vestan, I heard you command these men." Dust's voice was deeper than when Eric had talked to him before. He spoke with a confidence that didn't exist when he was around Eugho, yet it wasn't unauthentic. This was his element, these were his men.

Vestan bowed politely. "I serve under Geralt ... but yes, I command this base."

"Geralt, yes, I'll speak to him later." He looked around the base as he talked, eyebrows resting on the training equipment. "Fine work you've done while I've been gone. Looks good."

"Thank you, sir, but"—Vestan glanced behind him— "you were taken by the Royal Guard. When were you released?"

Dust let out a hearty laugh and patted Vestan on the shoulder. "I wasn't released, lad! A few friends broke me out during a transport.

I'm not surprised they didn't announce it here in Feos. You all would have come looking for me if they had."

"We would have." Vestan nodded in agreement. "We should have even been the ones to break you out. I'm truly sorry we didn't."

"It's not a simple thing to do. Besides, from what I've heard from Eric, you've kept yourselves quite busy."

"Eric?" Vestan turned to him and smiled. "I knew your appearance wasn't random. I thought I saw a bit of Dust in the way you fought, but I didn't allow myself to believe it."

Footsteps sounded behind Eric, and his stomach dropped. Both he and Vestan stepped to the side to allow Geralt space to enter the large room.

Dust scowled and crossed his arms. "Not often I see someone return from the dead."

"Nor from a life of imprisonment," Geralt countered. "But it seems the world is full of miracles."

"Who are you? Unless you still have a dozen holes in your body, you can't be the real Geralt."

The man bowed before Dust. "But I am. The physical body has changed, but the ideals remain the same."

"That isn't an answer," Dust said. "Take off your mask."

"I cannot afford to reveal my identity, not yet. But in time there will be no need for me to keep it hidden."

"Of course." Dust waved his hands. "After you've finished your schemes."

"You have no authority here, Dust. You have been gone a long time." Geralt walked past him, gaze fixated. "This is *my* rebellion now. For the moment, you are still welcome to join it. I cannot deny your successes under Nick's command. But if you continue to pry where you have no need to, then I shall have no choice but to force your leave."

Dust's scowl grew into a glare, and he looked at Vestan, who turned away.

Dust closed his eyes and took a breath. "Fine, then. You have a great deal of my old men in your service, and I don't want to abandon them."

"I'm glad we agree." Geralt started towards the doorway. "I have to take my leave for now, but feel free to make yourself at home, Light stealer."

Dust waited for the man to leave and then threw his arm up with a roar. "Are you all blind? And Vestan, what are you thinking?"

"He wasn't exactly wrong, sir. You have been gone a long time. We had to learn how to stay together without the Light stealers to lead us."

Dust leaned forward. "So much that you would turn to an imposter?"

Vestan winced. "He knew so much, about everything. And the way he fights is just like Geralt, move for move. He had resources, connections, eyes throughout the city. By the time he found us, we were hardly more than another collection of homeless. What choice did we have?"

Dust's expression softened, and he lowered his head. "I'm sorry. It was my failures that brought us this low."

"No." Vestan shook his head. "It is because of the enemy we fought. Even now we don't have the courage to challenge the Archduke, let alone the king. We failed by losing our will to fight."

Dust nodded. "Bankrupt nobles are hardly worth the effort. Why do you target them?"

"That is Geralt. He believes it will rekindle our spirit to have victories. He lists off which noblemen we should attack and then sets us lose. Until Eric arrived we would massacre every one of them."

"That will only teach bad war habits."

Vestan motioned to Eric with a grin. "That's what he says. And I agree. But what Geralt says goes. If we lose him, we lose our funding and resources."

Dust huffed. "As much as it pains me to say it, I agree that you do need to follow him for the time being. But don't lose yourselves in the process. Remember the true Geralt and his dream."

Dust started towards the door.

"W-wait!" Vestan stepped forward. "Where are you going?!"

"I cannot join, not yet. I cannot work for someone who stole my commander's name ... Eric will be more than enough to keep you all safe."

Eric's hands tightened into fists. *He's leaving me to do everything?*

"I don't blame him." Vestan sighed. "He's a commander of armies. We're a group of looters."

"But we're changing." Eric said. "He needs to help us change."

"Maybe he still will. But I'd give him a chance to cool down after that confrontation with Geralt."

Eric watched Dust until he disappeared up the staircase. "I guess so. I'll talk to him later."

Vestan started to ask a question about Dust, but the sound

went past Eric. His eyes were fixed on a lone man moving down from an upper room. He had a cloth wrapped around his eyes in the same way that Jeffe did when Eric had first met him.

A Huntsman?

Eugho had mentioned the Storm had one. But why was he coming down?

Eric started toward the man slowly as they both crossed the room toward the entrance tunnel. He was able to get a glimpse of his other side, where the man had his hand on the hilt of a blade.

Dust!

Eric quickened his pace but went just slowly enough that he wouldn't draw attention to himself. He followed the Huntsman up the staircase and into the alleyway.

There, the Huntsman followed Dust. Eric followed the Huntsman, who clearly had no idea he was there. There was something to be said for being immune to Bask.

He put each step down with care, to not make any noise. The Huntsman never noticed as he moved in for the attack.

Eric broke into a sprint. "Dust! Look out!"

Dust spun and reached for his sword as the Huntsman's weapon swung down on him. It was too late, and Dust had to step back and take the edge of the blow on his arm.

By the second strike, Dust was ready. His arm was weaker from the first attack, but he dug his feet into the ground and threw his weight to compensate. It caused his attacks to be reckless and clumsy, but he was able to defend himself.

Eric charged. The Huntsman turned at the noise that came with no Bask signature.

"Leave now," Eric called, "or face us both!" He reached Eric's side and lifted his sword.

The Huntsman stepped back a few paces and held his weapon defensively. "What are you? How are you hidden from my sight?"

Eric tapped the Huntsman's blade with his own. "Leave or be killed."

"Two against one." The Huntsman moved back another pace. "I have more coming. An entire squad. We're going to kill you no matter what you do."

"More like you?" Eric feigned the best laugh he could. "I doubt they'll have much luck against me."

The Huntsman started to back away. Eric pushed him back further as he feigned a charge while making as much noise as he could. The Huntsman leaped and sprint away.

Eric searched the sky for shuttles heading their direction. There were none.

"What was that?"

They turned to see Vestan approaching from the hideout. He looked from them to the running man, eyes wide as he held his sword half-heartedly in front of him.

"That was the Huntsman who guarded our hideout." He slid his sword back into its sheath and turned to them. "What happened?"

"He attacked me," Dust huffed. "Obviously, he was told to do so."

"That can't be right. He only answers to Geralt. I thought he welcomed you to stay with us."

Dust shook his head. "Shows us his true nature, then. He didn't seem too excited to see a leader from the past rebellion. He fears I could rival his command."

"He isn't like that, though." Vestan slowly shook his head. "He's always had our interests at heart. He wouldn't do this."

"He did. And there isn't anything we can do about it." Dust covered his wound with his hand and started forward again.

Vestan reached out to stop him, but Eric patted him on the shoulder, and he froze.

"Don't worry about it now." Eric said. "Geralt's dangerous, but he won't harm you or the rest of the Storm as long as you do what he says."

He jogged to catch up to Dust, the mask of confidence he wore melting away.

I hope.

Chapter Twenty-four

Soft clacking broke the night silence as Myr retraced her steps to her base. She looked at the ground as she walked. She should be on alert. She lived her life on alert. But tonight, she needed to think.

Everything about this city is odd.

Despite her repeated actions against his interests, Lord Cer hadn't once attempted to contact her since she'd arrived. She hadn't exposed herself unnecessarily, but her presence in the city couldn't be denied.

It was as if it did not concern him. She had a massive number of troops at her command, the ability and desire to enact justice against even Archdukes, but Lord Cer seemed to view her as unimportant.

And why should he view her any other way? She hadn't been able to acquire any information about what Lord Cer was doing. The effects of his Bask taxing was obvious, yet she couldn't trace it back to him. His transports were clean, as were all his personal vessels. Any vessels that he or his men used bore no evidence of carrying large amounts of Bask.

But who in their right mind would work with him? He is stealing from anyone who's ever been loyal.

Myr let out a sigh and waved her hand at the door to her base. Her mind connected to the mechanism, and it opened to her signature. She stepped into her office.

She eased herself down at her desk, as she did every night, and fired up a screen. It showed all the work she had on the case. Maybe tonight she would see something more, maybe connect two things that she had missed before.

She found a new file among her working files. One that she knew she hadn't placed there herself. But that was impossible.

How could someone gain access to this? She lifted her hand, studied the king's seal etched into the back of it. It alone would allow her to access her systems. They could not possibly be broken into. No manner of manipulation could recreate what only the King himself could do.

Hesitantly, she opened the file. The screen filled with reports and charts, each with the names of nobles from Feos. These were men who had been killed recently without explanation.

Someone else is investigating?

She sifted through the files. They didn't offer any information she didn't already know; the nobles lost all their Bask and were forced to close their businesses. And shortly after, many had their homes attacked by the rebellion.

It was all linked, she knew that. But what did the person who'd given her this file have to do with it? If they were any part of the King's government they could have given this to her directly.

The last file contained a map of Feos. It had nothing other than a time and a circle around a small section of the map, directly east of the Sky Port.

Could it really ...?

In all her time in Feos, she had never gotten a name behind the Bask taxing. Alonius Cer wasn't doing it alone, but whoever he was working with was hiding himself so well that it seemed he had a ghost for a partner. Who had given her this information, and how did he or she come across it?

She turned off the system and rose. Right now, those things didn't matter. That meeting was going to take place in just a few hours, and this could be her only chance to stop all this before it goes too far. While there was still a city to be saved.

Myr reached for her switchblade and strapped it to her side.

How would you stop this, Eugho?

* * *

Twisting blues twirled around Myr as she lay flat against the rooftop of a small building. The blues were not visible to the eye, but she could sense their presence along with the Bask energy around her.

It was the artificial sense of the Huntsmen she wore, a difficult yet powerful method of surveillance that was arguably one of the most useful machinations of Bask. The Huntsmen mask would limit sight so that the user would not be overwhelmed. Most Huntsmen are blind and don't have anything to worry about, but a person with all their senses can get migraines if they use a mask too much.

A skilled soldier with the right technology would be able to feel her hunting, but her location would remain unknown.

Currently, there didn't seem to be any other Huntsmen about. She wore it to make sure her soldiers wouldn't be spotted by Lord Cer before the Bask transport took place. It seemed she had little to fear in that regard, or perhaps more so. Anyone who came within her range moved causally and never took a position that would be suitable for a Huntsman.

Where are they all then?

"How much longer?" she asked a nearby soldier.

"Only a few minutes until the scheduled time, Captain."

"Get ready."

As if on cue, a blinding light entered her field of senses. It was a cargo shuttle, nearly filled with pure Bask stones.

This much, and they aren't masking it?

She removed her mask, and her body struggled to adjust to the sensory change. It was painful—her senses seemed so much more intense than normal.

With as little noise as possible, Myr crawled over and peered just over the edge of the rooftop.

The cargo shuttle bore the insignia of Marquess Vant. Driven by the Marquess himself.

He came alone? Must be trying to save his reputation.

She looked down the street from the other direction. There, a small group of shuttles came into view. They were built for combat, and the men driving them were well armed. It seemed excessive, as the Marquess was unarmed and in ordinary clothes.

It was of no consequence to her. Her own soldiers outmatched and outnumbered Lord Cer's, or whoever it was who'd hired the guards.

She whispered to the other soldiers. "Wait until it is clear that the Bask is changing hands, then sound the call."

All shuttles stopped, and a door on the lead vehicle from the receiving shuttle opened. A lone man stepped outward. He wore a crimson combat suit that covered his entire body and had a long but thin sword sheathed behind his back.

Geralt?

She shook her head. He was dead. This had to be an imposter. But even that idea was strange. What did he hope to gain from this masquerade?

"Marquess Danton Vant," the crimson soldier said as the nobleman stepped down from his transport. "I assume you brought enough this time."

Danton shot him a glare but opened the side of his vehicle to reveal his cargo. "This is all I have left, my entire life's work. Is this now enough to satisfy you?"

"I hope so, for your sake."

The crimson soldier stepped forward to inspect the Bask, and then he waved a hand at his men. Immediately, the other shuttles pulled up to the side of the transport. The men inside moved the Bask from one vehicle to the others.

"This will be enough. You will have no more visits from me."

The two walked to the front of the shuttles. Danton looked back, and his face dropped as he watched the men unloading his treasures. "I won't, will I? Now that I'm useless to you, you'll send the Storm to finish me off."

Geralt waved a hand. "I see no reason to."

Danton laughed and turned away. "I'll be ready for them. I won't die like the rest."

Myr motioned to the soldiers behind her. One shouted and shined a bright blue light into the air.

Like ants out of a hill, Myr's men descended into the square. They caught the attention of the soldiers, who dropped the Bask and reached for their weapons.

Geralt reached for his sword and turned her direction. He locked eyes with her and lowered himself into a stance.

Fine, then.

Myr burst forward, sword drawn as she descended on the man in red. He lifted his blade to meet hers. His was made with a black-colored metal, and Myr realized her mistake.

Umbranium? Where did he get that?

The two swords clashed, Myr's entire being rippling with the vibrations of the black sword. The Bask within her revolted with a searing pain.

"Guard-Captain Myr ... of all people," the crimson soldier said. "I didn't expect you."

Myr parried the man's counter strike. Her men rushed to her side, but she held a hand to halt them. "Arrest everyone else! I'll handle him."

The man in red cocked his head to the side. "You will, after what you just felt? Interesting. I have always wanted to fight a switchblade wielder."

What does he think this is? A game?

Myr lifted her sword and waited for the man to attack. She couldn't afford for their blades to meet too many times. Every clash would be more painful for her than the first.

The man lunged at her and stabbed downward. Myr couldn't retreat, so she moved forward. In a blue flash of light, her sword transformed into a short saber. She used the flat side to redirect his attack.

The two metals slid against each other with a high-pitch scraping. The Bask churned inside her faintly, bearably. Myr threw her weight into the man, aided by a small burst from her jump pack.

With a grunt, the man was thrown off balance, his deadly blade thrown with his arm to the side. Myr tossed her switchblade to her other hand and attacked while keeping the man from bringing his sword back with her right hand.

Her switchblade molded forward with her strike, the saber straightening into a rapier for the lunge. It was halted at the man's armor momentarily, before piercing through and into the flesh at his side.

It wasn't a fatal wound. Myr needed answers. She pulled back, drawing her sword out quickly, and faced off against him.

"Surrender," she said. "This is a fight you cannot win."

The man stumbled backward, grasping his side with his free hand. "That was a good blow... But I cannot surrender."

"Lord Cer is insignificant compared to the King, stranger. No matter what he has threatened, it is nothing compared to what the King can do."

The man shook his head with a laugh. "He hasn't threatened me, Captain. And soon your 'King' will be nothing more than a memory."

He tossed a couple of pulse bombs in her direction. Myr had anticipated the attack and lifted her hand, firing the lifter on that hand at full strength. The force pushed the orbs off in either direction, so that their explosions didn't affect a soul.

Myr clenched her fist and fired the hook shot mounted on her forearm. It clamped on the man's leg and pulled. His feet were yanked from under him, and he slammed into the ground.

A current shot through the coil into the man. It wouldn't be as effective through his armor, but it was enough to incite a roar as he struggled to escape. He slammed his blade a few times into the coil with insignificant effect. Finally, he gave up and fired off his own jump pack.

Myr released the coil from her arm before she could be pulled up and detached her crossbow from her back. Wasting no time, she fired multiple tranquilizer bolts at her target.

A small shield opened from each of the man's arms, barely blocking each of the bolts that rained came upon him. He started back downwards and used the lifters on his hands to slow his decent as he neared the ground.

Is that how this would be?

Myr reached for a particular pack of bolts. Force rounds, bolts that would shatter any shields that the man might be carrying. Some of his bones would shatter, but if he blocked this shot as well as he had the last, he should survive.

"Captain!" A man called from behind.

She readied the shot.

"Guardians are coming!"

Myr's froze.

"About time." The crimson soldier stood straight. "I'd say we both leave this fight for now, unless you want everyone here to die."

No! Not now! Not when I'm so—

A sickening crash sounded behind her, and she whirled around to see a cloud of dust. Something massive had just landed behind her.

She fired her force round into the dust and bolted in the other direction. "Everyone! Retreat now!"

Her soldiers abandoned their prisoners and followed Myr. Lord Cer's men called after them. Bound, they were helpless as the abomination in the dust cloud unleashed its fury upon anything that was near.

Their cries were cut short as the sound of thunderous attacks met the flesh of the helpless guards. With how little time they had to react, Myr knew that some of her men would be caught as well, and anyone who was wouldn't survive.

Curse all of this! Is Alonius even a human?

Myr and her men reached her shuttle, still hidden in an alleyway, and clambered inside. Jak was in there already frantically managing the video feeds of all the soldiers. He breathed a sigh of relief upon seeing Myr's face.

"How many made it out?" She asked as she leaped into the driver's seat.

"Fourteen. Almost everyone, Captain."

Almost.

"There shouldn't have been any casualties. How did Lord Cer react so quickly?"

"He didn't have to." A soldier entered the shuttle and sat down with a thud. "He had the Guardian hidden in a false wall. They chose that spot for a reason."

The last of the survivors boarded her shuttle, and she took to the air.

The clearing was still clouded with dust, the Guardian gave it no time to settle as it continued its wild attacks. All she could see was the occasional whip-like metal tendril that showed itself as it flung yet another body through the air.

She turned the shuttle toward the outer city. With her engines maxed, she rocketed away from the chaos.

"He was one step ahead of us, *again*." She slammed her fist into the dashboard. "We *had* the collector. I was a moment away from apprehending him!"

"We know what he looks like, at least." Jak offered,

"We know what color his armor is! Everything about this... He takes every precaution possible."

Jak looked her in the eyes. "But you're smarter, quicker. He won this time, but you'll best him. It's just a matter of time."

Myr turned away. "I've wasted too much time already. Today Lord Cer sent a Guardian to kill us. An Archduke attacked the King's men. Lord Cer no longer has the right to control this city."

Jak gasped and leaned in. "Captain, there hasn't been a war between the King and an Archduke since—

"We're falling back to the Capitol. Call ahead and tell them to prepare the Interceptor."

Jak repositioned himself and turned toward the rear of the shuttle. "Yes, Commander." *This has gone unchecked far too long. It is time to end it.*

* * *

Aeia sat next to Eugho in the command center. It felt odd that her part of the mission was complete. She wanted to be out there with the Shadows, even though she knew her novice skills would only get her in the way.

All she could think about was what could go wrong and how she would be powerless to help sitting here.

Eugho seemed completely calm, focused on his work at the desk. He noticed her glance and looked up with a reassuring smile.

"They won't get caught. Meckea's Shadows are the best I've seen. They're probably safer than we are."

"About the same," came a familiar voice.

The shadows from every corner of the room moved toward the center, each taking the form of a person as they stepped into the light.

"Welcome back, Meckea." Eugho smiled. "What did you see?"

"Geralt." Sestes spoke first. "Or at least a man wearing his armor. He matched the description Aeia gave as well."

Eugho scowled. "That is very unwelcome news. I believe that is the same man Eric saw leading the rebellion."

"The same man is doing both?" Aeia cocked her head to the side. "But wouldn't that mean..."

"Yes," Eugho nodded. "Lord Cer has gained control of the entire city. Even those who think they are fighting against him."

Brunst shifted. "The best battle is one avoided. Alonius is keeping anyone from taking up arms against him."

"Almost everyone." Eugho tipped his head forward with a smirk. "Meckea, what happened when the captain confronted him?"

"Myr defeated *Geralt*"—she scoffed at the name the imposter had taken— "with ease, but she was interrupted by a Guardian. She retreated with her men, and they seem to be heading back to the capitol."

"Very good. Then we should see the Royal Guard mobilizing in a matter of days."

"Is... that a good thing?" Meckea asked. "All of Feos will become a war zone."

"It will. But that's what I intended from the start. Only two powers match that of Lord Cer. Archduke Orlan to the east and the crown itself. And a battle between Archdukes would simply be intervened by the King's army."

Aeia leapt to her feet. "I thought we were going to save Feos!"

A frown formed on Eugho's face. "You saw for yourself, Lord Cer is manipulating every part of Feos to his will. No rebellion will work, and arresting him will not stop his corruption. That leaves us with only one option."

"I don't believe it." Aeia slowly shook her head. "This can't be your plan."

"Then believe *this,* Aeia," Eugho said. "I know Myr. I raised her. She will not harm an innocent if she doesn't need to. This is the safest way to win back the city. And once Lord Cer is gone, the city will be under the protection of the crown."

"Don't deceive the girl." Brunst scoffed. "Sure, Myr won't kill anyone she doesn't have to. But Lord Cer will kill everyone to save himself. War isn't pretty. But you have to accept that if you want to change anything."

Aeia scowled. *I don't. I will save anyone I can.*

She turned to Eugho. "I'm going to Eric. That man in crimson is his commander. He has to get out before the army arrives."

He nodded. "Brunst will go with you. You'll need his protection."

She started to protest but stopped herself. Things were becoming too chaotic for her to travel alone safely.

"Thank you." She turned to the soldier. "Let's move quickly. Who knows what Geralt will do now that he's been discovered."

Chapter Twenty-five

Aeia pressed her finger to her beacon to let Eric and Dust know she was arriving. They were still a bit far off, but she hadn't told them she was coming.

"I hope they aren't at the rebel hideout," she mumbled. "What do we do if they are? They could get caught before we can warn them."

Brunst shrugged. "It was your plan. Didn't you consider that?"

She flushed and looked at the ground. "I just hoped that they wouldn't be."

"Relax, kid, I was kidding. It's a lot better to try and fail than to not try at all."

She still watched her feet as they walked. "Have ... have you done that before?"

Brunst let out a sigh. "What, fail? Plenty of times. It's a part of life. Especially when you work with Eugho."

She looked up and cocked her head. "What do you mean?"

The soldier laughed. "The man's a tad ambitious, if you can't tell. Even when he was the Guard Captain he would undergo missions as risky as this one. They don't always work out."

"Can this mission fail?"

"Every mission can," Brunst noted. Sometimes it doesn't matter how much work you put into something, it can always fail. But the more you focus on that, the more likely it will."

"I see. I've put all my faith in Eugho. I've never even considered the possibility."

"And that's just as dangerous. Don't plan on failing, but make sure you are always prepared ..."

Brunst grabbed her shoulder, and his immense strength stopped her. He scanned the tops of the surrounding buildings, eyes narrowed.

"What?" she whispered.

"Huntsmen, and a lot of them. They're searching for someone."

"Dust," she whispered. "If any of them saw his signature they'd know it was him."

Brunst nodded. "His signature is very well known among Huntsmen. And he is one of the last people Lord Cer wants to invade his city right now. But that's not our only problem."

He pointed to her. "These Huntsmen work for Lord Cer. They'll know your signature, right? As one of Lord Cer's Void Jumpers."

Aeia froze. *No. They'd know even more about who I am. Signatures between family are similar. Could they see that I'm ...*

He directed Aeia back the direction they'd come from. "What do you know about Shadowing?"

Aeia looked from rooftop to rooftop, eyes wide as she tried to see them. "M-most everything. But I'm not good yet."

"It will have to be enough. Do you have the implant?"

She nodded.

"Shadow me, *now*."

Aeia swallowed hard. This was the most difficult part for her, the skill of hiding behind someone else's signature.

She activated her implant. She could feel the energy of Brunst next to her, the unique wavelengths that made up his personal signature. Once she had a clear view, she looked at her own.

The two were wildly different, a challenging task for even an experienced Shadow. But she tried anyway.

She took control of the Bask energy she radiated. Manipulating it, imitating it. She had to get her flow to be as little as possible while matching the signature of Brunst. If done correctly, it would make them seem like one person to a Huntsman. Too much energy, no matter how it appeared, was a giveaway that there was a Shadow in the area.

Her Bask energy struggled against her will. It wanted to flow as it pleased. Each attempt she made to control it failed after a few moments.

"Are you done yet? He will be able to sense signatures soon."

Aeia closed her eyes tighter and followed Brunst by holding onto his sleeve. "Please be quiet, this is difficult."

It's no different from Void Jumping. It's all about control.

With a deep breath, she calmed herself. She rejected the world around her and focused only on the two Bask signatures. They came in line with one another, and their wavelengths became one.

The shadowing complete, her implant activated again. It took over the process for her and would retain it for a few minutes.

"Done."

Brunst stepped in front of her and reached for the hammer at his side. "Good. They'll know you performed a shadowing, so stay back and keep your face hidden. He can't know who you really are."

She complied, pulled her cowl over her head, and stepped behind Brunst.

Two men dropped from the rooftops, slowing themselves to a soft landing in front of her and Brunst. Both of their eyes were covered in a permanent binding, and they had small crossbows out and ready to fire.

"A Shadow and a Knight?" one asked. "What are you two doing in the bad part of town, eh?"

Brunst gripped his weapon tighter and pulled back. "I have no reason to answer you, Huntsman."

"This area is under investigation." The other spoke up. "Anyone here is a suspect. Tell your Shadow to reveal himself, or we will have to fire."

Brunst rushed forward at an inhuman speed and swung his hammer. Its head extended outward on the end of a coil and slammed into one of the Huntsmen at full speed. His chest caved in at the blow, and he was flung across the street.

The second Huntsmen jumped back and yelled into his communicator. With his free hand, he fired a quick shot at Brunst. The bolt flew at Brunst's chest and pierced his clothes. It stopped with a loud *thunk* as it met his armor. It fell to the ground harmlessly.

Brunst charged him, his hammer retracted back to its original position as he ran.

The Huntsman fired another shot, this time at Brunst's head.

Brunst lifted his arm, and the bolt pierced the thick flesh.

Now the huntsmen were only at arms' length, and Brunst swung downward with his hammer. It came down on the Huntsmen's head. Despite the helmet, it was a lethal blow, and the man dropped.

Aeia gasped as Brunst pulled out the bolt in his arm. In only a minute he had killed them both. People she feared due to their strength and power were helpless against him.

He waved for her to follow and ran down the street. She did, pushing herself as hard as she could to keep up with the Knight. Each of his footsteps shook the ground. More huntsmen fired at them. Brunst put himself between Aeia and the attackers.

He reached beneath his shirt and pulled free his chest plate. It had a handle on the back so that it could double as a shield.

Brunst repositioned his shield after each blow. The small bolts bounced off the thick plate, and the Huntsmen abandoned the barrage to move in.

The Knight stopped and pulled free his hammer again. The Huntsmen lowered their bodies and spread out. They moved in with swords drawn to attack from all sides.

Brunst backed Aeia into a wall and glanced at her. With a smirk, he rushed forward to attack the Huntsman directly in front of him, leaving Aeia exposed.

"N-no!" She gasped and looked for a path of retreat.

There was none, and a few of the Huntsmen broke off to apprehend her. Their eyes were covered, giving her no path to enter their minds. She was left with only a dagger as protection.

She pulled it free and held it out. The Huntsmen rushed in with their swords.

Aeia lifted an arm in protection, only to see a flash of gray before her. A lone man appeared in her defense and struck outward at both Huntsmen at once.

Surprised and unprepared for the newcomer, they took the full force of his blade.

Suddenly her entire body felt to come alight with fire until her being burned and contracted. She looked herself over. There were no flames, or anything visible that was causing the pain.

"Sorry." She recognized Eric's voice. "I had to use an umbranium sword. It was all I had time to bring."

He lifted her and sprinted away.

She forced an eye open, despite the pain. Eric smiled apologetically, his face turning red from the exertion.

"Let me know when you can walk again. This is actually pretty difficult."

She smiled and tested her hands and legs. They responded better. The pain was receding. "I'm okay."

He dropped her to her feet.

She scowled. "I'm not that heavy."

Eric panted and raised an eyebrow. "Trust me, *everything* is heavy when you're running like that."

She looked back in the direction they'd come from. "Brunst?"

It was Brunst who answered. "I'm fine." He joined them, running from an adjoining road. "The pulse bomb I used wasn't lethal. We need to hide."

Eric nodded. "The safe house is just ahead."

The group ran down the street and into an abandoned shop. They moved to the back, where a doorway was hidden in the wall. Eric went for a switch hidden under a floorboard, but Brunst opened the door with a wave of his arm.

Aeia moved inside, followed by the other two, and the door shut behind them.

"There," Eric let out a breath. "They can't sense you in here."

"Hopefully not." Dust appeared from another room, arms crossed. "We'll soon find out how good of an engineer Sale is."

"Yes, but there's something more I'd like to know." Brunst retrieved a medical kit. "Why is every Huntsman in the city after you, Dust?"

"I made the mistake of showing my face to the rebels. I was not able to guide them away from the Geralt imposter, and I assume he wants me dead before I can."

"I'm beginning to think that the Storm is more than it seemed," Eric added. "Geralt could be directly connected to Lord Cer himself."

Aeia reached into her pocket and retrieved a small storage device. "He is. This is footage Meckea gathered during the most recent Bask transporting. The Storm's leader is the man leading that as well."

Dust accepted the device and connected it to a screen, and the video started. He stared, and his jaw dropped. "I knew they were connected, but I never expected this! What does he gain by keeping the guise of Geralt during the taxing?"

"He uses the Storm as a means of extortion. If they pay the Bask, they live. Anyone else is killed in a rebel attack."

"That poses a problem, then." Dust scowled. "Eric, you haven't been killing the nobles. Lord Cer won't appreciate loose ends."

"Geralt spoke to me about that," Eric said. "He was adamant that they need to die. What will Lord Cer do if we don't perform the way he wants?"

Aeia looked Eric in the eyes. "He'll kill you. I've seen it before."

Eric glanced toward the door. "I need to warn Vestan."

Dust waved a hand. "We aren't going back, Eric. Not after what happened today."

"I *have* to," Eric said. "The mission isn't finished yet. We don't know who's leading the Storm. It isn't Nick Barrier, and we know it's not a Light stealer, all of them are dead except Dust. It's somebody who knew both Alonius Cer *and* Nick."

Dust threw up his arms. "But no one like that ever existed! Nothing short of reading his mind will tell us how he knows so much!"

"I agree." Aeia nodded. "Which is why I came in person."

Dust and Eric turned their gazes toward her.

"I haven't seen the man's face yet," Aeia said, "but his eyes are exposed. Take me with you tomorrow. If I can get a moment with this 'Geralt,' then I can get to the bottom of this."

Eric's interest morphed to concern. "Aeia—"

"It's fine. I can handle it."

Brunst growled. "You didn't say anything about that at the base. We were supposed to be warning Eric."

Aeia offered Brunst as warm a smile as she could. "I know, I'm sorry. You've done more than enough. I won't ask you to come."

He scoffed. "Nice try. As if Eugho would let me walk back alone."

"Hold on," Dust said. "Even with your ... gifts, how do you plan to approach him? He's working directly with Lord Cer. He has a squad of Huntsmen on call. They know all our signatures now. They won't let us get anywhere near the hideout."

"Well, *two* of our signatures," Brunst corrected. "Eric can't be seen. Aeia needs someone trustworthy to shadow."

Dust shot a glance to Eric, who shook his head. "I want to get Vestan out of there, not involve him further."

"As long as Geralt is hiding behind his mask, there's nothing we can do to stop him. Vestan wants to fight against Lord Cer. It's his fight too. We need to use him."

Eric rubbed a hand over his face. "Fine. But he needs to be brought in."

"Fine with me." Dust nodded. "That boy needs to be on the right side again."

Eric looked at Brunst, who said nothing. Then he met Aeia's eyes. She had no objections, either. As long as they'd let her do what she did best, she'd do it however they wanted.

"Good." Eric nodded. "Geralt will be returning to the hideout tomorrow. That will be our chance. I'll bring Vestan as soon as I can, so, Aeia"—he focused on her— "be ready."

Chapter Twenty-six

Eric lead Aeia and Vestan as they marched through the night. So far, their plan seemed to be working, none of the Huntsmen had confronted them.

"We're approaching the hideout." Eric said to Aiea.

The group stopped. Vestan looked wary, but he'd promised his help, if only to uncover the truth. He faced Aeia. "What am I supposed to do when we confront Geralt?"

Aeia smiled. "Nothing. I'll handle it."

She closed her eyes. Her face lost all trace of emotion. "Your signature is so soft, Vestan. The Shadowing is easy." "Let's make this quick," Eric said. "I don't want the shadowing to fail while you're still inside the hideout, Aeia." They entered the doorway and moved down into the hideout. A lot of people were about today, more than usual. Almost none of them were equipped with weapons or armor. Eric only recognized a few.

"What's going on, Vestan?" Eric said. "These people weren't here earlier."

Vestan shrugged. "They are from the different Storm hideouts around Feos. Perhaps a meeting of sorts?" Something felt off. Eric wasn't a leader of any substantial rank, but he felt like he would have been informed if such a meeting were taking place.

He shot a glance at Vestan, who looked as concerned as Eric felt. Eric pushed the group a bit harder. Eric looked to Aeia for confirmation, then pushed the office door open.

Geralt was standing at the back of the room as if waiting for them. His armor was different than it had been before. Sill red, yet the design had changed. More weapons were attached in various places, and it seemed thicker and more durable.

But the most important change—his eyes were now covered by a visor.

"Welcome, Eric, Vestan. I see you've brought a friend. What can I help you with?"

Eric looked at Aeia, who shook her head. He focused on Geralt and stepped forward.

"We came for answers, Geralt. You've been hiding a lot from us."

The man waved. "You no longer need to call me that. I've come to realize that a hero of the past is not what this world truly needs."

"I see," Eric said. "If you're not Geralt, then who are you?"

"My name is Victor. You should recognize it, Eric, the name comes from your world ... as did my father." Victor pulled his sword slightly out of its sheath. "This blade, this armor, this name ... All of them belonged to my father, the man who died fighting an impossible war eleven years ago."

This man is Nick's son ...?

No. Furthermore... "An impossible war?" Eric scoffed. "You're leading a rebellion just like him!"

Victor shook his head. "We both know I am not. My plans do not involve this rebellion. After tonight, the Storm will no longer be needed. Alonius Cer has gathered all the Bask he needs. There will be no war, not this time."

"So, you were helping him?" Aeia stepped forward. "Why? Lord Cer is a monster. This whole city is collapsing in on itself, and you helped him? After what he did to your father?"

Victor waved her words away. "I bear no love for Alonius Cer. But his plan, or at least the one part of it I intend to let him accomplish, is vital to the salvation of this world. My path is different from my father's, but my desired result is the same. I wish for a world without Bask stones. And if that is not possible, then the next best thing is a world without a man in total control of them—a world without the king."

Victor paced. He circled them as he walked. Eric stepped closer to Aeia. Vestan could defend himself, but Eric would ensure Aeia was protected.

"The nobles," Victor said, "even the Archdukes, can be killed. People often forget that there were once *seven* provinces in Nont. But an invincible, immortal King is what keeps this kingdom the way it is. As long as he is alive, there can be no change."

"You ... you can't kill the *king*," Aeia's words rolled out slowly, terrified.

"Maybe, maybe not. But Alonius bears the greatest threat to him, and that's why I would work with one demon to slay an even greater one."

"All this to kill the king?" Eric shook his head. "What happens to the Storm when you've accomplished your purpose? What will they do when you no longer need them?"

A hum started in the distance. The sound seemed to be getting louder.

"That ... that is the greatest evil I will do." Victor started towards the back of the room. "I must stand by and do nothing as Alonius Cer disposes of them."

The hum increased in volume, and Eric's stomach lurched as he considered what it might be.

"What did you do?" Eric growled.

Victor glared at him. "This war will not end death. The sooner you learn that, the sooner you can become the leader this world needs."

"Me?" Eric stepped backwards. "What are you talking about?"

"My father waited for you, Eric. Waited for over twenty years. He understood his shortcomings and did all he could to prepare the world for your arrival. That was the last wish he left me, to seek you out when you appeared. Little did I suspect you would find me first."

Victor reached towards Eric. "You must come with me. Everyone who remains here will die."

"I won't become your weapon." Eric gripped the hilt of his blade and pulled it free.

"Well, I asked." Victor shrugged as he looked up. "It's not that I ever thought you'd be the hero he said you would be."

Eric stepped towards him. "Aeia, Vestan, tell everyone to evacuate. They aren't equipped. They won't stand a chance."

The two nodded and rushed back into the training area.

Victor made no move to stop them. "It's too late. And I'm not fighting you today. I'm leaving through the back door—it locks from the outside, by the way."

Eric's stepped forward. "You'll lock everyone in? These men who've fought for you without question?"

"They've done their part. It would have been impossible without them. But now, their purpose is done."

This man, this son of his friend... How could he treat human life so callously? Eric stared at the man before him. He struggled to comprehend what Victor had just said. And then, it came all at once. Anger took him over, and he surged forward, his blade poised.

Umbranium met umbranium, the ghostly *clang* echoing off the walls of the small office. It did nothing to either of them. Nor would any of their other weapons. It was a battle of strength and skill.

Victor stepped back, repositioning his blade so Eric's would slide down its face and away from him. Then he tipped the blade forward off the momentum, which forced Eric into immediate retreat.

He followed with a quick jab at Eric's gut. Eric met the blade and redirected it away before jumping forward to ram a shoulder into Victor's chest. Victor stumbled back a few steps, which gave Eric time to follow up with a downward slash.

Victor defended against his attack, but it was ill-prepared. Eric's blade broke through and grazed Victor's armor as he struggled to move out of the way. Insignificant damage was done, and the two fighters found themselves on equal footing once again.

The both moved forward as they met each-other's blows. Eric moved in ways he didn't know he could, his muscles remembering every lesson he'd been taught. He stayed on the defensive, and the veteran Victor could not break through.

Eric was stronger. Not by much, but he could feel each of his attacks having more effect than the last. Slowly, he gained the advantage over Victor.

Eric started his full-on assault. He moved past Victor's defense and slammed a fist into his side. It had devastating effect, more than Eric thought it should. Victor stumbled back with a hand covering his side. He bent forward and held his sword held between them in a weak attempt at protection.

Eric swung hard and slammed his blade into Victor's. Victor's sword flew free of his grasp, and Eric grabbed hold Victor's arm and twisted it, forcing Victor to his knees.

"Stop this!" Eric yelled. "You can't win!"

Victor growled and slammed a hand against his chest. His suit shifted. Some of the red portions of armor on his back opened, and a jump pack rose out. Victor launched forward, out of Eric's grasp, before Eric could do anything. He rolled across the ground, before the lifters on his hands slowed him to a stop.

"I will not fight you any longer," Victor said. "It will only lead to both of our deaths."

"If we fight together," Eric said, "we can still save them. They don't need to die for nothing!"

"And neither do you. Help me save this world." Victor straightened, met Eric's eyes. "Eric, help me. My father believed in you. Perhaps I can too.

Eric raised his sword. "I cannot stand by and watch innocent people die."

Victor backed toward his hidden door. "This will remain unlocked for one minute. You have until then to make your choice."

"No!" He lunged forward, but Victor made it through the door. If he followed, he'd be separated from Aeia and the Storm.

He gritted his teeth and turned back.

There is no choice.

Chapter Twenty-seven

Aeia shouted and pushed against one of the rebels. She did little more than annoy him. She looked at Vestan, who was having as little success. The men had become too rowdy in their celebrating and ignored them.

She shouted as loud as she could, but it was drowned out by the crowd's noise.

This can't happen! They're all going to be killed!

The ominous sound of screaming outside the door finally got their attention, and they hushed.

Hundreds shouted in terror outside the hideout, accompanied by the sounds of combat. The men rushed to the weapon stores but found them mostly empty. They realized what was happening, but it was far too late. They moved away from the entrance as far as they could.

The screams outside slowly began to die down until it became all but silent.

The seconds passed slowly, the silence disturbed by hopeful murmurs from the rebels. Aeia knew there was little hope.

The doors exploded from their hinges and were sent flying across the room. They crashed into some men just to the side of Aeia. She could hear the cracking of their bones. She let out a scream that was lost in the shouts of the rebel's terror.

Aeia lifted her arm as dust and splinters rained on her. She looked through slanted eyes as dozens of fully armed soldiers entered the hideout. They bore Lord Cer's insignia on their chests.

Panic rose in the crowd. Aeia, smaller than the rest, was defenseless as the soldiers moved in. She watched as they slaughtered every man without mercy, regardless of whether or not they were surrendering or fighting back.

They didn't stand a chance.

An arrow flew past her face and plunged into a cowering man at her side.

She had to escape.

She searched for a way out of the massacre, but there was none. Soldiers poured in from every possible entrance, even from hidden doors on the sides of the room she hadn't even noticed. The enemy soldiers knew everything. Victor had condemned all these men to die.

A soldier moved in on her. She pulled out her dagger and lashed out at him. He was not expecting any fight from a girl, much less one her size, so he was unprepared for her attack. She left a gouge on his cheek before moving in and stabbing him in the side.

He howled and rolled backward as he scrambled away. This drew the attention of two more soldiers, whose faces twisted in anger when they looked at her.

Trapped, she was left with only one choice. She jumped. Hurling her consciousness into the mind of one of the soldiers.

She entered, moving through the void as quickly as possible. As expected, she was soon surrounded by the whirlwind of colors and patterns. This time, however, she wasn't going to create a castle. No, that move was designed to allow her to be there without harming the host's mind.

Instead, she created a house of glass, a more realistic version of a person's mind. She built her body as strong as she could. She didn't care this time about being caught. The soldier's mind wouldn't last long enough to harm her.

Grass appeared beneath her feet, and she charged forward, rocketing herself like an arrow straight through the fragile building.

Immediately, she felt a pulse as the host's mind wavered. It had no defense against her.

This was her curse.

She smashed the walls and supports that held the mind together, causing it to cave in on itself. Soon, even the grass and whirlwind began to disappear. Soon, only the void would remain.

Finished, pulled out with ease less than a second after she had first Void Jumped. The soldier she'd attacked collapsed, which caused the other to stumble in confusion. He looked up at her in horror. She hadn't kill the man, but his partner didn't know that.

Anger flared in her stomach at the terror on his face. "Scared? Didn't know there'd be someone who would *fight back?*"

But before she got riled up, a sensation filled her body. It cooled the flame in her stomach as if an icy wind had washed over her.

Her body was following all the training she'd had, pushing her emotions aside.

I am a tool.

This was her purpose, the thing that separated her from others.

She dropped the second soldier in an instant with another Void Jump. It was simple, so easy for her. There wasn't a man here who could resist her strike.

She dropped two more, her mind quickly remembering the steps. It became easier each time.

This was her training, to remove all enemies of her master, Lord C---

She blinked.

Enemies of who?

She looked at the insignia of the man she had just rendered unconscious. The world began to clear, the icy tendrils loosened their grasp on her heart.

But with that, she lost her ability to control herself. She looked around. For every soldier she had dropped, three more had filled the room. She couldn't fight them all.

Fight anyway. If you don't the rebels will all die.

It was no good, the words meant nothing to her in her current state.

"I can't keep fighting!" she cried to herself. "I can't do it alone! I can't stop this from happening!"

She watched the innocents being cut down. There was nothing she could do to stop it.

I'm nobody, just a weapon. I can't....

No. She was wrong, she *could* do something. These men weren't the king's soldiers, they were personal guards. And the person who owned them...

There was one thing about her that she just might be able to use, just *one thing*. Ironically, it was the part she hated most.

Her last name.

A soldier eyed her cautiously. His expression changed to worry when she started to approach even though he was twice her size.

She locked eyes with him, which caused the swing of his sword to fall clumsily. She ducked below his sword, her new plan giving her strength, and dashed around him to the men behind.

They came down upon her like a wave. She wouldn't fight them. Instead, she lashed out her weapon in a quick and completely controlled manner, evading attacks from all directions as she maneuvered to the entrance of the room.

There was a trail of soldiers behind her now, but that didn't matter. Just a few more feet...

She slipped from one of their grasps and ducked between the legs of a tall man. He was the last guard, and she was directly in front of what appeared to be the commanding officer.

She locked eyes with him, refusing the urge to jump. He glanced at her, and she closed her eyes and screamed. "STOP! You don't realize who you're fighting!"

The soldiers tailing her caught up. She could feel them behind her, assumed they were preparing to attack.

Their commander lifted a hand to stop them. "And who is that?"

Aeia opened her eyes. There was only one way out of this. She had one thing left she could use, something she has refused to acknowledge as long as she could remember. But it was true, and it was her only hope.

"My name is Aeia Cer! Lord Cer's only child!" Her voice boomed louder than she had thought possible. The massacre died down, and soldiers turned to her. The noise faded out until all she heard was the clunk of swords as their tips hit the stone floor.

She glanced to her sides. All eyes were on her.

"Lord Cer doesn't have a daughter," the commander said. "Or any children at all."

"He had one. I am the daughter of Alonius and Alora Cer. You won't know who I am, but the Huntsmen outside will."

Aeia had been shadowing Vestan all this time. She focused and disconnected the shadow. Visibly, nothing changed, but she knew the Huntsmen would notice.

"How did you...?" The man scowled and waved for men to surround and protect her. He turned and tilted his head down to speak into a communicator. After a few moments, he raised an arm.

"Pull back! We're taking her!"

Chapter Twenty-eight

Eric ran into the main room. Bodies were everywhere. Those who lived struggled to care for the wounded with what little supplies they had.

But there were no attackers.

It's over? Already? He looked for Vestan and Aeia. *How could we have won?*

He spotted Vestan caring for a man and ran to him.

Vestan's face showed of pure dread when he spotted Eric, and he rose to meet him. "Aeia, your friend. She gave herself up to stop the fighting."

"*What?*" Eric grabbed Vestan's shoulders. "But... how? She's a Void Jumper yes, but I didn't realize—"

"And, the daughter of Lord Cer. The Huntsmen confirmed it."

Eric's eyes widened, and he stumbled back. *She was ... all this time?*

They'd never talked too much about their pasts. Was that why? Did Eugho know that when he'd brought her in?

Eric turned and started toward the door. "We need to move everyone out of here before they change their minds and come back."

Vestan nodded and shouted his command. Retreat was slow, and quite a few had to be carried, but before long they were able to make it into the streets.

The conditions were even worse outside. While it looked like most had been able to escape, the corpses of the unfortunate made a layer of bodies around the entrance.

Eric carried one of the last of the injured outside. He kept his vision as high as he could, and tried not to step on anyone as he walked. He approached Vestan and gently laid the young man down.

"Do we have any transports to move these people?"

Vestan frowned. "Only a few. I've sent people to retrieve them. We'll be short on space. Should we worry about the injured from the other side?"

Only a few of the soldiers had physical wounds. The rest seemed to be unconscious for no reason.

"If we can, but our men have to come first."

Vestan nodded. He looked away, wiped sweat from his brow, and looked back at Eric. "I would have left them."

I wanted to.

Brunst approached, gripping the hammer on his side. "They offered no mercy. I don't see why you should."

"We aren't like them," Eric countered. "We don't have to sink to their level."

Brunst shrugged. "Your choice. Where is the girl?"

Eric closed his eyes. "She gave herself up to stop the fighting."

Brunst flared, grabbed Eric by the collar, and yanked him forward. "And you *let* her? Do you realize what that means? Aeia *cannot* be returned to Lord Cer. The entire plan fails if she is!"

"The *plan*? What about Aeia!" Eric yelled back. "And besides, I was trying to stop Geralt from getting away! Where were *you*?"

Brunst pushed Eric away. The force caused him to tumble to the ground. "We need to return to the base. If Jeffe can intercept them, we might still have a chance."

Eric climbed to his feet.

Remember the mission.

A chopping sounded in the distance. The three looked to the sky, and Eric unlatched the crossbow from his back.

He set his sights on the vehicle as it grew closer. It had no windows and only two rotating propellers that were connected to its sides by a thick bar. It came to a stop above them and hovered there.

What is ...?

Eric looked at Brunst, whose eyes were locked on the shuttle in the sky. He narrowed his eyes and raised a shield warily between himself and the vehicle.

He doesn't even know what it is.

A loud clank echoed, bringing everyone's attention to the shuttle as its body came loose. Its pointed end dropped straight down as the rest of it went completely upright. A seam appeared on its smooth front, and twin doors opened.

It revealed a massive figure, the silhouette of a man. He was still deep inside the vehicle.

Eric looked at Brunst. All color drained from the warrior's face. His mouth parted. Then his features twisted, and he backed up.

"Guardian!"

A flash of green rippled through the silhouette, its massive limbs coming into motion with the first pulse. It stepped out of the shuttle and dropped like a cannonball into a cluster of men.

The ground boiled and vibrated beneath Eric. A cloud of dust rose after the shock wave. Eric dropped to the ground with a howl, but the noise he made was drowned out by the thundering noise.

Dust filled his eyes. He covered his face, but it did little to help. He stumbled about the ground and struggled to get back to his feet.

As the air began to clear, Eric struggled to rid his eyes of dust as he looked at the source of the shock wave.

The figure rose from a crouching position, standing more than eight feet tall. It seemed like metal, coil woven through coil tightly. The only solid piece was its head, which coned to a point that gave it a more helmet-like appearance. Altogether it had the appearance of a massive man covered in armor.

Protruding from its back were six long coiled tendrils of metal, each of which pinned a man to the ground. Everyone seemed to have pierced straight through its victim's heart with improbable accuracy.

Nothing moved. Every man stood frozen with fear.

This can't...

A lone man cried out in terror. He scrabbled at the ground in an attempt to escape. His outburst was cut short, his chest pierced with a tendril stretching from the machine ten feet away.

An uproar built. Men ran in every direction.

But the guardian's long tendrils retracted and shot back out, slaying soldier after soldier.

One astonishingly brave soul faced it. The guardian struck with a punch that sank into his unprotected chest with a sickening crack. The man fell aside as if swatted like a mosquito.

The machine moved toward Eric. He raised his sword, frozen as scrambled for a plan.

Should I try to fight it?

He looked at his sword, a weapon he had been impressed with in the past. Now, he might as well be swinging a plastic spoon.

Eric watched as one of the beast's tendrils rocketed toward him like an arrow. He braced himself for the blow.

Instead of a lethal wound, Eric merely felt ice cold metal as it brushed against the side of his neck. He opened his eyes to see that the tendril had missed. It hit another man who had been cowering behind him.

The coil reeled back in, and the guardian stepped past Eric without having noticed him.

It didn't see me?

Eric looked at his chest. Unharmed.

Could it be?

His shocked body fought against his movements, but he turned toward the machine. It didn't look as it attacked, it seemed to just *know* where its victims were. It must not have been using sight as its targeting method. It must have been using Bask!

Eric charged, his sword raised. When he caught up to it, was he unsure of where to strike. Its limbs were thick, so his blade wouldn't be nearly enough to cleave one off.

A tendril shot out to the side and headed straight for Vestan as he followed Eric, shield raised.

That won't be enough!

Eric struck down on the assaulting tendril with his full weight and strength. His blade cut into the Umbranium with a loud clanging that reverberated through the streets.

The tendril twisted. The Guardian lost all control of it, and it flailed and coiled. It smacked Vestan's shield with enough force to cause the man to stumble backward.

The machine froze and reached out to grab the tendril with a hand. As it examined it, the tendril regained its shape. The guardian retracted it. Once it was coiled completely, the guardian turned.

Eric's body tensed as the guardian looked around for the surprise attacker. Its faceless head scanned the battlefield, sometimes looking straight at Eric. But not once did its gaze ever linger on him.

Eric crept behind it and struck again. His blade collided with the thick metal of the Guardian's leg, doing little more than carving a splinter off.

The guardian whirled with an outstretched arm and swept the area. Eric dropped onto his back, the Guardian's limb grazing the tip of his nose, before Eric rolled to the side and back to his feet.

Its reactions are almost human. Eric paced around the machine. *Is it being controlled from somewhere?*

Still not knowing where he was, the machine swung at the side Eric had not moved to. Its massive arms did nothing more than flail harmlessly in the air.

It gave him time to think, finally, of a way to bring something so large and strong down. He needed something heavy, something bigger than the Guardian is.

The green energy that pulsated through the machine seemed to originate from the center of its chest. Eric could assume that its power source was there, *if* that helped at all, as that was also where the machine's armor was thickest. Eric was going to need a lot more than what he carried to pierce that.

What could do it, then?

A small click sounded, followed by an explosion of pure Bask energy. Another went off shortly after as Vestan threw the few Pulse Bombs he had at the machine. It didn't appear to do any lasting damage, but it caused the guardian to stumble backward, nearly stepping on Eric as he scrambled to get out of the way.

That was more than enough to get its attention back at Vestan, it near-instantly sent tendrils his way again.

But the machine was stopped once again, this time by the strike from a hammer to the back of its head. The force caused even the guardian to stumble, and it nearly tipped forward.

Eric turned, saw Brunst.

Brunst attacked again, and his hammer extended out as he swung it down. One tendril lashed out and redirected the hammer head away, while another flew like an arrow. Brunst raised his shield and took the blow head-on. It was enough to stop the initial force of the attack, but the guardian continued its thrust. Cracks soon began to form on the shield's surface, the tendril's point digging deeper and deeper.

As it pierced through, Brunst let go of the shield and grabbed the tendril with both hands. His muscles bulged as he forced the tendril away from his chest.

Eric heard metal sliding against metal, and he turned back to the guardian. Another tendril snaked out of its back and launched at Brunst. The same one that still had a chunk carved out of it.

Eric swung his blade at the weakened spot with all his might. A loud *snap* echoed, and the tendril fell lifelessly to the ground.

The guardian pulled back a few steps, still struggling with Brunst. It lashed out at Eric's position with its four remaining tendrils.

They slammed deep into the ground around him, but they didn't touch him.

In one motion, it abandoned its attack on Brunst and used the tendrils to launch itself at Eric. As Eric rolled toward it, the machine slammed into the ground just behind him.

It caught itself with a hand and hopped to its feet. It looked around for Eric and felt around with its tendrils.

Eric attacked it in multiple places as he danced around the machine. It swung its limbs and snapped back at him. Nothing hit, and Eric watched its movements and noticed subtle patterns. It didn't react like a machine, and he could read it like any other opponent.

Soon, it was growing fiercer, *frustrated*. Its attacks soon became reckless as it desperately tried to pinpoint Eric's location.

And then, it froze.

Eric did, too. Something had changed, and he needed to figure out what.

It resumed with a new focus and changed its patterns. It waited for Eric to make the first move, and attacked in the places it thought he might go.

It's figuring me out. He gritted his teeth. *I have to act fast or—*

A blur of motion flew past his face, and a tremendous force rammed into him. Despite his armor, his chest cracked, and his whole body was hurled across the clearing.

Eric's world spun, his mind struggling to figure out what had just happened.

A burning sensation started in his chest and spread throughout his body. A pain greater than he had felt before.

I was hit...?

He couldn't move, his limbs ignored his frantic calls to action. His eyes were open, yet he only saw a rapid blending of color, white splotches appearing on the edges.

Am I dying?

He couldn't fight it. The control he had over his body had been stripped away, leaving him as a spectator. All that was left in his world was pain and the growing whiteness.

And then he felt it.

Subtle at first, a strange sensation covered his body. Warm, welcoming, the feeling prodded at him. It was nothing like he had experienced before, yet somehow it was familiar, like it had been there for some time, and he had only now noticed it.

The white in his vision faded, changed to blue. He saw it everywhere, emanating from every source. The clearing and everything in it radiated this strange aura... an aura that was now calling to him.

"I can help you," it seemed to say. *"I can save you."*

It prodded at his mind, his heart. It soothed the pain of his wounds, caressing him like a child in their mother's arms.

What are you?

The answer trickled into his body, relieving the pain.

Eric welcomed it. The aura seeped into his body slowly, cautiously, as if trying not to overstep its bounds. As it did, the chill of the air lessened. The control over his limbs started to return. It was restoring his life, making him stronger than before.

His whole body filled with the aura, which seeped into him from every direction. His left eye became enveloped in it the aura completely, and his sight instantly regained focus and clarity.

It traveled deeper before reaching the center of his chest pressing on his heart, the final barrier.

"Let me in and together we can fight."

Let it in? Eric hesitated. He felt like he had let something in already in the past. The memory was so faint ... but he had given allegiance to Him back then. Would he be betraying Him now?

The aura made that thought seem false, as it continued to restore his body.

This can't be bad... can it?

But what was it?

Eric scanned the street the people, the shuttles, the walls, the Guardian, all of it, was filled with this aura, this... energy.

Alarms sounded in his head. *This must be...!*

This world—all the technology in it, the trees, the animals, and the people themselves. They all needed one thing. The people were all fighting to control one thing. There was no other explanation.

This is Bask.

Like the removal of a disguise, he saw the aura for what it truly was. He felt it past the mask. He was *not* being given control over his body, it was *taking* control of his body. The *gift* the energy gave him was a Trojan horse, a way past his defenses. He had almost given himself up as an eternal slave to the energy's might.

The aura sensed his resistance and became violent. The soothing turned to fire, every crevice it had seeped into felt as if it had just been set alight.

Eric rolled across the ground, fighting it. He threw one hand over his burning eye, while the other clawed at his chest, trying to tear away the presence.

Get out!

The energy no longer asked for entrance to his heart. It tried to break down the door. It poured in harder and harder, barraging him with waves of force.

He fought hard, yet his mind was tossed about in a sea of it. Bit by bit, he began to cave under the pressure. Bask started to break down the barriers of his heart, pouring in more of itself with each small victory. Eric couldn't fight it much longer. He was going to be a slave just like the rest.

He dug into the ground at his sides. He tried to call for help, but he couldn't move his mouth at all. He was left only with his mind.

Help me! Please!

He wasn't sure what he was doing, or how anyone could possibly hear him. But someone *had* to. He couldn't fall to it, not after everything he'd done. He was supposed to be free from it, and help those who were its slave. If he lost his freedom, what help could he possibly be?

"Eric."

The voice was so powerful, yet so soft. He recognized it. Like he had heard it a thousand times yet had never been able to truly hear it.

The world seemed to slow. For the moment, the attack against him halted. The presence of the Bask was still there, yet something kept it from his innermost heart.

"Eric, stand up."

The voice was strange. There was no specific sound or tone. In fact, he wasn't hearing it at all. It was as if it was speaking directly to his soul.

Who are you?

"You know who I am."

A memory flitted, a thought reemerging that had been untouched for years. It was impossible though, wasn't it? This wasn't even earth. How could he be here?

"You finally called me. I have been waiting for you."

What? He squeezed his eyes shut. *You were waiting ... for me?*

"Your world is to be a world of love, Eric."

Tears started down his face, sadness, anger. *I don't understand! My world, and everyone in it, are gone! Where is your love in that?*

"It is not gone, but it does need me. My people have strayed far from me. They have forgotten what love is. Look now to the creation you never left."

Eric opened his eyes. His blurred vision saw the stars above him. Were they the same? Could he have been so blind? Could the answers to all his questions been above him the entire time?

These *were* the stars he'd studied as a child, the stars his mother pointed out to him. He had been so focused on everything that had changed, he'd never looked to see what was the same.

It was right there.

"Do not give up, Eric."

The attack resumed, the searing pain renewed. The last barrier of his heart weakened, and Eric was not able to keep it back. The Bask pushed its way inside with the intent to consume, control. It rippled at its victory. Its single foe within its grasp.

But Eric's heart was already occupied.

The aura reeled back, startled by the other Presence. It lost its foothold in Eric's body, and fought back. This time, he was not fighting alone.

The reigning Presence surged with Eric, expelling the energy from his body. The seemingly unstoppable might of the Bask proved useless compared to Eric's ally. Together they did one great push and threw the energy out completely.

A massive force burst out from Eric in every direction. The energy that covered everything quivered together in one great reaction, a scream of pain.

The Presence now filled Eric, giving him the ability and the courage to stand once more. His wounds still hurt, and the burning sensation caused by the Bask still lingered inside. But now he knew he wasn't alone. With the Presence, he could fight.

The fighting around him had stopped. Everyone, including the Guardian, looked at Eric.

Eric could still see the blue aura radiating off everything through his left eye. The only place the aura had no foothold was around Eric, the energy shying away with each movement he made.

He pulled himself to his feet and moved over to where Brunst was crouched.

"How are we supposed to kill that thing?" Eric said.

Brunst blinked shook his head. "We know nothing about the guardians. Only Lord Cer has them. I've never heard of one being defeated, just beaten until it retreats."

Eric pulled himself upright. "They retreat?"

"Eventually. They do seem to have some sort of self-preservation instincts."

"We can use that." Eric put his blade back into its sheath and handed it to Brunst. "Trade me swords. Also, give me any pulse bombs you have."

He took it warily and shot Eric a glance. "My sword is a carving blade, and it requires Bask. I can't use yours either, one swing with it, and I won't be able to move."

"I know." Eric fastened the pulse bombs to his belt. "But can you use it just once?"

"If you're asking if I'll die ... no, but it definitely won't be pleasant."

Eric pointed at the center of the Guardian. "One strike straight in the middle. If you can lodge it in there, I'll handle the rest."

He turned back to the guardian. It had turned its attention back to those it could see and attacked them.

Eric pulled Brunst's blade from its sheath and lifted it. It was heavy, cumbersome. He couldn't see energy radiating from the blade itself, but as soon as he touched the hilt, he could feel the small Bask stone within. The Bask inside the blade reacted to Eric and cowered like a frightened animal. It had nowhere to go. It was at his mercy.

Eric called out to the stone with his mind. A connection was made, but only in one direction. The Bask heard his call, but could not—*dared* not—try and enter Eric.

The blade came to life. The metal moved up and down faster than Eric could see, heating up while moving so quickly.

Eric turned back to the guardian. It was facing him, looking straight at his blade and moving forward.

Eric switched the blade off, and the guardian lost its dim beacon. It sent tendrils out to feel the area in search of him.

You can see that, can't you?

Eric stalked around the guardian, giving it a wide berth. He inched to where Vestan was hiding near the hideout entrance. The man still stood, mouth agape, as Eric came closer. "What did you *do*? The entire... *everything* shook when the Bask left you!"

"I'll explain later. For now, our priority is to kill that thing."

Vestan glanced toward the monster, then back at Eric. "You have a plan, I hope."

Eric pulled the crossbow off his back and handed it to him. "I doubt even this thing will be able to cut through the Guardian before it can counter like last time. So, I want you to get anyone who will fight to help shoot that shuttle down when I lure the Guardian below it." He motioned to the Guardian's carrier, which still hovered above the street.

Vestan raised an eyebrow. "The impact will hardly be enough to destroy the guardian, Eric. All that will accomplish is a longer walk home for it."

Eric turned back to the guardian, which was nearing their location now. "Just trust me."

He stepped toward it, blade in hand. The monstrosity loomed over him as he drew close. He honed in, planning his moves as he traveled the final few steps.

Eric picked up a stone and tossed it at one of the tendrils on the opposite side. A soft *tink* echoed as the stone met the metal, and the guardian slammed all its tendrils into the area surrounding the rock.

Eric turned on his blade. Just as the guardian retracted its tendrils, Eric drove the blade into its back. The metal screamed, the twisted coils giving way to the blade that wedged in the crossing tendrils.

The guardian lurched, not daring to extend its tendrils. If it tried, Eric's blade would carve into them. It reached back frantically before twisting wildly to attack.

Eric pulled the blade out and hopped back as the guardian pounded the ground with its large fists in a fit of rage.

Eric danced across the street as he flicked his sword on and off. He only gave the guardian glimpses of light as it tried to chase him. They neared the transport in the sky, and Eric shot a glance to Brunst.

Eric turned on the blade and tossed it up and over the guardian. The blade drew its attention and launched its tendrils after the blade. Eric used that opportunity to move directly in front of the machine. With one motion, he activated all four of the pulse bombs on his belt at once.

A massive burst of energy exploded off him, seizing the guardian as all its limbs were overloaded with the energy. As soon as the explosion faded, Brunst hurtled in with the blade raised high above his head. He brought it down in full force into the machine's chest, where it slammed with another burst of a different energy.

Both the guardian and Brunst reeled back.

The soldier stumbled backwards and collapsed.

The guardian was more resilient, and Eric had to throw his weight in a tackle to cause it to finally tip backwards.

"Now, Vestan!"

Dozens of bolts flew into the sky at the transporter. They tore at the engines and sheared them apart. Both engines failed at once, and the transporter started to fall.

Eric pushed away as hard as he could and rushed over to drag Brunst away.

The transporter, a great hammer, came down on the guardian into the umbranium blade, the nail, lodged in its chest.

The transporter crumpled and burst into a thousand scraps of twisted metal. Eric collapsed from the shock wave, debris raining on his body.

He threw his arms over his head and waited for it to stop.

All went quiet.

Eric turned toward the scene. Some of the monster was still visible under the wreckage, but it no longer moved. The green energy that had pulsated through its body was gone.

One by one, the survivors returned to the clearing. They warily approached the wreckage and checked for life. Eric joined them and moved a few pieces of debris to investigate.

His sword was stuck through the Guardian's chest, penetrating whatever it was that gave it life. It would no longer be a threat.

Eric looked up at the growing crowd. They all looked at him in wonder as they approached the scene.

Vestan came to his side. He threw one arm in the air and cheered. The victory shout echoed throughout the square.

Chapter Twenty-nine

Eric motioned for the others to stand back and reached for his blade. He yanked and pulled. Somehow it was still intact, and he finally wrenched it free.

From on top of the wreckage, he looked inside of the guardian. As expected, the core was made of a sort of Bask. While it had once given an unusual green energy, it now was completely lifeless.

At least it can be killed.

Eric sheathed the blade and turned to the others. They had their victory, but he still had something to do.

"I have to go to Lord Cer's fortress."

The victory on Vestan's face melted away. "*What?* That's mad! Did you see what a single weapon of his can do?"

"Aeia needs help. She can't be forced to live the life she did before."

"She's Cer's daughter!" a man called. "Why would we help her?"

Eric clenched his fists and turned toward the man. "She gave herself up to save us. We would have been annihilated if not for her. We can't leave her now."

He looked among the men. There were tired, wounded, and frightened. How could he blame them for not wanting to seek out more trouble?

What normally would have been anger in his heart was replaced by compassion. "This city is falling into chaos. You should do what you can to protect your families."

I need to find a shuttle. It can't be too different from a car, right? It's my best bet to get to Aeia in time.

As he started to leave, he felt Vestan clutched his shoulder. "The only way our families are safe is if we stop the archduke. And last I heard, he prefers to stay in his fortress."

"One last fight then?" Brunst groaned as he struggled to his feet. "If there is any time to attack, it is now."

He lifted his communicator as he limped toward them. "I just got word. The Royal Guard showed up outside the city. Without the Marquess guarding the border, Lord Cer will have to send his own men to stop them. That's a lot less men to guard his fortress."

"The Guard Captain is here?" Vestan smiled and raised an arm to his soldiers. "Lord Cer will pay for this cowardly attack! Gather every survivor, every weapon from all the Storm bases! Everyone who will fight for our city will march on Lord Cer's fortress! We no longer have the imposter calling himself Geralt. He betrayed us. The true Geralt was lost ten years ago."

He turned to Eric, his eyes burned with fiery determination. "But we have someone far better. And he needs our help."

* * *

Aeia sat in the corner of the prison cell, her arms wrapped tightly around her legs as she stared at the door.

Artificial light still shone below it, and she could occasionally hear footsteps as someone patrolled the hallway outside. Any minute now, someone would barge through the door and force her back to her father's house.

A fate even worse than death. He had only ever sought to use her as a weapon. Jumpers were some of the best assassins, if they were controlled.

I'm used to it. I really am just a tool.

That was the only reason Eugho had brought her along on his missions. Even to him, she was just a tool to be used. No one would miss her, much less come for her.

She tightened her grip around her legs and hid her face.

Her life would be what it had been before. Only now her father's grip would be unbreakable. She would have no second opportunity to escape.

At least...at least she had gotten the first chance. At least Eugho had given her the chance to see the world. The chance to save those she cared about. It was something. She even got to help some people, convince them that a better world could be possible.

They can do it. I know they can. The nobles can't control the people forever.

If only everyone could be like Eric. Maybe then the rebellion would have a chance to win.

Eric. She thought she'd saved him. The soldiers had fallen back to ensure she was returned to her father. But a guardian shuttle passed them on their way back.

He can't fight those. No one can.

She fought tears. She didn't even know why she was so sad at the thought. She had only known him a few months.

He was so kind to me.

And she was the one who got him killed. She had known what she was doing when she brought him to the village that day. Ever since she'd met him, she'd known he was a good person who would help their cause.

But she'd used him, the same way others used her. She knew that he would help, and so she'd asked him to, when he had nothing to do with any of this.

I'm a monster, just like I've always been told.

Frustration boiled up in her. It was the same feeling she often got when forced to do terrible things as a jumper—the same things she would be doing again shortly.

It ended so soon.

That short breath of freedom hadn't been nearly enough. She wanted to feel it again—help everyone feel that way. But it was impossible now. Her father would never let her glimpse freedom. She probably wouldn't even be used as a Void Jumper.

Tears of both sorrow and anger streaming down her face, she stood and looked out the barred window.

"Whoever is out there, don't give up! Keep fighting, and we'll win!"

No response. Not like she'd expected one.

Just like before, she was waiting for the world to magically change on its own.

I still hope for that? After all that's happened? She laughed at herself. *Still foolish as ever. Nothing will ever change.*

Their plan had seemed perfect, right until it had collapsed around them. They couldn't create an army to fight Lord Cer. The so-called army was killed alongside Eric. Even if the Guard-Captain were to stop Alonius, how would that change anything? Feos would be placed in the control of a new Archduke, and the world would continue as it had before.

How can we fight this? How can we save a world so far gone?

She looked out the small window again. After all this, the world still looked the same. Nothing had changed, nothing would change. The world was going to stay the same forever. Like Eric had told her, it was covered in darkness, and it would stay that way.

And yet, just like before, even after all their work had gone unrewarded, she found that tiny sliver of hope inside.

"Go away!" She sobbed silently. "I don't want to hope anymore."

It seemed even worse off before Eugho found me. I thought that I was just going to fade away, never leaving my father's grasp.

"Stop!"

People found me, cared about me, dreamed the same way she did, dreamed that the world could change.

Aeia dropped to the ground, covering her ears in a futile attempt to ignore her own thoughts. For once, she wished for the peace that the other Jumpers got. The peace of not having to worry about the world, the peace to just simply... exist.

She'd be sent back into training. She wouldn't fight it this time. There would be no point.

I am just a tool. I thought I could be more, but that only ended up hurting people.

The sound of scraping metal echoed through the room, followed by a deep thud as the door to her cell was unlocked.

Aeia hopped to her feet and whirled around as the door slid open. Blinding light shone into her otherwise dark room. She couldn't see specifics, but she saw the silhouettes as two men came into the room.

"Lady Aeia, your father has requested your presence."

She didn't recognize the voice. And why was he talking to her like that? She looked about the room and back to the men. "Do I have a choice?"

"It was a request, my Lady. He is... very clear in his decisions."

When has he ever requested anything?

Aeia pulled herself to her feet and followed the men. It was either go now, while he was in a good mood, or wait until she was dragged in.

Chapter Thirty

"Welcome home, Aeia."

Aiea didn't put on her mask. This time, she would force her father to look at her, at the *real* Aeia. She was a different person.

"What do you want?"

Alonius let out a huff and shifted in his seat. "You've changed while you were gone."

Aeia narrowed her eyes and lifted her chin. "I was never complete."

"Of course not. I never intended for you to be."

Aeia stepped back. "What?"

"Regardless of what people say, I do plan for the future. You are my only heir."

Her mind filled with more and more questions. She tried to push them back. This monster was Alonius Cer, possibly the most hated man in all Nont. Any reasons he had for anything would be twisted.

"But that is not important right now. It is nearly time. If our city is to take the next step, I'll need you here as well. I trust that you can still perform?"

"I won't do anything for you. Never again."

Alonius rose and walked around his desk. "You were found at one of the rebel hideouts we raided last night. Their goals are shallow and short-sighted. This world cannot be changed with the sword, not like they think. It must be destroyed in the way it was created. This world has not been like this forever. Rules were established with the kingdom, rules that would ensure its survival. You cannot win if you continue to abide by them."

Aeia shook her head. "I don't care about your delusions."

Alonius smiled. A thing she hadn't seen since she was a small child. It filled her with disgust, he was *not* the same man he was back then. The creature before her shouldn't even be considered human.

"Whether you care or not does not matter." He hummed in a soft voice. "You do not know it yet, but you, my daughter, possess the power to break the rules of this world."

"You cursed me!" She spat the words. "Your abominations won't be missed when you're gone."

Alonius's face shifted to rage, and he stepped toward her with a hand raised. He was interrupted when the door burst open and the commander who'd brought her stepped into the room.

"Lord Cer! We're under attack!"

"*What?* By who?"

"It's the rebellion, my lord! The Storm is at the front gate!"

Eric!

Alonius strode toward the man, his glare piercing. "They should all be dead! Did I not give you orders to execute them all?"

"I sent a guardian, my lord. I just got a report that it was killed!"

"My guardians *cannot be killed*. Send every man to the gates. Unleash the rest of the guardians! Not one rebel leaves this place alive."

"No!" Aeia pulled on her father's arm to force him around.

He gripped her neck with both hands. He was far stronger, and it took him little effort to slam her against the wall. "You and your rebellion forget what you are! I created you ... and them! You are still of use to me, but they are no longer needed. They are lost. You cannot save them!"

But he was wrong, because she *could* save them. *Everything* came back to her father. If he was gone, then all this fighting, this death, would go with him.

She looked him in the eyes.

"You would dare threaten use your power against me? I gave it to you!"

You gave me this curse. The curse that is strong enough to remove anyone without a trace. No matter who, or where, they are.

381

Aeia jumped.

*   *   *

She pierced the void like an arrow, shooting straight through into Cer's mind. She felt unstoppable as she built the castle.

He oppressed me all these years, making me think that I was helpless against him! I can win!

The castle complete, she leaped into one of the windows.

Make this quick, before he finds me.

She had never moved as fast as she did now, navigating the halls without setting off a single alarm.

But she stopped when she noticed something strange. A new hallway, one she hadn't prepared, was opening. At its end, a single doorway.

His mind will not have caught up yet. He can't be changing things yet.

Which meant that his mind was prepared to do this, somehow.

He knew I'd jump?

The thought was terrifying. Though there was nothing behind these doors that would be able to harm her. So, what could he be trying to show her?

A message? A memory he wants someone to see?

It was too odd to be ignored.

Pushing the door open, a warm summer breeze washed over her carrying the familiar scents of Manor Cer—before her home had been turned into a fortress.

As she went further inside, the host's vision cleared to show her father overlooking the city of Feos on a balcony she'd spent many evenings on herself.

She gasped at the sight. The city showed none of the signs of her father's corruption. Not a single warship could be seen in the skies, only trade vessels of noble houses who had long since ceased doing business with Feos.

And yet, her father was filled with worry and disappointment. The view was not warm to him.

But why? Things were good then.

"Alonius." The voice came from behind, and she turned at the same time her father did.

A hooded man was crouched on the far side of the balcony atop the railing.

"You have a gift. I did not hear you coming once again, my friend."

The man dropped his feet down, sitting on the railing, before pulling back his hood to show another recognizable face. A young Geralt, not a single wrinkle on his face, his hair without a single silver strand like he'd borne the day he'd died fighting the king.

Aeia guessed that this memory was older than she was, that it had occurred years before her father began his descent into madness.

"I suppose." Geralt sighed. "Though from my position, I doubt I'll ever find my stealth useful. My job is to be seen more than anything."

"A shame." She saw the green, amusement, swirl around Cer. "You would make quite the shadow."

"So I've been told, but I'd much rather be hunting them. I prefer force when finding out the truth. Spying is a last resort, though I will not hesitate if I have to."

A deep gray, shame, rose in her father, and he lowered his head. "I did not mean to hide it from you forever."

"Why hide at all? We share the same goals."

Cer lifted his head and looked Geralt in the eyes. "Because my plan has a terrible price. And I knew that you would not approve."

"We knew there would be sacrifices, Alonius."

He shook his head. "Not like this."

Realization crossed Geralt's face, the life draining from it. "You couldn't possibly mean ..."

He turned back towards the city, clasping his hands behind his back. "Tell me, what do you see."

Wary, Geralt stood by his side. "Feos."

Her father nodded. "We've met here countless times, overlooked the city as we made our plans. After years of work, can you notice a difference?"

There was silence for a long time. "No."

"Neither can I. Every day I come out here. Every day I expect to see something different. And yet the world never changes."

Aeia gasped. *He's had the same thoughts I have?*

"It's a small hope I carry. But hope alone will solve nothing. The world needs something drastic to happen if anything is to change. Someone has to take action."

A reddish orange, determination, rose within Alonius, a will and purpose she had no idea her father carried.

"I have to be that man," Alonius said.

"A man cannot change the world. Not alone."

"Then I shall have to become something different."

Geralt grabbed her father by the shoulder and turned him until they were face to face. "You've said that before! But what of your wife, Alora? What about Aeia? This path does not only affect you."

"And that is why I need you. Watch them for me. In a matter of days I will no longer be able to trust myself with them."

Geralt's face darkened, and he stepped back. "They will not be harmed as long as I live."

Geralt hopped back onto the railing, preparing his jump pack. "But I cannot say the same for you, should you go through with this."

The memory faded as Geralt shot off the balcony.

Aeia couldn't process what she had just witnessed. Her father worked with Geralt? He spoke of changing the world, but then made it worse? Did he think that Feos was any better than it had been before?

The man she saw in that memory couldn't have been the same one she saw today. He spoke like he actually cared for her well-being, yet he'd put her through torture and forced upon her the worst curse she could imagine.

But... she knew him. She remembered the kind father she used to have. Where had that kindness gone?

She stepped into the hallway to look for another door. Suddenly, the stone she stepped on gave way.

The floor beneath her collapsed, causing her to slide to the shimmering field where she'd arrived.

The castle was dissipating into the air as it fell.

Time to go.

This had been a bad idea in the first place, she knew that now. She tried to pull out.

The exit closed off. Her connection with her own body was being barricaded. She'd been found out.

While she had expected mass armies or weapons forming in the field, she instead only saw a single man.

It looked like her father, except much younger, close to the age as he had been during the memory. Except he didn't have that life in his eyes. They were as cold as he was now.

"You shouldn't have come inside, Aeia. You grew too confident, and it will cost you."

She stared, dumbfounded, at the second presence.

"How are you here? This is *your* mind!"

"You think I would teach you *everything*? Jumpers are dangerous enough as it is. There have to be some... safeguards."

"I'm stronger than you think. I've learned a lot this past year."

He shook his head. "It doesn't matter. You're foolish. I needed you alive. I need you to carry on in my place if I fail."

"I would never take your place! No ending is worth what you're doing."

"Then you too are no longer needed."

The ground shook beneath her like an earthquake, only more rhythmic.

She looked at her father for an explanation, but he didn't change his icy glare.

He stepped back, and the ground lifted him up so he was on a mound. Then, she turned and saw the source of the shaking, the front line of a massive army.

"Thousands of men are at my command in Feos. *This* is what you are trying to fight against. You saw first-hand the consequences of your rebel meeting. And that was not even a fraction of my strength."

The army halted just behind his pedestal, preparing to charge.

How can he control his subconscious like this?

"Tell me, before you die, what you were trying to accomplish? Have you ever seen anyone defy me and live? Not even the King can stand against me any longer."

She looked at her feet. *Why did I do all this? Why did I think we could win? I should know more than anyone...*

Yes, she knew better than anyone. She'd had every reason to give up years ago, but she hadn't. And because of it she saw something great begin to form.

"Hope." She looked back up, standing strong against the force. "I always felt... No, I always *knew* that this isn't how the world is supposed to be."

"Hope ..." he repeated. "The world will not change with hope, girl. The world will change only by someone who will use any means necessary." The slightest of smirks crossed his face. "I could never understand a girl with such power surrendering herself for the weak."

"I *do* understand. I know that nothing will change without sacrifice, but what good can possibly come from what you're doing?"

"Good, or not. It doesn't matter." He dropped from his mound and walked towards her. "I am going to take this world."

And with that, the army charged.

Aeia waited for them to get close. When they did, she leapt backwards so that their spears stabbed harmlessly into the ground where she had been a moment before.

But that only left her more exposed, and a flurry of arrows approached her like a storm cloud.

She remolded her body, transforming herself into a bird and flew through the storm of death.

By now, her mind should have retaken to its training, covering her in the icy grip, and turning her into an unstoppable machine.

But the change never came.

She focused as hard as she could, twisting and turning between the attacks of her father's subconscious.

But it was relentless, and she was getting nicked by the arrows. The attacks sheared off feathers and cut into her body.

Can't outrun it...!

She transformed to her normal form and tried to harden her skin, taking the brunt of the blows head on.

It worked! The arrows hit her but bounced off with negligible effect.

She landed on the ground, and the wave of arrows dissolved into nothingness. She looked up and saw not another wave, but a single form.

Her father crashed into her, plowing his forearm into her neck. The attack was so fierce that had she not been on the defensive, he would have crushed her mind in a single blow.

"You're strong. You've always been," he said, his glare burning into her. "You were supposed to be my weapon, the tool to keep the lords beneath me in check."

Her mind reeled, struggling to regain itself, her father's strength threatening to tear her apart.

"I'm... not a tool!"

Her strength returned, and she pushed against him with all her might, effectively breaking him off and throwing him into the air.

But it was no use. He twisted in the air and landed unscathed.

His army caught up and washed around him like a flood.

They were upon her again, but this time she knew that running would pointless.

She stopped, concentrated on creating a particular weapon, a long and heavy blade.

Using her mind's strength, she wielded it with no trouble, slashing the weapon with a force that sent the first line of men flying. The second followed.

There were an overwhelming number of soldiers, but she knew how the subconscious fought. She ducked between the blows, and hurling the blade around, her small body becoming a whirlwind of metal.

Arrows were fired again, but this time she made no effort to get away, instead, charging straight into their ranks blade first, the arrows fell to the ground behind her.

She couldn't defeat them all, she should have already lost—she knew that—but she had to keep going until...

Her father appeared again, his own personal sword modeled in his hand.

She saw him coming this time and mounted a counter offensive against his attack. They crashed against each other.

The power of their consciousness equal, their blades met in perfect opposition as they fought, though Aeia was working harder, thanks to the soldiers' attacks.

Battling a mind is like a sword fight. Each attacker tried to find weak points while also trying to defend. And much like in a normal battle, a single wrong move could cost a warrior his life.

But like a sword fight, there are many ways to win.

She parried an attack before pulling back and planting her feet, her sword raised high next to her face.

It was a terrible position for the broadsword she was using, and her father saw her weakened state and lunged.

Just what she wanted.

As she started her thrust, her blade transformed, turning into a rapier. The resulting attack was much quicker than Cer had anticipated.

He stumbled, trying to back away, but her blade caught his shoulder and tore through the flesh.

The look of shock on his face was more than satisfying. It twisted into rage.

He leaped back a few feet, holding his wound. "Where did you learn *that*?"

She smirked. "You think I idled by this past year? I've been very busy, father."

"Only one man used a weapon like that, and he died years ago."

She took advantage of his confusion and tackled him, rocketing both high and out of the army's reach.

His grip tightened. She could feel his focus returning as they flew, and she wasted no time in rolling away as they crashed to the ground.

She hopped to her feet, only to see him charging at her once again.

She planted herself against the blow, both blades straining against the massive strengths of their wielders.

As they both reached the climax of their strength, a deafening thud pulsed through the field. It shook the area, stunning her as she tried to figure out what had happened. She looked to her father. His face was expressionless as he gripped his chest.

His... heart? But I never—

An arrow narrowly missed her. The army had caught up.

She leapt high into the air.

Only this time, no arrows followed.

Cer jumped up in pursuit, grabbing her by the throat and slammed her back to the ground.

She struggled, trying to pry his hands from her neck. But it was pointless. He had her completely pinned.

She looked into his eyes and saw nothing but hatred.

"Why?" She gasped. "Why have you always hated me? You were kind once! I used to love you, father!"

She saw a flicker of something in his expression.

"You are cursed."

"You cursed me!"

He narrowed his eyes. "I tried to *save* you! But your curse proved too powerful! Death is all that remains!

"That's a lie!" She cried out in rage, throwing him off.

She rolled a few feet, grabbed her fallen weapon, and charged him before he could recover.

For once, she proved faster. He was defenseless, and she pointed her blade at his throat.

He froze, even his army slowing to a stop in a large circle around them. They didn't dare move forward.

"Go ahead," he said. "Do it."

She searched his face for any deceit and found none.

"Do it, I said. If you think it will help your goals."

She didn't say anything.

He moved closer until the blade pressed against his skin, arms open wide. "Don't you want to stop me? So, kill me. It will make things easier for you. You might even to be able to convince the other archdukes that you're the rightful heir."

But still she stayed silent, returning his glare.

"That's why you came here, isn't it?" he said. "Why else would you jump into my mind?"

"Not to kill." She pulled her blade back an inch. "If I could just ..."

"Just what?" He spat. "My captain is still in the room. He will apprehend you no matter what you do. Nothing short of killing me will solve anything."

He moved forward again, pressing his throat onto the tip of her blade until it started to bleed. "And when I awake, I will not show you mercy a second time. Either you kill me, or you die."

Her mind swirled in confusion. She had vowed never to kill again. And this was her own father.

She didn't want this.

"No?" he said. "All right then."

He created another blade and swung at her.

She grabbed his wrist and tackled him. He was much weaker now, and she could feel his strength ebbing.

Unfortunately, hers was too. She had been away from her body for far too long.

"You think to change the world without bloodshed?" he said. "You think that anyone will listen to someone who doesn't have the strength to kill?"

He started to force her back, the tip of his blade getting closer and closer to her neck.

He was giving her no choice now, it was kill or be killed.

He's a monster! Remember all the things he did to you! Think of the massacre!

The strength in her arm began to give out. Last chance.

"It is true, *daughter*. I will show you! I will take this world the only way possible... Straight through the bodies of anyone who stands in my way!"

She cried out, thrusting with everything she had left.

And then, nothing.

The fighting stopped, he stopped struggling against her.

Did... I...

The mind began to collapse. The world was falling apart around her, the massive army vanishing as quickly as it had appeared.

I... couldn't have...

She dropped her blade, and it dissolved into nothingness.

But, that was... different. It wasn't like the other times!

The ground below shook, reminding her that she had to leave immediately. She pulled out as fast as she could, the void threatening to swallow her along with him.

* * *

She dropped to her hands and knees. Feeling the cold stone beneath her again.

I can't believe... I...

She looked up to see what she had done. The scene was not at all what she'd expected.

Instead of the lifeless, yet otherwise unharmed body of a jump kill, she instead saw a long bolt protruding through Lord Cer's chest from the back.

What?

She looked around and saw the captain. He seemed as surprised as she was. They both turned to see a man perched on the windowsill, a crossbow in his hands.

Her mind couldn't process it. She couldn't even try. "Eric?"

He shot her an apologetic gaze and aimed at the captain. "Move and you'll receive the same."

Aeia started towards Eric, her feet barely able to move beneath her. "But ... why?"

He hopped from the windowsill and positioned himself between Aeia and the captain. "I saw you jump into him."

She shook herself. "You were trying to save me?"

"I knew you could beat him. But I... I didn't want you to have to do it."

Anger, confusion, sadness. She didn't know what she was supposed to feel.

"I'm sorry," he whispered.

Tears formed. Thoughts, memories assailed her. She needed silence.

"Surrender," Eric called to the captain. "Your leader is dead; the nightmare is over. No one else needs to die today."

Hesitantly, the captain pulled free his weapons and dropped them on the ground before raising his hands. He lifted his arm to his face and spoke into his communicator. "This is Captain Eran. Lower your weapons. Lord Cer is dead. We have lost."

Epilogue

She had dreaded this day for weeks. The realization had come to her only few days after taking on the currently-unofficial position as Archduchess of Feos.

Many of the low-level officials were eager to follow Aeia's leadership. They had assisted her in searching every inch of the fortress for hidden storerooms her father might have built. It was a quick process, since many members of the Storm had volunteered as well after Eric's endorsement of her. They seemed to be willing to do anything the 'Hero of Feos' told them to.

And it was all for nothing.

Dressed in an outfit *slightly* more extravagant than she would normally wear, Aeia found herself having to force each step she walked down the hallway. What would the crowd say? Would they assume her lying and riot? If they did, could the small force of soldiers loyal to her stop them from rampaging the fortress themselves?

Lost in her worries, she didn't notice she had stopped walking altogether until the appearance of another person came into view. The mere sight of his kind face lifted her fears for a fleeting moment.

"Eric, I can't do this."

"Coming from the woman who took on Alonius Cer by herself? This is only an announcement. And with all the wealth you have poured back into the city by selling the fortress furnishings, people will love you."

"It's not enough!" The words spilled out in a shout that she had never heard coming from her mouth. "People are still dying in Feos. I will never march them out like my father did, but have you seen the streets? A body can be seen on every block!"

"Faults of your *father*, Aeia. When you said you were becoming Archduchess, I thought you were joking. And I've never heard you joke before." He sighed and leaned against the wall. "Only you would volunteer to take the mantle Alonius left behind. You should take your victories as they come. The fact that you aren't chasing people from their homes is an improvement."

"An improvement? I want to save this city, Eric."

"That can't happen in a few weeks. You should know that better than anyone."

"He's right, Aeia."

They both jumped as a hand appeared in the windowsill before Eugho climbed through the window and pulled himself into the hall. "I've been fighting to save Feos for *years*. What you two accomplished in only a few months is simply astounding. But you must remember that while Alonius is gone, the damages of his rule will affect this city for many years to come. At least we know they aren't going to be any worse off than they are now."

Aeia lowered her head. "It doesn't feel like that. The Storm and the soldiers still clash, the other Archdukes deny my legitimacy, and the Royal Guard are all but quarantining us. The city is in more chaos now than it was under my father's rule."

"Which is why our team remains vigilant. You aren't alone, Aeia. Not since the day we met in that alley."

"Even less since you saved me from that forest," Eric added as he held out his hand. "We'll get through this."

She took his hand. They were right. No matter what happened now she wouldn't be facing it alone.

With Eric by her side she marched to the balcony. The murmurs of the crowd below grew as she stepped outside.

Before her was the largest gathering of people she had ever seen. They filled the courtyard and spilled out the front gates. The sea of blue hair was dazzling, only out-shined by the looks on the people's faces that took her breath away.

Hope.

Please, even after what I have to tell you, don't give up hope.

"People of Feos." The words came out as barely more than a whisper. She could hardly breathe under the eyes of so many. She was used to being in the shadows, being ignored.

They need answers.

Aeia sucked in a deep breath and shouted across the masses. "As you all know, Alonius Cer is gone. He can never hurt anyone again."

She closed her eyes for a moment before continuing. "He stole from us. He stole our food without payment. He stole our homes for his soldiers. And worst of all, he stole the Bask that keeps us alive."

"Give it back then!" A woman from the crowd shouted at her. The rest voiced their agreement.

Aeia winced. "Most of the charging stations are still stripped bare and useless. I know that you all came here hoping I would replenish them."

Cheers came from the crowd. She noticed a couple, hair turned almost white, hug each other.

Aeia gripped the balcony tighter. Tears formed in her eyes as she tried to force the words out. "As if to strike one final blow against us, Alonius didn't leave a single clue as to what he did with all that Bask. I don't know where it is."

The crowd began to murmur louder. The faces of hope shifted into fear and anger.

"We searched this fortress. We even had help from many of the officials that served under Alonius. Whatever his plans were for the Bask, he did not share them with anyone."

"Liar!" A man shouted. "You just want it all for yourself!"

"Yeah!" Another agreed. "Cer's are all the same!"

Aeia swallowed hard.

"He shared his plans with one man! with one man. The man who claims to be Geralt worked with Alonius to transport the Bask. We will stop at nothing until we track him down and demand that the Bask … the life of the city… is restored to us."

Made in the USA
Columbia, SC
07 March 2020